FIGHTING FOR JEN (SPECIAL FORCE: OPERATION ALPHA)

COUNTERSTRIKE, BOOK 5

CARA CARNES

Dear Readers,

Welcome to the Special Forces: Operation Alpha Fan-Fiction world!

If you are new to this amazing world, in a nutshell the author wrote a story using one or more of my characters in it. Sometimes that character has a major role in the story, and other times they are only mentioned briefly. This is perfectly legal and allowable because they are going through Aces Press to publish the story.

This book is entirely the work of the author who wrote it. While I might have assisted with brainstorming and other ideas about which of my characters to use, I didn't have any part in the process or writing or editing the story.

I'm proud and excited that so many authors loved my characters enough that they wanted to write them into their own story. Thank you for supporting them, and me!

READ ON!

Xoxo

Susan Stoker

CHAPTER 1

Three months ago...

Banner "Razor" Nilon parked his motorcycle beside his VP's and inhaled the early morning air. Faint scents of garbage permeated the air behind Cholo's. His gaze swept to the city dumpster at the back end of the small lot. East side Austin had undergone a significant makeover the past decade—or so he'd been told by locals when he and his motorcycle club had settled in the thriving city just under a year ago.

It'd taken longer than he wanted for the Scythe MC to quietly cement themselves within the area, but they'd managed. Now they could focus on what mattered—vengeance and redemption. All of his brothers had taken blows they shouldn't have during military service. Most had been unrightfully dishonorably discharged.

Razor would make it right. Somehow.

"They're waiting," Frenzy said. The man never pulled his punches, which was why he was the Scythe's VP. He'd keep Razor focused on the objectives. He always had.

"Let them wait. Which of you wants to tell me why the

fuck we're bothering with this?" His gaze sliced to Sandman, his Sergeant of Arms.

"We fell on their radar thanks to that fuckwit Guerillo," Sandman said.

"And how did that happen? We haven't been on anyone's radar since we got out." Fuck. The entire point of forming an MC was to operate beneath everyone's notice. How else could they investigate corrupt military personnel and right wrongs while tending the emotional damage they'd suffered?

"Counterstrike is solid, more so than any other group we've run across, mainly because they've hooked up with The Arsenal," Sandman said. "Don't get Anarchy started about that crew. Chatter within the private paramilitary arena hails them as the best around. They've taken a lot of corrupt dicks out like the trash they are without hesitation."

Razor grunted. He admired that shit, mainly because that's exactly what he wanted to do. No. Needed to do. None of them wanted to waste their lives chasing phantoms. They'd served their time and gotten kicked in the head in return.

"Cholo and Mingo have both signed on with Counterstrike," Frenzy said.

Razor scowled. When? As if sensing his inquiry, Sandman added, "Last week. Their cousin ran across Guerillo's activities in Golden Crescent. Counterstrike waded in, as you know."

The entire world knew. Media had blown the story wide open. Even though the FBI and other government agencies had already taken over the remaining investigative work, the media vultures made sure everyone knew who'd taken Guerillo down: Counterstrike.

"We're an unknown in their city," Frenzy said. "And we can't afford to ignore that this is very much their city."

Fuck. Razor got off his bike and made his way to the back

door of Cholo's. The crazy little shit had become a burr in the Scythes' asses, one which popped up frequently. He and his brother had a strong street rep even though neither were in a gang. No. The local gangs were all leery of Cholo and Mingo—a fact Razor not only admired but fucking appreciated.

Yeah, he'd have this "meet" with Counterstrike for Cholo and Mingo. Then he'd get back to what mattered—his Scythe brothers.

The typically busy restaurant was vacant when he entered. He paused in the entry a moment as his eyes adjusted to the low lighting. Two men sat facing the door. Twins, unless Razor was seeing double. A gorgeous brunette sat between them. She pulled her long dark hair behind her ears and licked her full pouty lips as he approached.

Well, then. Maybe this meet wasn't so bad after all. He sat across from the three unknowns but didn't bother sliding over. Neither Frenzy nor Sandman would sit as long as he was in an unknown situation. Crazy fuckers thought he needed protecting.

"Razor," the twin on the left said. "I'm Ethan Davenport. This is my brother, Milo, and our sister, Jen. We own and operate Counterstrike."

Billionaire do-gooders who'd exited the military and shifted from spec ops work to helping domestic violence victims and anyone else who needed someone in their corner. Anarchy and Sandman had spent hours drilling Davenport history into his head.

"I respect what your group does, but what the fuck am I doing here?" Razor asked, keeping his gaze on the beauty in the middle. She shifted restlessly between her brothers.

"Funny," Milo said. "That's what we wanted to know. Why are you in Austin? What are you doing?"

"Living the dream," he quipped. Sarcasm laced each word as his gaze sliced to the twin on the right. "Why do you care?"

Sandman cleared his throat. The sound thundered within the silence, a brick-to-the-head style reminder Razor needed to mind his manners. Whatever.

Ethan's cell phone rang. The device lit up where it sat on the table. The man looked down. Eyebrows raised, he clicked Answer. "Now's not a good time, man. I'm in a meet, but you knew that."

"I did." Razor stilled. Why was Tex phoning Ethan?

"Fuck," Frenzy spat angrily.

So much for Tex staying out of their business. The former Navy SEAL had inserted himself into their lives shortly after Razor formed the Scythes. He'd offered his assistance, but none of Razor's crew had wanted to involve the man in whatever wars they'd wage. The work he did was too important for him to be mired in Scythe troubles.

"There's a lot I haven't shared and probably should have," Tex said. "Razor and the rest of the Scythe MC are solid. They're brothers who got done wrong."

Fuck. "We don't need or want a character reference, man," Razor said. Anger mottled his words. "This isn't a job interview."

"No, it's a distraction neither of your groups need. I'm wading in and cutting the posturing off at the knees." Tex's voice boomed through the phone. "Details are theirs to share when and if they want, Ethan, but I back Razor and his crew. Whenever, however, and wherever they want me to when their stubborn asses decide to tap me in."

"Good to know," Milo responded. "That still doesn't tell us why they're in Austin."

Because two of their quarry were nearby—one south in San Antonio and the other north of Austin. Neither would be a focal point for a long time because it'd take time to handle those particular infestations. Other parasites required immediate attention. "It's centrally located and no local MCs to worry about."

"You need better intel, then. There are lots of MCs in the area," Ethan said.

"None we'll need to worry about." Razor shrugged. "We have a reputation, one we earned quick. Very few crews have the balls or numbers to mess with us."

"How's that possible?" Jen asked. Her sexy voice wrapped around Razor.

When Razor didn't respond immediately, Sandman waded in. "Razor's gramps was in a club, a big one with a strong reputation. We're linked to that crew and several others. Altogether, we're several thousand strong with more than half being well-trained former military."

Razor shot his SoA a look, then honed in on Jen. "Does that answer your question, beauty?"

Milo growled. Amusement rolled through Razor when the woman glared up at her brother. Fuck yeah, she wasn't a withering wallflower who wanted anyone fighting her battles.

"I'll cut through the bullshit foreplay. We aren't a threat, nor will we get in your way," Razor said. "What you're doing is a worthy cause, one we not only support, but would be willing to assist with, should that ever be needed." Not that Counterstrike would deign to work with anyone dishonorably discharged.

Razor's gut soured. Too many of those he'd fought and bled beside had turned their backs on him. He'd learned to expect nothing from anyone beyond his Scythe brothers. Not anymore.

"We won't be needing your help," Milo replied.

There it was. Confirmation.

"I see I'm wasting my time," Tex said. "One of these days

you boys will pull your heads out of your asses and realize you're two sides of the same coin. Let me know when that day comes."

Damn. Razor hated pissing Tex off. "We done here?"

"Yeah," Ethan said. "Stay out of our way and mind your manners. We don't tolerate trouble in this town."

Cholo and Mingo approached. Razor's jaw twitched as the silence thickened. "Good. Neither do we, which is why there's a new law in town. The Scythe MC is that law where the gangs are concerned."

"What does that mean?" Milo growled.

"Just what he said," Cholo replied. "Sorry I'm late. I was on the phone with leaders from the local gangs. They all phoned Mingo and me to rant about our boy here. Apparently there were some very intense *conversations* last night." Amusement filled the man's words. "You've got brass balls, man. My brother and I have kept those crews on leashes, but we've never choke-collared them."

"Rules are simple," Sandman said. "No peddling their shit to kids, no turf wars, and anyone who wants out gets that out. They violate any of those laws and they won't live long enough to reap the benefits."

"Not sure that's a smart play on your part," Ethan said.

"Then we'll agree to disagree. You do your thing to rescue people in trouble, and I'll do mine to keep them breathing." Razor stood. "I'm not your enemy, but don't fuck with us."

He made his way toward the exit, opting to do so with a casual stroll. Although he had no doubt Counterstrike was a solid crew, he had no intention of being their ally, even if they miraculously wanted to.

"That didn't go as well as I'd hoped," Cholo said, making his presence known as they exited the restaurant.

"Respect, man. You and your brother are solid as far as we're concerned," Razor replied. "But those two are cut from different cloth. To them we're nothing but dishonorably discharged scum."

"You're wrong," Cholo said.

Razor ignored the man and got on his bike. He had a club to protect. Nothing beyond that mattered.

* * *

Two and a half months ago...

Razor's gaze swept through the thickening crowd shoved into a confined area thanks to barriers set up by the police. His skin pricked with unease as he found the Davenports at the top of the steps with a few other upper echelons. He recognized Mrs. Cumberland and the state's Attorney General from the media coverage surrounding the Guerillo debacle.

The case against Guerillo's second-in-command started several days ago and all three of the Davenports, along with several of Counterstrike's operatives, had testified today. Jen stood between her brothers. Another brunette he recognized as Cholo's cousin stood to Ethan's left with Hazard, one of Counterstrike's main operatives.

His skin crawled. They were too exposed. The three men's gazes swept the thickening crowd, their unease palpable as they moved the two women a couple steps behind them. One of the twins whispered to the Attorney General, who shook her head and pointed toward the media, who'd taken over the area at the base of the stairs.

Shit. They wouldn't get gone until the AG got her fifteen minutes of fame.

Not our problem.

Then why the fuck was he here?

"We've got trouble brewing," Sandman said.

"No shit," Razor replied. "They're fish in a barrel."

"Yeah, and I've gotten three calls from the local gangs. A San Antonio crew was spotted heading this way," Sandman said. "They wanted us to know."

Fuck. "Did we get a description of their ride?"

"Rides. Four vehicles," Sandman replied. "Low riders. What do you want to do?"

"Send the descriptions to everyone. Take them down. Get me their leader here," Razor ordered. So much for keeping a low profile today. He'd brought enough Scythes to cover the area in case shit went down. There'd been too much coverage leading up to today for him not to worry about a potential threat.

"Counterstrike probably has coverage," Frenzy said.

"Doubtful," Sandman said. "Most of them were stuck in court. Cholo's mentioned they're seriously short-staffed right now and covered over with cases. What few operatives they had not testifying today are likely not in town."

"And local cops won't handle anything like this well," Frenzy added.

"Star formation in the area," Razor ordered. "Get vehicles here. Now. I don't give a shit what."

He charged toward the stairs and shoved his way through the media. Sandman remained at his six because the stubborn bastard wouldn't ever leave his side.

"What are you doing?"

"Whatever it takes," Razor growled. He took the steps three at a time and was halfway up when both Davenport twins noted his approach. They visibly tightened, closing ranks in front of their sister.

Fuck. His thoughts drifted to the beautiful woman too often. He'd spent hours poring through intel Anarchy had gathered about her and her brothers. The work she did was beyond amazing.

"What the hell are you doing here?" one of the twins asked.

"Saving your stupid asses," Razor replied. He glared at the Attorney General. "You want your fifteen minutes for the media vultures, but this shit is done. A San Antonio crew is about to roll in and paint these streets."

"What?" The other twin grabbed his arm. "Are you sure?"

Razor glared at the man's hand. He was about to reply, but gunfire sounded from behind him. He shoved the two men backward. "Inside. Now!"

The entire group turned and ran toward the building's entry. The metal detectors went off when he ran through them, but he ignored the rent-a-cop and continued forward. Razor grabbed his cell and hit the call button. Frenzy picked up on the first ring. "Two rides. South exit." He hung up and motioned toward the rear exit. "That way."

"We need to stay here," the Attorney General said.

"You're choice. Counterstrike is gone," Razor spat. "You aren't turning their testimony into a funeral pyre so you get your face in national media."

"I told you we shouldn't address the media today," Mrs. Cumberland said. "You should've listened to me. This man is right."

"He is," one of the twins said. He stopped when they arrived at the back exit. "What's the plan?"

"You leave. We deal with this shitshow and you'll probably need to bail our asses out when the local cops try and blame us." Razor grabbed his secondary weapon and gave it to the man. "Just in case."

"Thanks." The man took it. "Stay close to me, Jen and Bea. Milo and Hazard, same for you."

Razor glanced at Sandman, whose jaw twitched. He pulled his secondary and handed it to Milo.

"I can't believe you came here armed," the Attorney General said. Her face reddened.

"And I can't believe you didn't have armed officers with us," Jen said. "Either shut up or go away."

Ah, she was a little spitfire. Nice. Razor clicked answer when his cell rang. A man's voice sounded on the other end. "We're pulling up, Prez. Make it quick. We've got company coming from the west."

"Move out. Stay alert. Incoming." Razor exited first and directed his attention westward as two SUVs pulled up. Two prospects exited both of the vehicles and drew their weapons as a black low rider careened around a corner.

"Aim for the tires," Razor ordered. "No kill shots."

"Fuck," Ethan growled as he crouched beside Razor and took aim. "Get in the vehicles!"

His phone rang. He threw it down on the ground beside him and hit the speaker button. "A little busy."

"Jumper's got overwatch. Get in the fucking vehicle," Frenzy ordered. "Sandman, drag his ass there if you have to."

"Don't even think about it," Razor warned. "Get everyone else in."

"On it," Milo said.

Sandman darted forward and crouched behind the second vehicle. Smoke bloomed from the target car as five armed men exited. Razor aimed and shot the first in the shoulder.

"Get to the car, Davenport. Jumper, no kill shots." He barked the latter order into the phone and hoped the former sniper was on the call.

"Like I'd be messy, Prez," the man said. "Get to the car. You're covered."

Razor grabbed his phone and Ethan's arm. He shoved the man toward the second vehicle as the first careened from the curb and headed east. Sandman and Jumper had the situation covered. Four of the five men were down, clutching their injuries. He shoved himself into the car behind Ethan. Sandman followed.

The prospect drove before the car's door was shut. Razor took his first deep breath. "We're clear. Status?"

"We've got three of the four vehicles detained. The fourth squirted, but we have crew following," Frenzy said. "Half of ours are in cuffs."

Fuck. That was the last thing they needed.

"Not for long," Ethan said. He grabbed his cell and hit a button. "Everyone okay?"

"Yes," Jen said. "We weren't the ones reenacting a wild west showdown. What can I do?"

"Tell whoever's driving to take us to the police station," Ethan said. "They're arresting Scythes."

"Idiots," the woman spat angrily. "I'm on it."

Razor couldn't help but chuckle along with Ethan. "She's a firecracker."

"She is." Intensity resonated within his gaze. "Not sure what you were doing there, but thanks for the save. We were assured APD had the scene contained."

"Clearly not," Hazard said from the passenger's seat. "How did you hear about this?"

"Local gangs saw them roll in," Razor said. "One of the new rules. They spot anyone from outside in town, they have to alert us."

"That sounds like a pain in the ass," Ethan commented.

"You have no idea," Sandman said. "But it paid off today. We've got the leader and several of his crew. The others were turned over to the police."

"Who then arrested the good Samaritans who did their job." Ethan coiled his fist. "That's happened to our operatives before. We'll get it sorted."

"You've got a choice," Razor said. "Do you want to go with

us to speak with these idiots, or would you prefer not being involved? Turning him over before he answers my questions isn't an option."

"We're with you," Hazard replied.

"You had exit transport ready," Ethan commented.

The prospect chuckled. "Not exactly. This is more of a loaner."

The billionaire sighed and withdrew his phone. "I'll assume the other is as well."

"That's a good assumption," Sandman said. "We were only there cause Razor had a gut feeling shit was gonna go sideways. His gut's never wrong."

CHAPTER 2

Jennifer Davenport honed the rage rolling through her into a steely weapon and directed it at the Chief of Police. "Let me get this straight. These men not only saved the lives of potentially hundreds of citizens today but did so in a way where no one was killed and you have the audacity to stand behind the decision to arrest them. On what grounds?"

"Carrying concealed weapons and discharging them in public." The man shifted his attention to the Scythes standing in a group. Still cuffed. "We have yet to ascertain their involvement."

"Their involvement," Jennifer repeated. "This is how we're going to proceed. You are not only going to release all of these men, but you're going to apologize and thank them for their selfless efforts on behalf of the city." She blasted the Attorney General with a withering look. "You'll both do this immediately or I will give the media outside fifteen minutes of fame you will not want to be a part of. Then you'll both be personally dragged into the most epic lawsuit this country has ever witnessed. And I guarantee the entire country will witness it. I will rain the fires of hell on this city and you both."

"We're more than justified to act as we have," the Attorney General said. "Their records will speak for themselves."

"Oh, they will." Jennifer took a step forward, into Penelope White's personal space. "They are all heroes who served this country. Bled for it. Do not think for one second I won't make that known. You know who I am. What my brothers and I do. More importantly, you know who helps us. They have the resources to shine the real light on who these men are. One call and that happens. Then your actions will speak for themselves. Arresting the valiant men who risked their own lives to save your witnesses. And you."

"Ms. Davenport." The police chief cleared his throat. "I see you're somewhat passionate about this. Let's discuss it in the morning."

"That is not happening." Jen motioned toward the Scythes. "You have ten minutes to remove those cuffs and make your apologies. Then you are both marching outside and thanking them publicly for their work today. If you don't, I will go out there and give the performance of a lifetime. You both know I was raised in the limelight. I'm good at crying on cue. Damned good."

She let the threat loom a few beats before she took a step back and directed her attention at the strangers who risked their lives to save her today. "Thank you for saving me and my brothers. My friends. I'm sorry you're seeing the worst of this city right now. I can't assure you it won't happen again, but I do promise I will not ever let it stand."

Crossing her arms, she raised her brows and regarded the Chief of Police and the Attorney General. "What's your decision? Before you tell me, you should know both of my brothers will likely be here soon. If you think one Davenport billionaire crying on camera is epic, just wait until she does it while clutching her two heavily military decorated and media cherished big brothers."

"You wouldn't dare," Penelope said. "You hate media attention."

"I hate bullshit like this even more, so much so I promise every cent of Davenport money will be solely invested in destroying you both if you dare take this unbelievably wrong action." There's no way any judge would ever let this arrest stand. There was zero evidence against the Scythes, aside from the video footage from the scene. "Have you even run their records yet? Have you even bothered to ask if they have concealed carry permits?"

She glanced over at the men. "Raise your hands if you have the necessary permits to carry concealed." Every hand rose. She smiled and redirected her attention. "You can thank me for doing your job later, Chief."

The man's lips thinned. "We've perhaps been a bit rash in our decision to arrest them, but we've yet to ascertain their involvement."

What a pig-headed blowhard. Footsteps sounded behind her. Ethan and Milo both entered, along with Razor. Her body heated when her gaze swept the sexier-than-sin man, whose gaze was on his men.

"You good?" Razor asked his crew.

"Oh, yeah," one of the men said. "Best entertainment we've had in months, Prez."

Razor chuckled as his gaze moved to her. "I bet."

"As entertaining as this may be, Chief, you should know Counterstrike requested the Scythes provide security on our behalf today." Ethan slid the lie out easily. "Since Mrs. White refused to let us carry concealed within the courtroom and the operatives not testifying today were unavailable, we had to seek outside assistance."

"Is that right?" The Chief of Police's eyebrows lowered. "I find that highly convenient."

So did Jen, but she could make the paperwork exist. "Careful where you trudge, Chief. Calling us liars is opening yourself up to another lawsuit, and I do love all that legalese. There's nothing better than sitting down and typing out page after page of it while I sip on a glass of wine and envision crushing anyone who dares to call my brother a liar."

Razor chuckled. He put an arm around her waist. "I can perhaps understand how you arrived at the misguided notion we were somehow involved with today's events, sir. We did, after all, manage to apprehend the majority of today's assailants before any of your officers even drew their weapons or realized there was a problem."

"And how was that?" The chief crossed his arms. "You failed to notify us of a threat?"

"So you could what?" Jen shook her head. "There wasn't time. How long between getting word there was a problem to it being an active situation?"

"Minutes," Razor pulled out his phone. "I'd have to look through the calls to verify, but she's right. There wasn't time."

"How did you come about this information?" Penelope asked.

"I was concerned for the safety of the Davenports and the other Counterstrike operatives," Razor replied. "As such, I expressed that concern to a few people and asked they notify me if they saw anyone suspicious in the area. They did, and let us know."

"And you happened to be in the area," the chief said.

"Like my brother's already mentioned, Counterstrike hired them to provide a protective detail." Ethan crossed his arms.

"You chose to parade them in front of the media rather than see to their safety," Razor said. "Don't put your faulty decisions on me. Neither of you put their safety above your personal desire for attention. This is your penance, and perhaps a lesson."

Damn. Jen couldn't help but embrace every word the man spoke in a confident tone that belied any argument.

"I kind of hope they arrest us," one of the Scythes said. He shrugged. "I want to see our little dragon there rain those fires of hell she promised."

"Is that right?" Razor's gaze locked onto her.

"I may have promised the lawsuit to end all lawsuits as I cried on cue between my brothers for the media." She shrugged. "I have my moments."

"She's really good at crying on cue," Ethan commented. "And Milo and I are excellent at supporting her in front of the media. We've had an entire lifetime to practice."

"There's no need for that." The police chief motioned toward the Scythes. "I can see we had a gross error in judgment. My sincere apologies." He glanced down at his phone. "There is one unfortunate point to discuss. It seems one of my detectives thinks there may have been a high-powered rifle used in the altercation at the rear of the building."

Damn. Her pulse quickened when she recalled the loud gunfire erupting around her. Her mind raced for an explanation, but Milo spoke before she could.

"One of operatives, Chatter, was in the area on another assignment," Milo said. "He heard the gunfire and took initiative to assist our exit. I'll gladly have him come and answer whatever questions you have, but he is one of the men your SWAT teams calls when they are shorthanded."

"Oh, yes." The chief tugged on his uniform. "Of course. I forget more than a few of your operatives have been assisting us when needed. I'm sure that won't be an issue."

Jen hated how easily her brothers lied—and so well she often couldn't even tell when it was not the truth. She couldn't protect them when they put their neck on the line like that. "I believe we are done here. I'm sure these men would appreciate being uncuffed and released. They've sacrificed enough of their valuable time as it is with this mess. I trust this sort of false assumption about them won't happen again."

"They are not authorities, nor is Counterstrike," Penelope said. "This sort of situation wouldn't happen if you remembered that."

"And it wouldn't happen if you did your job," Razor said. "I won't ever apologize for protecting people. Funnily enough, I could've sworn you wouldn't either." His gaze cut over to his men. "Prospects are bringing over vehicles to get you back to your bikes, which had better not have been damaged if they were impounded."

Jen made a mental note to follow up with that as she followed her brothers and Razor out of the room. Exhaustion plagued her steps as the adrenaline she'd been relying on dissipated. The testimony alone had been enough to deal with. A gunfight? Yeah, she could live an eternity without another one of those, thank you very much.

No one spoke as they made their way out of the police station. Two men in Scythe cuts stood beside three motorcycles, which gleamed in the late afternoon sun.

"Thank you," Razor said. "For defending my men so valiantly."

"It was the right thing to do," she said. She looked into his intense gaze and licked her lips. "And thank you for being there and saving us." If he wouldn't have… A shiver ran through her.

"Your brothers had already sensed a problem because of the large crowd and your exposed position. They'd already put themselves between you and any potential threat." He offered a slight smile. "You would've been safe."

"But they wouldn't have been," she whispered. "Thank you."

Razor nodded and headed toward the motorcycles.

"Razor." Ethan's voice startled Jen. Razor turned. "Thank you. We owe you."

"We need to follow through with the shit he got out of those gang members," Milo commented.

Jen tightened. "What did he find out?"

"Someone hired them to hit us today," Ethan said. "Guerillo, or someone working for him."

Damn. Jen had hoped the threat from that ring they'd taken down was over. "Will this be an active problem?"

"No," Milo said quickly. "We'll make sure it isn't, but we shouldn't have any gangs attempting drive-bys. The Scythes have this city locked down tight. No one will enter it and pose a problem, or they'll be on their radar."

"Then why did this one?" Jen didn't want to imagine the power Razor and his crew held. How feared they had to be to control that many people. "I know The Arsenal looked into the Scythes and so did your friend Tex. Are we sure they're solid?"

"They are," Ethan said. His expression turned grim. "They just operate from a slightly darker handbook than we do, which isn't necessarily a bad thing. It makes them not only respected but feared."

"More than us with the street crews," Milo admitted. "Come on. Let's get you home."

* * *

One month ago...

Jen tugged her blue blouse and wished for the umpteenth time she'd opted for slacks rather than the snug jeans she'd donned. *You shouldn't even be here. Turn around and leave.*

Determination filled her as she made her way into the small bar. Music filled the area, a rock song if she wasn't mistaken. It'd taken a lot of creative questions and sleuth skills to ferret out this location. Fortunately, Mingo and Cholo were talkative around their cousin, Bea.

God. Bea had been a lifesaver the past few weeks. Jen hadn't ever been this busy. Counterstrike was covered over in cases because of all the media attention lately. While she was glad people now knew there was a resource that could and would help, she hated how many cases they had to temporarily turn down.

Too many people needed their help and wouldn't get it. She clutched the two folders she'd put together as she made her way toward the back of the small club. If Cholo was right, the higher ups in the Scythes frequented this establishment.

This is so stupid.

Yep. Ethan and Milo would kick her ass if they found out she was here, but someone needed to help these two women. If Counterstrike didn't have the time, then maybe the Scythes would.

Face it. You just wanted an excuse to see Razor again.

Ugh. She couldn't deny that part of her brain. She'd become a bit obsessed with the sexy biker. He exuded the same lethal badass vibes as the Counterstrike operatives but, unlike them, he made her entire body heat with an awareness she hadn't felt in ages. When he looked at her, she felt…

Exposed.

No, she felt like a woman, one stripped bare of her legal persona and overprotective big brother armor. Razor didn't strike her as a man who'd shy away from going after what he wanted and, unless she'd read him entirely wrong the few times their paths had crossed, he wanted her.

Feminine laughter echoed from the darkened corner she

approached. Dread curdled her bravery a few beats. This was a terrible idea. *Turn around.* Soft shafts of life fractured the darkness when she took another step forward. Long, red hair bobbed up and down as a large hand gripped the curly mass.

"Looking to join in or take her place?" The husky whisper against her ear jolted her half a step forward. Her arms scissored out to prevent a fall, but a firm grip steadied her at the waist. "Sorry, beauty. Couldn't resist." A husky sigh rushed warm heat against the shell of her ear. Tingles ignited across her skin. "Fuck, you smell good."

"Razor." Her back pressed against a hard chest. "Sorry. They told me you were in the back."

"Someone's got a sense of humor. They won't ever give my location away, but they will send wayward little lambs to my VP or SoA." Amusement filled his voice as his hand stroked along her hip. "You here looking for an adventure? I doubt your brothers would approve of you dirtying yourself by showing up here all alone."

Jen gulped. Getting dirtied up sounded a bit fun, thrilling even. "You make that sound like a bad idea."

"Oh, it isn't." He chuckled, bathing the heated skin along her ear with another bout of breath once more. "I'm sure it would be one hell of a ride."

Images assailed her as the visual cue "ride" took on a life of its own. This wasn't why she'd come here, but maybe it should've been. *Face it, Jen. You wanted to see the dirty-minded biker again. Alone.* "We need to talk."

"Is that right?" He huffed and loosened his grip. "If that's what you want."

She wanted far more than talk but took a steadying breath and turned to face Razor. Scruff covered his masculine jaw, adding another layer of don't-fuck-with-me to his already lethal vibe. Would the scratchy whiskers feel good against her skin?

"Keep looking at me like that and we'll have a problem," he warned. "There's talk, and then there's talk, beauty. You aren't ready for the kind of conversation I want to have."

Oh, she was. So ready.

"Come on, little lamb. Let's go into my lair." He took her hand. Warmth seeped into her skin as he guided her to an empty booth across from the one the man and the redhead occupied.

Razor steered her into the booth, facing her away from the couple. Amusement broadened his full lips into a grin when their gazes locked. "What can I get you? Whatever you want."

Jen shivered at the implication and squeezed her thighs together. *Focus*. Razor reached over the narrow table and ran his hands through her hair, which had lost most of its curl during the day. Warmth spread through her, pooling between her legs as his fingertips glided from the tips of her hair and across to the button just above her cleavage.

Intensity resonated within his dark gaze as he flicked it open. She leaned forward into the feather soft contact as he traced along the exposed skin. Stroking up and down a couple times. His gaze wandered to the newly opened area. Although it was still a modest amount of skin, the fact her cleavage now showed just enough to be scandalous in a work environment quickened her pulse.

"That's better." He leaned back in the booth. "What can I do for you?"

So much. Jen shifted against the leather bench. "We have more cases than we can work right now. A few medium priority ones have fallen through the cracks." She shoved the two folders toward him. "I think these are two the Scythes could handle, if you're willing."

She intentionally referenced the Scythes, needing the distance it offered. It'd be too simple to tumble into his sexy gaze and let the sexual attraction between them take over.

Amusement glinted across his handsome face a moment. He opened the first folder. Jaw clinched, he flicked through the papers. "Fuck." Leaning forward, he slammed the folder shut, then went to the next. "Define handle. My idea of dealing with these fuckwits probably won't match Counter-strike's."

Jen suspected it would. Ethan and Milo never messed around when it came to abusers. None of the operatives did, which was why she was always one of their first calls after they'd addressed an issue. It'd taken a few trips to the county jail to bail a few of them out to find the acceptable line. They couldn't help people in need if they were in lockup, after all.

"As long as they make the first strike and do enough damage to be photographed afterward, I can explain away reasonable damage on an operative's part," she explained. "You are all highly trained. Bruising and some blood are well within the limits. Broken bones and anything requiring a trip to the emergency room before they're hauled into jail, not so much."

His mouth upturned into a half-grin. "I'm thinking you could explain away a lot."

"I can and I have." She motioned toward the files. "These two women are wanting assistance relocating. They both have family in the area, so this is more of an escort detail than a problematic extraction."

"The jargon is cute coming from you."

Cute? She wrestled with the word because it was the last thing she wanted to be when around Razor. Her gaze darted toward the couple still writhing within the shadows. "Travis and the other new operatives he took down to The Arsenal should be returning in a few days. I can see if they can handle these two requests."

"We'll handle them. That'll free them up to take on the other cases you've likely set aside for them." His lips thinned. "How long's the waiting time between initial contact and action?"

Too long. Even a few hours was too many in Jen's opinion. "It's improving. Forty-eight hours if there's only a minimal threat level. We're working on securing more safe houses. Anyone in immediate danger is taken to one upon leaving our office. We don't take risks with their lives."

"Even though you're covered over with cases. Tell me you don't participate in these removals."

"On occasion I do," she said. "Never alone, though. I can handle myself."

"I'm sure you can." His gaze swept across her. "You shouldn't have to, though." He tapped the files and let out an ear-piercing whistle. A wince flashed across his face. "Sorry, should've warned you."

He held the files up as the shadow in the booth across the way surfaced. Frenzy glanced down at her, then directed his attention to the folders.

"Get with Sandman. Organize two groups, one for each file. Roll out in an hour," Razor ordered. "Make contact with them first."

Frenzy nodded. He perused each folder's contents a few moments. His lips thinned.

"Nothing broken. No need for emergency rooms. No physical contact unless they attack first." Razor glanced up at Frenzy. "Assign a prospect to each final location for forty-eight hours afterward. Phone me once each woman is secured."

"On it. Gladly." Frenzy charged through the bar, motioning to tables of Scythes as he went.

"You've done this before," Jen commented. "Or something similar." The club members reacted too calmly, with precision. They filed out of the bar in an organized fashion, tossing money on the tabletops as they departed.

"We adapt quickly." He set both hands palms down on the tabletop. "Do your brothers know you're here?"

"No, but it was the right thing to do."

"It was." He leaned forward. "You have any more, let me know. Give me your phone."

Jen's hand shook slightly as she offered her phone. He smirked and held it up toward her so it would open with her facial scan. Then he made himself at home as he leaned back and tapped away. Awareness zinged through her as she watched him. His cell chimed. He put hers in her hand, then pulled his out and repeated the process. Hers chimed.

"Call me anytime, beauty."

Jen nodded. "Thank you." She stood, pausing long enough for her legs to not wobble. "Have a good night, Razor."

CHAPTER 3

Three weeks ago...

A night of limousines, caviar, and ballroom dancing was the ultimate hell as far as Razor was concerned, but he'd made a promise to Ethan and Milo Davenport. The billionaire twins, and former spec ops soldiers, took on the bulk of the media frenzy following the shitshow a few weeks ago, so the least Razor could do was drag his fellow Scythes to the charity gala.

Saving them from a drive-by shooting had been the right move, but had created a thunderstorm, one which fed from the Guerillo take down a couple months earlier. Thank fuck Counterstrike handled the media vultures.

Tonight's charity event was an intentional redirect, moving attention from what they'd done to what they intended to do. It'd also cast the spotlight on Austin's upper echelon as they donated to the cause. Holding the event at their family's mansion was a smart move. From what Razor had heard, everyone wanted to see the place they'd heard so much about.

It was massive and…cold. Nothing like Jen, or her brothers.

"You think they have that fancy champagne with gold dust in it?" Jumper asked.

"Shut up, you're showing your country bumpkin," Sandman said. "That's not a thing."

"It is too a thing," Jumper argued. He adjusted his suit jacket again. "Swore I'd never wear one of these things until I was getting married or buried."

"The latter can still be arranged," Frenzy warned.

Razor chuckled as he guided his most trusted Scythes along the shadowed recesses of the ballroom. Couples danced and twirled around in outfits costing more than a normal person's mortgage. Servants glided in and out with champagne and fancy finger foods.

Fuck. "How long did we agree to stay?"

"Three hours," Sandman said. "We have two hours, fifty-seven minutes and," he glanced at his watch, "sixteen seconds of our sentence remaining."

Right. Razor's gaze slid through the thickening crowd until it landed on the beautiful brunette who haunted his thoughts too often. Her dark hair was curled and put up in some fancy updo that elongated her neck. Her sexy smile activated his lizard brain from across the room.

She'd appeared a few times since that first night. The flirtation and banter between them remained at an acceptable level, although the urge to haul her across the table and onto his lap rode him hard.

"Run far away from that temptation, brother," Frenzy said. "Billionaire beauties like her won't slum it with our kind."

Razor grunted. Jennifer Davenport was the sexiest temptress he'd ever met, but also so much more than that.

She'd stowed her rich upbringing to help her older brothers form Counterstrike.

A long line had formed along the left side of the ballroom and snaked across the back entrance. Everyone wanted a moment of conversation with her and her brothers—likely to suck up since the three rarely offered an opportunity for high society shit like this.

Frenzy was wrong. Jen was the most down-to-earth, real woman Razor had ever met. A fierce warrior within her own right. Her battlefield was a courtroom and, from what he'd seen, she took on any battle and almost always won.

"Fuck, boss man has it bad," Sandman commented.

"Shut it," Razor warned.

The Scythe MC he'd formed as a new family for his military brotherhood was now on Counterstrike's radar. Jen's handoff of cases to them hadn't gone unnoticed long. Cholo approached first, followed by Ethan Davenport.

"I know she's been giving you cases we can't take on. Thanks for the assist. We owe you." Ethan's words from last week still looped in his brain.

Unlike Razor and the other Scythes, Counterstrike's operatives were touted as heroes. There was a thick line fed by blood, fueled by secrets, and inflamed by assumptions between the two camps. Truth and honor kept the Scythes moving forward. Blurring the firmly established line between his men and the Counterstrike crew could cause a huge problem—false hope.

Ethan's operatives might not have an issue passing cases to the Scythes on occasion, but that didn't mean anyone at Counterstrike respected the Scythes. "Dishonorably discharged" shoved Razor and his men into a cavernous ravine few would bother traversing.

But the few escorts they'd provided for Counterstrike's

clients had given a lot of his men hope that someone gave a damn.

His gaze swept through the ballroom out of habit. A skinny pale waiter caught his attention. The man's short, spiked orange hair stood out like a beacon as he worked his way through the crowd. "What the fuck?"

"Problem?" Jumper asked.

"Skeet," Razor said. "Get him outside for a conversation. That little shit shouldn't be here."

"He won't be working this crowd alone," Sandman said.

"Find the others," Razor ordered. "Round them up and bring them to me. There's a rose garden east of the mansion. I'll be at the water fountain. Quick and quiet. No reason to worry the rich idiots."

He navigated his way to the exit nearest the garden. Fuck. Warning Ethan and Milo wasn't an option since they were neck deep in brown-nosing assholes right now.

As if sensing his thoughts, Frenzy spoke. "Cholo is probably around here somewhere hiding out like we are."

Right. The street-smart man who'd amassed a crew of local business owners and concerned citizens to combat local gang activity had somehow become a regular presence within the Scythes' daily lives. He and his brother, Mingo, popped up wherever Razor went.

He pulled out his cell and typed out a message.

Fountain in the rose garden east of the mansion. Potential problem we're handling.

He pocketed his cell and charged toward the fountain. Fuck. Bullshit was the last thing he wanted to deal with tonight—or ever.

"Hey! What the fuck, man?" Skeet's high-pitched voice sounded from a narrow walkway. Jumper and Sandman appeared and shoved the idiot and three others to their knees.

Skeet's eyes widened when they landed on Razor. The other three whimpered.

"Skeet."

The man gulped. "R-Razor. W-What are you doing here?"

"Funnily enough, we were invited. Were you?"

"T-They needed waiters," Skeet said. "Just doing our part, you know?"

"Want to try that answer again?" Razor grabbed the man's orange hair and yanked hard. "Last chance."

"Okay. Okay." He held his hands up. "I shouldn't have come."

"That's the understatement of the century," Frenzy remarked. He looked over at Sandman. "Did you pat them down?"

"Yeah," Jumper answered as he tossed a small bag to the ground. It thunked near Razor's feet. "They must've just gotten started."

"You really thought you'd get by pickpocketing here?" Razor kept his voice low despite the anger rolling through him. He punched Skeet's face. "Call a prospect. Get a van over here. He can take them to the compound. We'll deal with these idiots later."

Jumper nodded. "I'll stay with them until the van gets here."

Razor took the bag and glared at Skeet and his idiot crew. Footsteps sounded from the left. He looked that direction as Cholo and Hazard appeared.

"Problem?" Hazard asked, his intense gaze on Skeet and the other three men. The former spec ops soldier had probably figured out the situation, but Razor nodded.

He held out the bag. "I recognized Skeet. We rounded up his crew, but we could have missed one. Small-time pickpockets and identity thieves."

"Shit," Cholo said as he took the bag.

"Open up a lost and found near the coat check area," Hazard told Cholo. "We'll announce some things were found in the bathrooms and in the ballroom near the end of the event."

Smart. "We'll handle Skeet and the others."

"Good. Filing police reports for this would spread like wildfire with the media," Hazard said. "If you need help, let us know."

"Not that we have time to breathe much less help with anything," Cholo commented.

Razor suspected the situation hadn't improved much. The Scythes would do more, but he knew better than to offer. The ball was in Counterstrike's court.

"I can get a few prospects here to cover for those four if you're shorthanded now," Razor offered.

"No. This makes sense. Bea mentioned there were more waitstaff than we'd expected," Hazard said. "We thought the place we hired had sent extras intentionally."

"Thanks, man," Cholo said.

Razor offered a chin lift as the two men left. Jumper and Sandman guided the four idiots they'd apprehended toward the parking lot. He motioned for Frenzy to head back inside because he needed a few moments alone to calm down.

He stared up at the inky sky. A few random stars shone, but he knew there were more. That was one thing he missed about the sandbox. The stars had been brighter over there, as if offering refuge from the hell they'd been in.

"Rough night?" The breathy inquiry drew his attention to the beauty who'd camped in his thoughts and refused to leave.

"How much of that did you see?"

"Enough." Flashes of long, sexy leg teased him as she approached. The royal blue dress stopped mid-thigh and fit her curves like a second skin. "You always pop up when we need it. Like a modern-day Robin Hood."

Razor chuckled. "Skeet was the Robin Hood since he was stealing from the rich. That'd make me Sheriff Nottingham, and I'm far from the law, beauty."

Pink stained her cheeks. "I don't know. You know your way around weapons and ride off into the sunset on a motorcycle like the Lone Ranger."

"You've got all your fictional characters mixed up." He sat at the fountain. "Are you hiding or just retreating from your fans?"

"Like any of those pretentious pricks give a damn about me and my brothers. They want to be seen with us. Attention whores."

Amusement rolled from him. "Careful. A reporter could be lurking."

"Let them. I have nothing to hide," she said as she sat. "I saw you looking up. Are you a star gazer?"

"Not anymore."

"That's one bad thing about the city. No stars to guide us." She glanced up, her full, red lips pursed. "They're brighter in the hill country. I sometimes study them when I go see my mom."

He'd read all about Jen's mom and the center the Davenports founded. She'd suffered a severe TBI at the hands of her husband. "I admire what you and your brothers have done. Counterstrike is a solid organization. You should be proud."

"It's never enough, you know," she whispered. "For every one person we help, there are ten more who won't ever get help."

"You're making a difference. That's all we can hope for. Leave this world better than we found it."

"Is that what you do?" Her dark gaze cut to him. "What makes Razor tick?"

"I have no clue. If you figure that out, let me know." He tugged a curl of her hair toward him and wound it around his finger. "You shouldn't be out here alone with me."

"Why not?" She leaned closer. "Do you have naughty intentions?"

Fuck yeah. So many. "You're a temptress."

"Maybe I just see the man you try hard to hide," she whispered. Her fingers slid down his shirt, then back up. "You've got a little blood right here."

"It's not the first time I've gotten dirty," he admitted. "It won't be the last. Men like me aren't for beauties like you."

Her sexy eyes narrowed. "That's not your call."

Blood surged to his dick. He threaded his fingers through her thick hair and tugged her closer. Their breaths intermingled as his heart jackknifed. Fuck. One taste. Just one caress of her mouth against his would make all the bullshit worth it.

"Jen!" The shout shook the dregs of lust off Razor. He surged backward as one of her brothers approached.

"Ethan," she said quickly. How the fuck did she tell them apart so easily? He'd yet to note any identifiable differences between Ethan and Milo.

His gaze slid from her to Razor. "What's going on?"

"Oh, the usual. Razor and his crew saved the gala from a pickpocket crew cleaning everyone out." Jen stood. "What are you doing out here? Where's Marisol?"

"Hiding out in the nook behind the dessert bar." Ethan grinned. "She said the baby needed chocolate."

"My niece has excellent taste. She probably smelled the imported yumminess in the fondu fountain. I think I'll go help her with that. I could use something tasty to stave my cravings."

Her sultry gaze roamed down him. Fuck. He shoved his hands in his trousers. "Cholo and Hazard have the property we got off Skeet and his crew. I'll be inside if anyone needs me."

Frenzy was right. Razor needed to stay far, far away from the temptation that was Jennifer Davenport. Billionaire beauties like her shouldn't be tainted by men like him.

* * *

One and a half weeks ago...

Police cars and an ambulance took up most of the circular driveway. Jen's pulse pounded hard as she willed the tears of anger away. Now wasn't the time to fall apart. There'd be time for that later.

No. There was never time to process the shit she saw. There was always another case, someone else in trouble.

She threw her silver BMW into park near the police cruisers and grabbed her briefcase. Details of what had happened were sketchy. All she knew was one of their newest clients was in trouble.

She headed toward the cluster of policemen and waited for the man in the suit to acknowledge her presence. "Detective. I'm Jennifer Davenport of Counterstrike. Two of my clients reside here."

"And your clients are?" Relief filled her when he didn't immediately push her away or spout the nonsense that they couldn't talk about an ongoing case. Yada yada yada.

Counterstrike finally had a strong foothold with the APD. They were respected for the work they did. She took a deep breath. "Cindy and her son, Samuel."

Grim expressions appeared when the two names were mentioned. Her stomach tightened. "What happened?"

"I can't give you specifics, as you know, but Cindy Greph's sustained multiple gunshot wounds. Her son has minor injuries that are being treated in the ambulance. We're waiting for child services."

Shock kept her muted for a few seconds. She'd spoken with Cindy three days ago. Her husband was violent. The woman had steadfastly refused Counterstrike's plea for an immediate removal from their home. She'd wanted to give him one more chance to get help for his rage issues.

Shit. She should have forced the issue and demanded she put her personal safety and that of her son as a priority. She and Milo had both argued that point, but the woman was determined.

She pulled out a business card with a trembling hand and gave it to the detective. "Please contact us in the morning once you have more information. I trust you haven't attempted to speak with my client yet?"

"No," the detective said softly. "He's too traumatized. We believe he witnessed whatever occurred here, so we will need to speak with him."

Jen nodded. "Certainly. We'll do our best to accommodate your request as quickly as possible. I'm sure you understand his mental health takes priority, though."

The detective nodded. "I understand and will respect Counterstrike's process."

Thank goodness. She pulled out her cell and hit the button to call headquarters as she made her way toward the ambulance. Field answered on the second ring.

"Field, I need a current listing of all available foster homes that are Counterstrike approved forwarded to me immediately," she said. "We have an eight-year-old boy who'll need placement. His mother was just murdered, likely by his father."

"Fuck." The man's muttered curses continued in a stream of creativity even she admired. "Give me three minutes."

It'd take longer than that for CPS to show up. She shouldered her way through a cluster of uniformed officers and stopped at the rear of the open ambulance.

A young woman worked on putting a small butterfly bandage on a cut along Sam's forehead. She paused as if sensing Jen's presence. "Can I help you?"

"Jennifer Davenport. I'm Sam's attorney," she said. "From Counterstrike."

The woman's gaze flashed wide. Sam trembled in the large blanket wrapped around his small frame. "He's in shock."

Jen toed off her heels and pulled herself up into the ambulance. She sat beside the paramedic and ran a hand down Sam's hair. "Sam, honey. Do you remember me?"

The boy's attention shifted to her. Tears ran down his small face as he nodded. "Miss Jen with the cookies and milk. Mom said I could trust you."

"That's right." She squeezed his shoulder. "We're going to figure all of this out, okay? The only thing you need to do right now is not talk about what happened here tonight without me there, okay? If anyone tries to make you answer questions, you tell them I have to be there with you."

The boy nodded. "He hurt her. He wouldn't stop." The boy cried. "It was so loud and there was so much blood. I tried to get to her, but she made me promise to hide."

"Ssh." Jen wrapped the boy in a tight hug and glared at the paramedic.

"I didn't hear anything," the woman commented. "I admire the work your group does. I wouldn't jeopardize the boy. Or anyone."

"Thanks." She pulled back and settled into a protective perch in front of the boy as the woman continued looking over his injuries.

Her cell phone chimed a few moments later. She thumbed through the potential foster families. They'd all volunteered their homes for children Counterstrike was helping. All the places had been kitted out with HERA drones and any other tech that'd help keep the families safe.

An older black woman appeared at the mouth of the ambulance just as the paramedic finished. Jennifer offered a tight smile. "Mrs. Woods."

"Ms. Davenport. I see you got here before me." Her concerned gaze swept toward the house, then back to Sam. "I take it he's one of yours."

"He is."

The woman visibly relaxed. Jen couldn't help but offer a small smile. She knew the work CPS personnel did was grueling, both emotionally and physically. Long hours. Far too little in pay. The emotional scars of what they saw, though…that was the true damage done to brave people like Mrs. Woods.

"Let's talk for a few moments," Jen said. She glanced at the paramedic. "Can I leave him with you a few minutes?"

"Of course."

"I'm going to be right outside, Sam. Okay?" She waited until the boy nodded. "We'll talk in a minute. You're safe. I promise you no one will hurt you, okay? If you get scared, call out for me."

The boy nodded again.

Jen jumped out of the ambulance and toed on her heels. She made her way to where Mrs. Woods was standing and knelt down to open her briefcase. She thumbed through the contents until she found the thin case file she'd started for Cindy and her son.

"How long have you been the boy's attorney?" Mrs. Woods asked.

"Three days," Jen answered quickly. "His mother came in for an initial intake but refused our pleas for an immediate removal from the home. She wanted to give her husband another chance to get help."

The woman's lips thinned. She'd likely heard that thousands of times in her career. How many people had fallen into the pitfall of another chance? Too many.

"I have all the formal paperwork."

"You always do. I wish everyone had someone like you in their corner," Mrs. Woods said. "It makes my life simpler, despite the grim circumstances. At least I know he'll be protected."

"He's protected because of you and what you do," Jen said quickly. "I'm just here to help in whatever way I can."

"That's appreciated."

"I'm afraid I don't have much information right now," Jen said. She offered the file. "Here's what I have for personal data on his mother, father, and Sam. No relatives on the father's side and Sam's mom was estranged from her parents. We've located them, but that's about all we've done at this time."

"We'll need to place him temporarily," Mrs. Woods said.

Jen pulled out her cell and forwarded the list Field had given to the contact number she had for the CPS worker. "We recommend any of these, preferably one of the top three. His father is extremely violent and likely responsible for tonight. Anywhere else would put Sam and the foster family at grave risk."

Mrs. Woods' lips thinned. Some of the social workers argued at this point, citing they knew their jobs better than Jen did—which was true. She wasn't a social worker. But she understood the underlying risks far more than anyone at CPS.

"Very well." She looked through the list. "I've worked with the Jamesons a few times. I'll contact them."

Jen nodded. "I'd like to accompany you until he's settled, if that's okay."

"Of course." It'd taken many cases to get that of course. Relief filled Jen.

Her gaze swept toward the house. *I'm sorry I couldn't save you, Cindy, but I'll do everything in my power to protect your son. We'll get you justice. One way or another, your husband will pay for this.*

She typed out a message to Field. *The Jamesons are up. Activate their system and let them know CPS will contact them shortly.*

Jen did what she could, but in times like these—where it ended in a loss rather than a save—it was difficult to accept. She rarely remembered those Counterstrike had helped to a new life. It was the Cindys who haunted her thoughts often. One day there wouldn't be any more Cindys. One day they'd do enough to prevent what'd happened today.

CHAPTER 4

Present day...

The only easy day was yesterday. Razor may have left military service, but the mantra had followed him and his Scythe MC brotherhood. Solidarity and respect were the blood and tendons but protecting those they cared about were the bones—which was why he and his crew were turning left into the neighborhood nearest the compound and following a South Sider.

Keeping the tentative peace between the gangs in Austin had become a Scythe job. They were a neutral crew with enough clout to enforce the peace—a peace that might be broken because of an idiot who'd pissed off the South Siders.

Fucking Dart. Trouble always found him. What few braincells he had left had apparently vacated the past few days because the man had gone too far tonight. Razor motioned for everyone to park in the street nearest Dart's rental. They'd already closed off the neighborhood so he wouldn't squirt.

Razor headed toward the sidewalk where Homer and two of his "lieutenants" stood. The fucker had no clue what the term truly meant. Dealing with the South Siders grated on Razor's nerves, but he didn't want a bloodbath in one of the neighborhoods the Scythes were protecting.

"You want to tell me what the fuck is going on?" Razor asked. Arms crossed, he glared at the short gang leader.

"Dart dipped his dick into the wrong girl." Homer glared at the house. "My cousin. She saw the error of her ways and scraped him off, but he's not taking no for an answer. He's gonna pay."

Shit. Sandman and Jumper settled into a protective stance to Razor's sides. "She in there?"

"From what we know, yeah." Homer touched the handgun in his waistband. "This isn't my style, man. We would've gone in and bathed the house in blood, but he's on your turf."

Razor grunted. They'd been working on extricating Dart from the neighborhood for a while now.

"That's a problem we're rectifying," Sandman commented.

"Jumper, take half the crew to the back. Make sure he doesn't squirt," Razor ordered. "The rest are with me."

"We aren't sitting this out," Homer said.

"Let us make initial entry," Sandman said. "If your cousin is in there, we don't want her hurt. We've got the skillset to get her out safely."

"So do we," Homer said with a chuckle as he looked over at his two men.

Arguing the finer points of former spec ops soldiers versus street thugs wasn't on tonight's agenda. Razor grunted his response and withdrew his sidearm. He motioned toward the house and approached.

He took the three squat steps up onto the porch. The hard pounding of fists against the wooden door echoed through the area. "Dart! Get your scrawny, coked-up ass up and open the fucking door!"

"Shit!" The shouted response boomed from the house. Razor growled his frustration and kicked the door near the handle. Wood splintered.

Weapon drawn, Razor went left while Sandman went right. They'd done this dance a thousand times over the years. Pale light splayed into the living room from the small dining area off the kitchen. A rat scurried across the discarded takeout containers and spilled beer cans.

"Dart!" Sandman shouted.

"Get out. I'll kill her. I swear I will." The man's voice was loud but edged with an emotion Razor recognized. Fear. Fuck. The only thing worse than an idiot was a terrified idiot.

Razor angled down the narrow hallway and turned left, weapon aimed at the bastard of the hour. A petite woman with long, brunette hair stared at Razor through terror-filled eyes. "What's your name, sweetheart?"

"Lupita," she whispered.

"Let her go," Sandman ordered.

"Can't do that. She wanted out. I'm getting her out." Dart shook his head. Oily hair knocked back and forth across his eyes as his hand trembled on the grip of the gun he pointed at Lupita.

"I changed my mind. Please. Help me." Tears filled her wide eyes.

Dart tightened his grip on her. "Shut up! You're lying. You wanted out. You begged me to help you. And I did. Then you fucking started lying saying you didn't want out. Bitch!"

"Shut up before I lose patience with you, Dart," Razor growled. "Lower your weapon and we'll talk this out."

"She's lying!" He shook Lupita with the arm he had around her.

"I can't leave. They'll hurt Tia." The softly uttered admission thundered through the room.

Tia. The old woman owned the nickname because she treated everyone like family. Every gang in the area loved the woman. How was she involved in this?

"Who will?" Sandman asked. "Your cousin?"

"No. He'd never hurt Tia." Lupita sniffled. "There's a new crew rolling in. They found me at the motel I was crashing at. They said if I wasn't a South Sider anymore then I was theirs. Muy mallo. Better the monster I know than them."

A new crew? Razor tensed. That's the last thing Austin needed. They'd barely brokered the peace between the existing gangs. "We'll figure out who they are and keep you safe."

A cockroach scurried from the closet behind Dart. Jumper emerged from the small space and shoved his weapon against the man's head. "Go ahead. Be stupid."

Dart cursed and lowered his weapon. Lupita darted toward Razor and Sandman. They both lowered their weapons as Jumper secured Dart.

"Lupe?" Homer's agitated voice rose from the living room.

The woman trembled. Razor put a hand on her shoulder. "You're safe. We'll protect you, but we need to talk everything through so we're all on the same page. Come on. Homer needs to see you, so he knows you're safe."

"He'll kill Dart."

"Probably. We'll figure it out," Sandman said.

Razor guided the woman into the living room and scanned the area. Trash littered the area. Cockroaches crawled around the sofa and end table. "Someone take pictures of this filth. If Dart survives his stupid choices, he's out."

One of the prospects pulled out a cellphone. Everyone's attention shifted to Homer as he drew his cousin into a hug. The woman cried.

"Cuz, you should've come to me," Homer whispered.

"I just wanted out, away from all this. I'm sorry." She sniffled.

Gang life was difficult to leave once you got in, but it was downright impossible for those born into it like Homer and Lupita. He empathized with the young woman's predicament. More importantly, he'd made sure his Scythe MCs were set up to extricate people like her if they wanted a fresh start.

"If you want out, we'll get you out," Razor promised. "That's what the Scythes do. You'll be free and clear."

"I can't. They'll hurt Tia."

"We'll sort that out," Sandman said. He reached for Dart.

Razor glared at Dart when he was shoved to his knees. "Time to start talking, idiot."

"I told you already. Lupe wanted out. I said I'd help. Then she fucking changed her mind, but I knew she was lying. So, I forced the issue." He glared up at Razor. "You would've done the same thing."

"Like hell I would." Razor punched Dart's face. "Tell us about the new crew she mentioned."

"I don't know shit about them. Skeet's heard stuff from the northside. They're recruiting heavily in the areas surrounding Austin." Dart spit blood onto the carpet. "That ain't my problem."

Fucking Skeet. He and his merry group of morons had spent three days learning a valuable lesson. It should've been longer.

"It is now," Sandman growled. "Your stupid ass shouldn't have been helping anyone get out of a gang. There's a process set up for that, one the Scythes handle. Not you."

"You really want out?" Homer asked as he drew back from Lupita. "Why?"

"I met someone. He's in Houston," she whispered. "But it doesn't matter. I've gotta stay here or they'll kill Tia."

"To fuck they will," one of the South Siders shouted. "Where are they?"

"Enough," Razor said, his voice booming. "No one is rolling on them until we have more information. We all agreed the Scythes would handle any outside threats."

"Then you'd best get on that," Homer advised. "My patience is thin. What about Dart? He needs a lesson in respect."

"We'll make sure he gets it," Jumper said. "Then he's out. I'll escort him to Austin's city limits myself."

"You can't do that!" Dart shouted.

"Watch us." Sandman motioned toward the door. "Get him outside. Have a prospect take him to the compound."

Razor waited until the living room emptied. Homer hovered near his cousin but maintained a distance. "Let's talk through the next few steps, man. I know this is hard, but we've gotta do what's best for Lupita."

"No shit." Homer ran his hand down his face. "Never thought my own blood would want out."

"I love him," she whispered. "We just wanted to be together. I had an out. He didn't. Please."

"You agreed to the terms of the peace agreement," Sandman said. "Anyone who wants out of any crews is allowed to move on."

"I know!" Homer shouted.

"I'm sorry." Tears streamed down Lupita's face.

"Don't cry," the man said. The hardened gangster fractured and drew his cousin into his arms. "We'll get this figured out. You're familia. That matters more than anything."

Razor analyzed potential locations to stash Lupita until they got more information about the new crew who had threatened her. None of them made him feel okay, except for one option. He pulled out his cell and thumbed through the contacts until he found Cholo.

The man was a king of the street. Now that Cholo was tied to Counterstrike, he held even more weight on the street. More importantly, the organization had a string of safe houses within and around Austin, all heavily secured. If they had one available, it would be the best place for Lupita.

"Yeah."

"We've got a situation I could use your help with," Razor said. "Homer's cousin wants out of the South Siders, but we've got an external threat. A new crew has rolled in. I need a safe place for her to crash until we get everything sorted and make sure she and Tia are okay."

"Tia? Fuck, man. She's an icon. Her old man started the South Siders. Her brother started the other gang a year later. There's no way she's down with tapping out," Cholo said. "I can believe Lupita, but not Tia."

"The new crew threatened Tia if Lupita didn't join them," Razor said. "We need to investigate them and neutralize any threat. Does your new group have a safe house we can use?"

"Yeah, but we're stretched thin on cases right now. It'll be on you to provide manpower."

Right. "Understood."

"You'll need to run by the Davenports and get the keys and entry info," Cholo said. "They landed a couple hours ago, so expect a hostile greeting 'cause they didn't want to be bothered with Counterstrike shit tonight."

Every meeting Razor had with the billionaire twins started off hostile. "Thanks, man. We owe you."

"I'm afraid I'll be cashing that favor in now."

Razor tightened.

"Jen's got a custodial case. The boy's father murdered the mom in front of him, but the criminal case is on hold—

which means the prick's parental rights are still in play for the time being. The kid's maternal grandparents are wanting custody even though they've never met the kid. Hell, they scraped their daughter off long ago."

"Not sure how we can help with that," Razor commented.

"The custody hearing is open court tomorrow. The bastard will be there. Jen's gotta bring the kid because the judge wants to talk with him privately so the decision can be made immediately," Cholo said. He expended a weary breath. "We don't have enough manpower to provide a security detail for her and the boy. I'm hoping your crew can handle that."

"Yeah. We've escorted more than a few abuse victims to and from court so they aren't alone. Send us the details and we'll be there." The Scythes may have just surfaced in Austin a year ago, but they'd run with another crew up north before that. Add in the other crews they'd forged alliances with, and Razor's club was a formidable force throughout the country.

"You'll have to talk Jen around to this."

Anticipation surged within Razor. The brilliant, beautiful brunette had been on his mind more than he cared to admit. Talking to her was far from a hardship. "I'll take care of Jen."

"Bea's worried about her," Cholo commented. "My cousin's tight-lipped, though, and won't say why. I think some shit's going down with this case Jen hasn't shared with us."

"I'll see what we can find." Razor clicked off and glanced at Sandman. "Call a church for dawn. We're escorting a kid to a custody case in the morning. Protection detail for him and Jen."

"And the safe house?" Homer asked.

"I'll get Lupita sorted. You can't know where it is," Razor said. He wasn't tight with Counterstrike, but he respected their cause and wouldn't jeopardize it by being loose with safe house locations. Even though Scythes had helped extract several people from violent homes, they'd yet to take any to one of the renowned locations that Counterstrike protected them at.

"That's bullshit." The man's jaw twitched.

"This isn't up for debate," Razor said with a growl in his voice. "Lock your personal shit down and man the fuck up. This is about your cousin."

"She'll be safe?"

"Yeah. We'll keep people there with her just to make sure." He glanced at Jumper as he returned from outside. "Are you in?"

"Yeah. I'll grab a couple others. We'll take her to the compound until you get the address to us."

Thank fuck Razor had a competent crew. Their initiative left him and Sandman open to handle the more serious problems—like a new crew rolling into Austin.

And a beautiful attorney who needed protection.

Razor pulled his motorcycle to a stop in front of a three-story house on the corner of a dark street. He was a bit surprised he'd rolled into the posh Hyde Park neighborhood after two in the morning without being stopped by local police. Folks in this area didn't tend to wander the streets this late at night.

Exterior lights flicked on and flooded the area. He winced as he moved toward the sidewalk. The large door opened and one of the Davenport twins exited. Lips thinned and eyes narrowed, he closed the distance and glared at Razor a few moments before shoving a folder toward him.

"Everything you need is in there," the man said.

"I appreciate it."

"We'll have someone watching surveillance if we can, but you're likely on your own. Cholo said this was for a relative of the South Sider leader. They don't know where this place is or we'll have a problem."

"Understood." Razor took the folder. "Our computer person, Anarchy, might have questions about patching into the security system."

"The number to contact is in the folder, but we're spread thin right now."

Razor nodded. He glanced over at the small bungalow beside the house. "Cholo's sending information to me, but is the kid here with Jen?"

"What the fuck business is it of yours?"

"Cholo asked us to provide escort and protection for your sister and the kid tomorrow." Razor shrugged. "We've done it a few times. Consider it a favor for a favor."

"Milo's gonna lose his shit when he finds out. And no, the kid isn't here. He's with a trusted foster family." Ethan's gaze swept to the cottage where his sister lived.

Which meant Razor was talking with Ethan. Good to know. Ethan had a longer fuse than his brother when it came to Jen, from what Cholo had said. "My crew isn't as savvy as yours, but if there's anything we can do to help with your other situations, let us know."

Razor almost choked on the statement. Most Scythes were former spec ops or well-trained former military, which meant they'd give Counterstrike a good run if the scales were balanced. But billionaires had access to way better weapons and slick toys than Razor and the Scythes did.

"That's appreciated. You've already done a lot by helping with those cases Jen's been slipping to you. We just need to get the second batch of noobs trained. Soon." Ethan expended a weary sigh. "What's the situation with whoever you're taking to the safehouse?"

"Unsure. She wants out of the South Siders, something about a man she met in Houston. A new crew has rolled into the area north of Austin. They threatened Tia if she didn't join them. We'll be investigating and neutralizing that problem."

Ethan grunted. "Fuck. Shit never settles, does it?"

"It's bound to one day."

"You need help digging into them, let us know. We're wired into some serious tech these days."

"I appreciate it. Anarchy's got quite a few contacts he can call on. We'll do what we can and reach out if that's not enough." Razor turned toward his bike.

"Razor." He turned to face Ethan again. "Goes without saying, but I'll say it anyway. If anything happens to her tomorrow..."

"It won't."

"Foster parents are dropping the kid off here at eight," Ethan offered. "I'll try and have a word with her about this before your crew arrives. I'm thinking that conversation is overdue if Cholo called this favor in."

"He mentioned Bea's worried about her. He thinks there's more in play with this case than Jen's shared with everyone." Razor shoved the file into the storage bin and straddled his bike. "We'll see what we can find out and let you know."

"Some friends of ours will be here helping us train the noobs this weekend. If any of your crew wants in, let us know," Ethan said. "I know you all are mostly former military. Refreshers help."

Razor wasn't stupid. Cholo had hovered around Scythe territory more than usual, which meant Counterstrike was still curious about the brotherhood. What they did. How good they were.

"I'll mention it in church in the morning." Church was a

term for a meeting with all the Scythe members. "I'll let you know."

Staying on Counterstrike's good side was a smart play, especially if it got Razor's brothers refresher training. They did what they could to stay sharp, but they lacked the slick toys. He waited until the man was inside to roll out. His gaze stayed on the small cottage longer than it should. The sooner he got a couple hours sleep, the better.

CHAPTER 5

"I'm scared." The whispered admission hung within the quiet surroundings a few moments.

Me, too, little buddy. Me, too.

Jennifer Davenport steeled her resolve and touched Samuel's shoulder. The eight-year-old had grown up faster than he should have, a fact she couldn't undo. Anger had become a constant companion since she'd taken on his case. "I'll be with you. No one will mess with you. If you get scared, flash the signal and I'll help. You remember it?"

Sam held up his tiny fist. "W-What if he wins?"

"He won't." The entire custody battle was utter bullshit. The boy's father had murdered his own wife in front of Sam, but he was presumed innocent until found guilty in the criminal court. That alone should've automatically given custody of the boy to his grandparents. Today was a mere formality, but little boys didn't understand red tape.

The grandparents were a whole other nest of worries Jen couldn't ignore. They'd rolled into town demanding immediate access to Sam and talked about him as though he were a possession. Assholes.

The judge should've ordered the private questioning of Sam to be on a different day than the custodial hearing, but Judge Harcrest didn't believe in wasting time and wanted a decision made today—which meant little Sam would be in the same vicinity as his slimeball father no matter what Jen wanted.

Sam wouldn't be allowed in the open court custodial hearing itself, which meant he'd be with Bea. She'd wanted one of her brothers there with her, or even Hazard. Heck, any of Counterstrike's operatives would do.

But they were too busy, which meant Jen and Bea were on their own today. All Jen could hope was that they could keep Sam safely tucked away somewhere until his time with the judge came, which would likely be either immediately before or during the actual hearing.

Either way, Jen would deal because protecting Sam was all that mattered. He was her client. With his mom dead and his father, hopefully, set to serve a life sentence once found guilty, the only people left in his tiny world were his mom's parents. Sam didn't even know the grandparents.

They'd scraped off Sam's mom when she'd gotten married to his father. Even though Counterstrike hadn't found anything negative in their background checks, that alone was an issue for Jen. They hadn't cared enough about their daughter to remain in her life despite her obvious poor choices, so how could they possibly love and raise Sam?

Days like this made her hate her work. No. They made her determined to do the best for children like Sam. If she didn't, who would?

"We should've let Cholo or your brothers deal with this bullshit," Bea whispered. "One bullet would make that bastard go away."

While Jen agreed to a certain extent, she had to believe

the court system wouldn't fail Sam. She'd lived and breathed the law so long that turning her back on it seemed wrong.

"He's seen enough violence for several lifetimes," Jen said. "We aren't contributing to it. This is his fresh start."

She'd accepted the operational gray areas of Counterstrike because she trusted her brothers and all the operatives who worked for them. They didn't take bullshit from anyone, which meant they did whatever was necessary to keep their clients safe. Jen had pulled them out of enough problematic legal situations since the nonprofit started to feel comfortable with what they did.

But situations like Sam's made her hope for easy resolutions that didn't end with a body bag. Call her crazy, but a little boy shouldn't have to deal with bullshit.

"Counterstrike's covered over in cases right now," Jen said. "We've got this."

Loud roars sounded from up the quiet street. Unease pricked her skin as her gaze swept toward the sound. Was that…

The thunderous growls encompassed the area. Early morning sunlight splayed off polished chrome as the massive formation of motorcycles came to a halt in front of the house. A few of them halted in front of her silver BMW while the rest remained behind it.

"What the hell?" Jen's startled inquiry fractured the silence when the metallic beasts grew quiet.

Her gaze swept over the men as they moved from their bikes and shifted into a formation along the sidewalk and up into the yard.

Sam's wide gaze latched onto the men and the motorcycles as his little body vibrated with…excitement?

Me, too, little buddy. Me, too.

She'd found herself thinking about Razor whenever she heard the roar of a motorcycle or caught a glimpse of one since the gala. Okay, since before the gala. She had a weakness for bad boys, a fact she'd steadfastly hidden from her overprotective big brothers.

And Razor?

Well, he seemed like a twisted mix of bad boy and kickass operative. She wanted to dig into the mysteries he tucked away behind a don't-fuck-with-me attitude.

"Oh, yeah. So Cholo called a bit ago," Bea whispered. "It seems we have an escort to and from court today. It's apparently a thing some MCs do for certain cases."

So that's what Ethan's cryptic text this morning had meant.

You've got an escort to court today. Play nice. Let me know if there's trouble.

The Scythe motorcycle club. Anticipation quickened her pulse as three of the men prowled forward. Although she visually scanned the one to the left and the far right, her gaze latched onto the tall, muscular man with long black hair and darker than sin eyes.

Razor.

Yep, she was definitely intrigued by the mysterious man who'd come into their lives when Bea's trouble happened. Saying she was intrigued was like calling the Pacific Ocean a pond. Yeah, whatever they were doing here wasn't good. She needed to focus on the custody case.

Muscular thighs clad in worn denim clenched as Razor crouched in front of Sam. His sexier-than-sin face shifted into panty-melting terrain when he smiled. He glanced up at her. "Jen. It's been a while."

Right. She should probably speak.

"Razor," Bea offered. "Who are your friends?"

Sandman and Frenzy. Jen bit back the response because she hadn't told her assistant about her routine visits to the bar. She hadn't told anyone, but she knew her brothers and Victoria knew. Nothing got past them.

He pointed to his left. "Frenzy, my VP." Then his right. "Sandman, our Sergeant of Arms."

"Who are you?" Sam asked.

"I'm Razor. We heard you're going into battle and we're here to help you out." He took a small leather bundle from Frenzy and smiled. "This is for you. From this day forward, you're an honorary member of the Scythe MC. If anyone messes with you, they mess with us."

"Cool!" Sam yanked his hand from Jen's and took a step forward. "Do I get a bike, too?"

Sandman chuckled. "When you get older, yeah. If that's what you want. What's your name?"

"Samuel, but my friends call me Sam." He shifted from foot to foot. "You can call me Sam."

Jen bit her lip and suppressed the frustration rolling along her tongue. While she had heard of motorcycle clubs offering safe escort and protection for abused children and wives, this entire situation should've been discussed well beforehand—not less than an hour before the freaking court case.

"Let's get you suited up, little buddy." Razor held the child-sized leather cut up and grinned when Sam shimmied into it quickly.

His small face split into a huge grin for the first time since his mom's murder. Warmth eased some of the worry inside her, but doubt crept in. Offering him this "protection" today might boost his self-confidence for now, but what would happen when they went back to their lives and forgot about him? What then?

"We'll have a formal ceremony and picnic for you soon," Sandman said. "Everyone's looking forward to meeting you."

"They are?" Sam's gaze moved to the gathered men behind Razor. "Wow!"

Razor, Sandman, and Frenzy stood. The latter's gaze locked with Jen. "We'll maintain a presence around the courthouse, in the corridors, and in the courtroom. When you're done, we'll grab burgers somewhere or whatever our little buddy is in the mood for. Then we'll bring you back here and go from there."

"You can't just..." Jen bit off the rest of the words and glanced down at Sam.

Wasn't this what she wanted? She'd wanted one of her brothers present today. Although Razor was far from being Ethan or Milo, he exuded the same lethal prowess, maybe even more so than the Counterstrike operatives.

Because he's a bad boy you want to climb like a tree.

"Please, Miss Jen. They can come with us, right?"

She knelt. "Are you sure you want them to come with us? You don't know them."

"I didn't know you either," the boy whispered. "Dad can't mess with all of them."

And there it was. His biggest fear voiced for all to hear. She touched his shoulder. "Your dad won't hurt you ever again. No one will. I promise you that."

"And Razor and the others can protect you, too," Sam said. "Dad's gonna be really mad. Real mad."

"I'll handle your dad, Sam. That's my job." Determination filled her voice as she stood. "He's not riding on a motorcycle. Not today."

"He'll ride with you," Razor said. "When and if he's ready, we'll start slow and make sure he's properly educated on riding with someone on a bike. We usually start with a sidecar first, but we'll come up with a plan."

"If you do this today..." The unspoken threat hung between them. They couldn't abandon him afterward.

"He's wearing our cut," Sandman said. "He's one of us until he decides otherwise."

Jen wasn't fully in the know about MCs, but she knew enough to understand the importance of a cut and what they'd given Sam. Protection. Brotherhood.

"Then we'd better get to court," Jen said. She squeezed Sam's shoulder. "Are you ready?"

"Yes!" He pumped his fist in the air.

Razor crouched down and pulled something from his pocket. He took Sam's hand. "There are a lot of evil monsters in this world, Sam. My brothers and I have fought them for a long time. We never fight alone, and you won't either. We might not be there in the judge's chambers today, but we'll be surrounding you and there in spirit. It's okay to get scared. When you do, squeeze this and know you aren't alone. Keep your eyes on Jen if that's easier, but you're a Scythe warrior now. He won't ever hurt you again."

The boy looked down at the small motorcycle and gave it a squeeze.

"We can't be with you when you talk to the judge, but your dad won't be there either," Sandman said. "We'll keep an eye on him. We'll also be in the custodial hearing since that's open to the public. Razor and I will stay with you and Bea while we wait for you to talk with the judge."

Sam squeezed the motorcycle again and nodded. His lips thinned. "He's gonna be real mad. He's already threatened Miss Jen."

Razor's eyebrows rose. Damn. She hadn't realized Sam knew that. "I'm not scared of your dad, Sam. I have a lot of people who'll keep both you and me safe."

Ethan and Milo were going to go apocalyptic when they heard about the threats. Plural. Sam's dad was a real piece of work, but Jen had dealt with assholes like him many times.

"Sandman and I will remain with Sam," Razor

repeated. "There's an army at your back now, though I suspect there would've been if your brothers knew about the threat."

Jen tensed. Now wasn't the time for that conversation. She nodded. "Then let's get to the court. She paused and looked at Razor. "Thank you for this."

"Do what's best for Sam. That's all the thanks we need." Razor whistled and made a motion with his hand. Everyone behind him converged to their bikes.

Jen tried to count how many but stopped at forty. Her mind reeled. It was a veritable army, just like Razor had promised. How had they organized this so quickly?

They're warriors.

Knowing she and Bea weren't alone today eased most of her worry. She had no doubt the custody hearing would go in her favor, not that she was pleased with either option for little Sam.

"Girl, you and I are having a long talk later. Threats? What the hell?" Bea asked.

"Nothing serious." The lie slid out easily enough. Bea had enough to worry about.

"And the eye candy? He's looking at you like he'd strip you bare and lick every inch." Bea wiggled her eyebrows. "But what's really interesting is how comfortable you are around him and the others. You've seen them more than at that gala a few weeks ago."

"They've helped a few people we couldn't," Jen said. "They're always willing to help anyone who needs it."

"That's so cool." Sam stroked the leather cut. "I'm one of them now. Wow."

She suspected he hadn't had many people in his short life he could rely on. She just hoped Razor and his MC weren't about to shred his young heart with the solidarity and protection they'd offered today. If they did? Well, she'd show

Razor and his crew exactly what happened when she got angry.

* * *

Unease settled in Razor's gut as his gaze swept the courthouse's long corridor. Too many people congregated with too few guards. He glanced at Sandman, whose head remained on a swivel. He'd likely sensed the same tension thickening the air.

"The judge thought my cut was cool!" Sam exploded with excitement as he sat on the padded bench in the nook nearest the court hearing. His little legs pumped back and forth as he chomped on the M&Ms Bea had given him moments ago.

Razor wasn't sure mentioning the Scythes was a good thing since most people had negative preconceptions about motorcycle clubs in general. Hopefully word had spread amongst the rich folk that the Scythes weren't a typical MC. They were about brotherhood and protecting their neighborhood, not drugs, whores, guns, or any of the other shit some groups exploited for money.

They'd opened a couple of shops when they'd first arrived. Word spread fast that they made damned good custom rides and overhauled pieces of shit cages, aka cars, better than anyone. Razor and Sandman hoped to open a personal security company and use the brothers not good with bikes or vehicles to man that endeavor, but it'd be a while before they had the cash to get it going.

"He was good to you?" Sandman asked Sam.

The boy nodded. "I didn't like talking about some of the stuff, but I did." He squeezed the motorcycle Razor had given him. "I told him I didn't know my grandparents and didn't want to go there. I want to stay with Miss Jen. Or you."

Razor tightened. The kid clung to them quick, likely

because he hadn't had many good role models in his world—which sucked since a crew of military rejects wasn't exactly a stellar model for anyone, especially a little kid.

Rejects. Anger surfaced within him whenever he thought about the circumstances that'd forced most of them out of military service. None of the higher ups had wanted to hear most of the reasons why behind some of their decisions.

While Razor hadn't been around for all of the situations, he'd heard the stories from his new brotherhood and believed them because the shit that'd gone down with Razor, Sandman, and Frenzy was enough for him to know bullshit brewed deep beneath Uncle Sam's surface.

He'd gather evidence and prove his men's cases eventually. Until then, they had a new brotherhood—one that wouldn't turn their backs on them for doing the right thing.

Heels tapped against the slate hallway. Razor's attention angled toward the sound. Jen approached, her steps confident despite her thinned lips and wary expression. Blood surged to his cock when he noted the snug skirt encasing her long legs.

She set her briefcase down when she arrived and crouched in front of Sam. An elderly couple arrived before she could speak.

"Is that him? Is this Samuel?" The elderly woman gripped her necklace. "He doesn't look anything like her."

"It's ridiculous you haven't allowed us to see him until now," the man said. "He's ours."

Sandman growled as he put an arm around Sam. Razor stood and put himself between the boy and the couple. The man took a step backward.

"Do you mind? This is a private matter. We don't need your kind involved in this."

"His kind?" Jen asked, her voice spiked as she rose. "He's done more for Sam than you ever have. Perhaps you should keep that in mind. You won today, Mr. Gentry, but you are far, far from being off my radar. Mind your tongue and your manners."

"Of course. Apologies," the man said. "We appreciate all you've done for our grandson, Ms. Davenport, but we can take it from here."

"Take Sam to the bathroom," Razor ordered Sandman. "I think we need to have an adult conversation."

"Come on, little man." Sandman navigated the boy toward the bathroom nearby. Sam's eyes widened the farther they went as he looked over his shoulder.

"What is the meaning of this?" the man asked.

"Mr. Gentry," Jen started, "we should discuss what should happen next. I'm sure you're anxious to get Samuel home and acclimated to his new life, but I'm afraid that might not be wise."

"Why ever not?" Mrs. Gentry asked.

"His father is still a very big threat," Razor said. "I'm Razor, by the way. I'm President of the Scythe MC. We're a motorcycle club that helps protect children in Sam's situation. While you were in court, my men have been surveilling the area to make sure you are safe when you leave the courthouse."

"Oh my. I can't believe Cindy got herself into this mess. When will it ever end?" Mrs. Gentry asked.

"I'm more than capable of hiring my own private security if that's necessary, but I doubt *that man* will be a problem once we're out of the area. He is restricted from travelling, correct?" Mr. Gentry glared at Jen.

"He is," she hedged. "But that rarely stops men like him. He's obsessed with getting his son back."

"He'll be in prison soon enough," Mrs. Gentry said.

"That's the hope. Sam will need to testify. He's the state's primary witness." Jen glanced down the hallway, then locked gazes with Razor. "Is the perimeter secure?"

"We have three potential threats being watched," Razor said. "Two black sedans, one white cargo van. None of them have moved since court began. We'd like to escort Sam and his grandparents, along with you, to a secure location. If anyone follows, we can make a plan from there."

"Absolutely not," Mr. Gentry said. He adjusted his tie. "We have a flight booked for New York City in three hours."

"I understand you are anxious to get home, but that is not a smart decision." Jen motioned toward Razor. "My brothers are both former spec ops soldiers, as is Razor here. If they say we should be more cautious and ensure he's not being followed, then that is what we will do. Need I remind you that I am still Sam's attorney? If I feel your decisions are putting him in imminent danger, I will not hesitate to drag you both right back into that court. Judge Harcrest was quite forthcoming as to his expectations regarding your grandson. He wants us to work together to keep him safe."

"I don't see how keeping him here any longer could be in his best interest," Mrs. Gentry said.

"We have many resources we can use in this area, far more than his father," Razor said. "There are safe houses with extremely good security. It might not mean that much to you, but it will to Sam. His entire world has been imploded. Taking a few days to get to know him while he's surrounded by people he knows and trusts will help in the long run."

The elderly couple looked at one another a moment. Mr. Gentry nodded. "Very well. I'll make a few calls and let everyone know we'll be delayed. One week. That's all I can give this…situation."

"That's better than nothing," Jen muttered. "But you are not in charge of this situation, Mr. Gentry. I am."

Fuck yeah. Razor suppressed the chuckle rising in his throat. Jen was a little spitfire.

Sandman and Sam returned from the bathroom. The boy huddled near Razor and glanced up at his grandparents. "Who are you?"

"We're your grandparents," Mrs. Gentry said. "We're going to stay here for a few days and get to know one another. Then we'll take you home where you belong."

The boy shook his head and wrapped his arms around Razor's leg. "I live here. I don't want to leave Ms. Jen and Razor and the Scythes. They're having a picnic just for me. Ms. Bea promised she'd take me camping with her son, Ryan. We're going to be best friends. I already know it."

"Oh boy," Bea whispered. She knelt to face Sam. "I know this is scary, but you're a brave boy. We're going to figure everything out, okay? How about we get out of this stuffy place and get those burgers and tater tots we promised you this morning?"

"With extra cheese," Sam whispered.

"That's the only way to eat them," Razor said. He glanced at Bea. "Your cousin's restaurant?"

Bea nodded as she pulled out her cell. "I'll let him know we're on the way. He promised to shut the place down for everyone except us. How many of your crew are coming with?"

"Forty-two," Sandman answered quickly. "We'll get takeout for the others, who'll be securing the safe house and surrounding neighborhood."

Frenzy had coordinated who went where early this morning before church. They had additional members they could call in if shit went sideways, but Razor doubted that'd happen.

"And the safe house? Should I call Ethan or Milo?" Jen asked.

"No, we've got this," Razor said. "You've done your part, beauty. Let us take care of this."

Pink stained her cheeks as she smiled. "Okay, smooth talker. Let's get those burgers. I think we've all worked up an appetite."

Mr. Gentry guided his wife toward the exit. Razor studied the couple and noted their ill-fitting clothes. The woman's dress was too loose, her shoes scarred from use. Her husband's suit was snug around the waist and the jacket was at least a size too large.

"What type of work do you do, Mr. Gentry?" Razor asked.

"I'm the CFO of a hedge fund," he said. "My grandson will want for nothing."

Right. Razor pulled out his phone and sent a text to Anarchy. *Find everything you can on the grandparents. Gentry out of New York. Something's fishy.*

Anarchy responded immediately with a thumb's up emoji. Fucker thought he was twenty, not thirty-two, but he was smarter than anyone Razor had met.

"Trouble?" Sandman asked.

"Inconsistencies." Razor pocketed his phone and motioned for the Scythes near the door to exit first. The Gentrys might think they were in charge, but they weren't.

Jen was. That thought stirred his dick. Nothing was sexier than a beautiful, confident woman.

"What's going on?" Jen asked, her voice low.

"I'm not sure, but I'm going to find out." Razor draped his arm around her waist. "What do you think of the Gentrys?"

"I think they're working way harder to get their grandson than makes sense since they scraped their daughter off so easily," she said, her voice sexy and low against his chest when she faced him. "Why?"

Razor glanced at the elderly couple who'd paused just outside the door. "I think a CFO of a hedge fund would have a suit that fits and outfit his wife with a dress from this decade." He shrugged. "I smell something fishy."

Her eyebrows furrowed. "Interesting. Maybe I should text Victoria and have her use HERA to dig."

Victoria was a former FBI agent who'd recently married Milo Davenport and taken over the operational and investigation aspects of Counterstrike. HERA was a state-of-the art security platform that ran drones and had access to every database around the world.

It was the brainchild of the women at The Arsenal, the best private paramilitary organization in existence. Counterstrike was working with The Arsenal, but Razor didn't fully understand in what capacity. All he knew was that Counterstrike could access HERA whenever they wanted—a fact Anarchy had bemoaned more than a few times. To say the man was jonesing to play with it was an understatement.

"I just told Anarchy to dig. Maybe he and Victoria could work together on it, assuming she has time," Razor said.

"She'll make time," Jen whispered. "I'll pass the basic background check I did on them to you. That'll give Anarchy a starting point." Humor filled her voice when she said the man's name.

"You find our road names funny?"

She shrugged. "My brother is Gemini, then there's Hazard and Chatter…so, yeah. They amuse me because I can't help but make up stories of how they came to be. Did you get yours while in the military or after?"

Curiosity danced in her gaze as it roamed down his body. Fuck. Such a temptress.

"Before, actually. My Gramps had an MC." Razor smiled. "I'll tell you about it later. Let's head to your vehicle. Stay behind me. Sandman's got Sam. My crew will surround us."

Jen nodded. "Thank you for today. I'm not sure I said that

earlier. Knowing Bea and Sam weren't alone made my job a lot easier."

"I'm glad we could help." But their work was far from over. The simple escort to and from the courthouse had expanded to a protection detail on yet another safehouse and an investigation into the grandparents.

CHAPTER 6

Laughter echoed around Jen. Bea's cousin had shut down the restaurant and greeted her and her Scythe entourage with open arms. The jovial cook had proclaimed Sam king of the day and given him a chef's hat to wear while he ate.

Sandman had remained at Sam's side when the grandparents insisted the boy eat with them so they could "get to know" one another. While Jen wasn't a fan of the elderly couple pushing that agenda now, there was only so much she could do.

She took a sip of her mint iced tea and studied the man quietly assessing her across the booth. Razor was such an anomaly—cut from the same military cloth as her brothers and their fellow operatives, yet not. He exuded lethal badass in everything he did and had a commanding presence. The simplest nod of his handsome face had entire tables moving to comply with whatever unspoken order he gave.

But he also exuded calm in addictive waves. She could spend hours with him knowing he'd handle whatever worries dared enter his terrain. Would he be that calm and confident in bed?

Or would he unleash the restrained beast she sensed lurking within him?

Oh boy. He was trouble in all caps. She had no business lusting after Razor, but she couldn't control the raw, achy need he awakened within her. It'd been too long since she'd had a lover, even longer since she'd been serious with anyone.

Get real. You've never been serious about anybody. The bar is so high most men couldn't even find it.

"You're thinking pretty hard." His full lips upturned into a smoldering grin. "Anything you care to share with the booth?"

"Not particularly." She dipped a fry into the pepper filled ketchup on her plate and silently wished she'd ordered enchiladas. She loved Cholo's burgers, but it was a sacrilege not to get Mexican food here because it was the best in the city.

Damn. Now she really wanted enchiladas and homemade tortillas. "I should've gotten enchiladas."

"It's not too late." He motioned toward the waiter bringing out piping hot plates of yummy Mexican food to a table nearby. "Which are you favorite?"

She feigned a gasp. "That's like asking which child is your favorite. That's unacceptable. But cheese with onions and extra salsa on the side are my go-to. With extra flour tortillas because they are the best in the city." She sighed and pushed her half-eaten burger aside. "Did you get that info to Anarchy?"

"I did. He's already gotten in touch with Victoria." Razor chuckled. "He probably broke a world record making contact. He's been salivating to work with HERA. We may have created a monster."

"Edge vetted him a while back and approved him to help us if there was ever a need." Jen shrugged when Razor's eyebrows lifted. "Mary, aka Edge, is always several steps ahead of anyone. You get used to it. At least, that's what Ethan and Milo say."

"So that's why Cholo asked for a list of our members. Have you met her?"

Jen nodded. "I have met most of the main Arsenal crew. They tend to appear and shake things up. It's fun to watch the Counterstrike crew train with them." She took another sip of tea. "So why did you start an MC when you left the service?"

"That's a complicated answer. The short version is that we all needed a new brotherhood. Most of us came back either haunted by the shit we did or jaded by the shit we refused to do and got in trouble for afterward." He folded an empty sweetener packet with his long fingers. "Most of our official military service records show us dishonorably discharged for one reason or another, as you know. The club gives us what we need. Brothers. Solidarity."

Jen tightened. Nothing sucked more than a dishonorable discharge for proud military vets, especially if it wasn't warranted. "I take it that's not the real truth. You said as much in the first meet you had with us."

"You're perceptive."

She shrugged. "I know there's a lot of bad buried within all the good. Ethan and Milo have shared a few stories. So have some from The Arsenal. Soldiers are more than their service file. Redaction hides a lot of the truth."

"It does." Razor glanced around. "Gramps formed an MC when he left the service. He said if he couldn't do anything else for his brothers in arms that he could at least give them a home. A new purpose. Most of them weren't exactly welcomed back with open arms. It was a different time back then."

"Vietnam?"

Razor nodded. "I learned the values of solidarity, honor, and brotherhood from them. Gramps didn't run his MC like most clubs are run. They got rowdy at times, but everything was centered around their family and brotherhood bonds."

"I know there's a stereotype for MCs. Drugs, prostitution, weapons."

"Those are the top ones, but there are more," Razor said. "We aren't one percenters and we're fully legal. Most of our income comes from the shops we run. We're hoping to branch out into personal security at some point because not everyone in our crew is good at repairing and building bikes and cars."

"It sounds like you have a solid business plan."

"That's more Anarchy's turf. He's our Treasurer and resident computer geek." Razor took a sip of his soda. "How did you and your brothers decide on Counterstrike?"

"I'm sure you've heard the rumors about my family." She paused and noted his nod. "Right. So, we didn't want anyone to go through what we did. It's easy to judge someone's choice to stay in an abusive situation. It's far harder to help them get out. Not everyone has the means to escape. Now they will."

He fisted his hand. "I should kill that son of a bitch for hurting you."

"There are worse things than death," she commented. "Trust me. Ethan and Milo exacted the perfect punishment for him. Carving up his carefully constructed empire bit by bit and crushing his aspirations until all he had left was the shell of the monster he is was perfect. Add in the fact his so-called useless children now have all that he did and that is my father's newfound hell."

"You make it sound like they did it all." He leaned forward. "I'm thinking you were the brains behind the plan."

"I did my part." And then some. Jen didn't talk about her

part in the "downfall" with anyone. Ethan and Milo wanted to take the brunt of that to keep her safe. Not that anyone would dare come after them. "Dad insisted I be an attorney. I'm thinking he regrets that demand."

Razor chuckled. "Blood thirsty is sexy on you. Half my guys fell in love with you at the police station that day." Awareness arced between them when he took her hand. "Do they chase away all the men? Is that why you're still single?"

"The work we do takes a lot of our time. Not everyone understands." She peered into his intense obsidian gaze and shifted in her seat. "I won't ever be the little woman who stays at home barefoot and pregnant to raise the kids and cook dinner."

"Anyone who'd want that for you is an idiot. You're brilliant in the courtroom. The guys who were in there sent me so many texts praising your work it almost blew up my phone."

Jen chuckled. "I was wondering who they were texting. The judge wasn't a fan."

"That doesn't surprise me. We have very few fans." His voice turned husky. "I'd like to take you to dinner sometime."

"Why?" She blurted the question out before she could process it. He couldn't possibly be hard up for dates. The man was sex on a leathery stick. Women likely begged for a chance to be with him.

Ugh.

Jen could face off against the best attorneys in the world and never doubt herself. Outside the courtroom, however, she was a hot mess. Personal relationships had never been a big deal to her. In all honesty, she was terrified to make the same mistakes her mother had by trusting the wrong man.

Love was a risk she hadn't been willing to invest in.

"Why?" Razor chuckled. He stroked her palm. "You're the most beautiful and brilliant woman I've ever met. You take on assholes in court and kick their asses without hesitation. And no matter how hard I've tried, and trust me, beauty, I've tried plenty, I can't get you out of my head."

Wow. Jen took a deep breath. "That's..."

"I've got no business wanting time with you. You're a billionaire and I'm a very dirty-minded biker with a shady military past that won't go away anytime soon."

How dirty-minded? She processed the possible options. Her nipples hardened.

Okay, Jen. We need words to fill that sentence in. Get with it, brain. Work, already!

"Think about it," he whispered. "I'd even pick you up in a car if you want."

"I'd want the bike I think," she said quickly. "I've never ridden, though."

Her legs and body pressed against his? Yes, please.

"We could do a scenic ride in the hill country and have lunch at this place I know. It's small and out of the way but has the best chicken fried steak I've ever had."

"I'll think about it," she said. Her mind screamed yes, but her brain shouted no. Now wasn't the time to get involved with the sexy biker. Nope. She needed to focus on figuring out what was up with Sam's grandparents and doing her part to nail his father for murder.

She wasn't on the investigative team looking into the charges, but she had promised to help however she could—which meant getting Victoria looking into the sick bastard.

Then there were the threats. She'd been threatened many times before, so much in fact that she rarely took them seriously. But the dead cat left outside her office the other day had been the straw that broke the floodgates to her fear.

She'd taken pictures and phoned the police, but there wasn't much they could do. She was a bit surprised the police report hadn't flagged in HERA and warned Ethan or Milo there was a potential problem.

The fact they hadn't come to her was all the evidence she needed that they were neck deep in other problems right now. She'd go to them if anything else happened, though. It was irresponsible not to.

"I hate to drag down our conversation, but I need you to tell me about the threat Sam mentioned earlier," Razor said, as if reading her mind. Tension filled her shoulders. "I promised to keep you safe. As far as I'm concerned, that extends beyond today."

"You have enough going on," she argued. "I heard Sandman mentioning some woman you're helping."

"The cousin of the South Sider's leader. She wants out, but an unknown outside party is trying to force her into their gang. We're working on getting info," Razor said. Shock must've registered on her face because his eyebrows rose. "What? You thought I wouldn't tell you?"

"Why would you?"

"Because trust goes both ways. If I want you to trust me with your problems, I need to man up and share mine." He leaned back in the booth. "I assume it's Sam's father. The boy assumed it was."

"I think so," she whispered. "It started with vague notes left on my car or in my mailbox at the house." She swallowed. "The last one was a dead cat left at our office with a note saying I was next."

"Fuck." He surged forward. "Why haven't you told your brothers?"

"I filed a police report. There's not much we can do. There's no proof it's him." She shrugged. "Besides, they're busy with other cases."

"I think we both know that's bullshit. You'd take priority." His fingers ran along her wrist.

"I will tell them if anything else happens. Until then, I'm being cautious." Situational awareness had been drilled into her by her brothers.

"Until then we'll be watching over you," Razor declared.

"That's not necessary." But knowing he wanted to protect her made her body tingle. A part of her liked knowing he cared enough to offer.

"I disagree. You have a choice. You either accept our protection or we go to your brothers and tell them about these threats. You're too important to risk." Determination settled in his gaze and firmed his kissable mouth into a grim expression.

Ugh. She hated that he was right. She did need extra help right now. What if Bea got hurt because she hadn't told anyone? What if a client got caught in the crossfire?

"Fine, but I don't want to interfere with your other work. Oh, and as long as you're helping me, then I'll help you." Surely there was something they needed legal help with.

"Fair enough." He smiled. "I'm looking very forward to working with you."

Oh boy. Anticipation beaded along her skin. Her pulse quickened. Yeah, she was looking way more forward to it than she'd care to admit. It'd been way too long since a man excited her this much—if they ever had.

* * *

Razor ignored the jibes from his brothers as everyone headed into the compound. He angled toward the far corner and entered the dark office. He thunked the Mexican takeout on the desk in front of Anarchy.

"Talk to me," he ordered.

"Fuck, man. This HERA system is wicked sick." Anarchy opened the takeout container and dug into the enchiladas.

Cheese with onions, just like Jen had mentioned. "Victoria said I could come over and help her dig deeper tomorrow, but I got to video in and observe as she got HERA digging into Sam's dad and his grandparents. Victoria thinks the system will find everything we need by tomorrow morning, but she did promise I could play around either way."

"Yeah. Jen mentioned Edge had vetted you a while back."

"What?" Anarchy leaned forward. The chair squealed its protest as the tall man hunched forward. "Edge? As in one half of the Quillery Edge? Wasn't that the crew your buddy mentioned we should contact about clearing everyone's names? Fuck, I'm stupid. Of course the Quillery Edge is behind HERA."

"Yeah." Razor crossed his arms. Tex had mentioned them a few times the past several months, each time a bit more insistent than the last. He hadn't wanted Tex burning any of his contacts or himself by looking into Scythe troubles, though. "They're at The Arsenal now, who is tied with Counterstrike."

"Right. So we do our part in keeping the pretty sister safe and then maybe we can have a meet and greet with the infamous Quillery Edge."

"Possibly." He wasn't going to use keeping Jen safe as a play to help his crew, though. No. Keeping the intriguing woman safe was his sole mission at the moment. "Jen will be helping us out with some of our situations. Try and get them sorted when you get a chance."

"Any particular ones you don't want her to see?"

Anarchy wouldn't share any of their service-related issues. Those were locked down tight where only Razor had full access. That left the mundane shit they hadn't hired an attorney to deal with. Custody rights. Pending divorces. Frivolous lawsuits against the club.

"No." He took a step toward the door. "She's a damned

good attorney. Let's not let this chance pass because we're worried about what she might think about us. Her brother and their operatives don't exactly operate in the standard operational zone all the time."

Anarchy grunted and ran his hand through his bright red mohawk. "Cool. Cool. I'll get everything ready. When's she coming in?"

"I'm not sure. Knowing her, sooner than you'll be ready." He chuckled. Yeah, he was looking forward to spending some quality time with Jen.

A ride into the hill country. The plan formed in his mind as he made his way back into the main room of the compound. Guys congregated around the two pool tables in the corner while a few got drinks at the bar.

As far as typical MC compounds were concerned, this one was pretty tame. Sure, they had wild parties now and then, but none were over-the-top crazy because men like him wouldn't give up control of an environment long enough to go completely wild.

He maneuvered to the corner table in the back corner and sat. Cholo leaned back in the seat across from him. The man's voice was edged with curiosity. "I heard you had an interesting day."

"Three potential issues at the courthouse. One black sedan attempted to follow us," Jumper said. "Anarchy ran the plates. It's a rental temporarily assigned to Gentry Enterprises."

"Gentry? As in the grandparents?" Sandman asked.

"Yup." Jumper thumped the table with his fists. "Looks like boss man here was onto something. They're fishy."

Razor grunted. Using the word "fishy" in a text shouldn't have happened. The twisted fuckers around him would razz him for weeks about it. Assholes.

"Has Frenzy finished a protection schedule?" Razor asked. "We've got two safehouses to watch."

"He's working on it now," Sandman said. "At least they're both nearby and in proximity to one another. I've already asked everyone to remain here at the compound as much as they can during their downtime."

The compound was an old warehouse that they'd gutted and added twenty-five small bedrooms to along the two back hallways. Each room had a full-sized bed and a dresser and not much else. Communal showers were at the end of each hall with six bathroom stalls. It wasn't much, and Razor hated asking his brothers to crash there, but it made sense from an operational perspective.

And fuck knows they'd all crashed in worse conditions.

"Anything on the new crew?" Razor asked. "I want that shit off our radar soon."

"I chased Skeet down. Fortunately, the fucker was still lurking where he'd been dropped off," Cholo said. "The tats he described mark them as an El Paso-based crew. A buddy of mine is gonna call with what he knows since that's his turf."

"Good. Once we know what we're up against, we'll schedule a meet with them, us, Homer, and..." he paused and glanced at Cholo. "I'm assuming you'll speak for yourself and for Counterstrike."

"That's the plan. We'll probably be better off leaving the other two gangs out of it. Fuck knows I'm gonna keep Homer's ass away. So that'll leave my brother and me, and your crew. Keeping the South Siders calm is enough to deal with," Cholo said. "Homer wouldn't want the other gangs to hear about this bullshit with his cousin anyway."

"True." Razor leaned back in his chair. "What's our turnaround looking like for the shops? I don't want these protective details cutting into our profits."

"None of us do," Jumper said. "There are enough men not working the shops to keep those who do off the protective rotation for a while. If it takes longer than we expect, we can fold them in. That's what Frenzy growled when he stomped toward his office."

The surly bastard was one hell of a strategist when he wanted to be. It'd been a while since they'd had to do schedules at all since most of the men tended to work around the clock without being asked.

"Ethan Davenport mentioned they were training some noobs this weekend," Razor said. "He invited us to participate."

"That's not a bad idea," Sandman said. "Fuck knows the equipment and shit we've gotten put together here only goes so far."

"Their set up is slick," Cholo said. "Most of you are former military, right?" Razor nodded. The man grinned. "Then that'll be right in your wheelhouse."

"Right, then if you could forward the info on that to me, Sandman, and Frenzy. Let us know how many we can bring out. We won't be in the way."

"He wouldn't have offered if he thought you would be," Cholo said. "He's likely vetting how good you are, especially since you've extended your protection of his little sister. Does he know about that yet?"

"No." Razor leaned forward and braced his elbows on the table. "There's a lot of shit he likely doesn't know about Jen."

"Talk to me," Cholo growled.

"I don't have many details. There have been multiple threats. She thinks it's Sam's dad."

"But she doesn't know for sure," Sandman finished. "We should get more information and look into it."

"Have Anarchy start with the police report she filed," Razor said.

"There's a police report?" Cholo spewed curse words in Spanish. "Fuck, man. This is not going to go over well when the twins find out. Patch was supposed to have HERA flagged to pull any reports involving anyone affiliated with Counterstrike."

"Well, you might want to follow up with him on that," Razor said. "Anything else?"

"Only the most important thing." Sandman grinned. "Little man's really excited about that picnic."

Fuck. Razor had already forgotten. "Right. Anyone want to coordinate that?"

"I'll do it," Jumper offered. "Think you can get us a decent discount from your restaurant, Cholo?"

"Yup. I'll get that done. I'll have to chat with the managers since I turned over daily shit to them. Just text me when and how much you'll need. I'll even deliver it myself if I'm invited." Cholo stood. "Later."

"Don't take all the party planning shit on yourself," Razor advised. "Use the prospects."

"I already planned to," Jumper said with an evil grin.

Razor patted the man on the back and headed toward his room. He and Sandman tended to stay at the compound more than the others, except for Frenzy who rarely left. Footsteps echoed behind him. He turned and looked at Sandman. "Problem?"

"That's what I'm trying to figure out. Is protecting Jen going to be a problem for you?"

"Why should it be?"

"You already know what I'm gonna say, man. Don't be a dick and make this hard." Sandman crossed his arms. "You're too close. Or, you want to be. Who she is. Who you are. That can't go anywhere good."

Razor grunted. He'd already considered the potential problem if he got too close to Jen while protecting her.

Remaining objectively neutral was vital. "I can't walk away from getting to know her, man."

They'd all sacrificed too much. He couldn't ignore the hunger Jen awakened in him, the desire to be close to someone again.

"I'm not asking you to. Just stay smart and let us have your six on this. Frenzy will kick your ass if you don't. So will I."

"Fine. Keep a couple of guys with me on Jen. Focus should be on the kid and his grandparents, though. We can call in a couple of the South Siders if we need to for Lupita."

"Like Counterstrike would be okay with that," Sandman said with a chuckle. "We've got this. No worries."

CHAPTER 7

Jen stacked all the recent threats and photos of the dead cat she'd taken in a stack and shoved them into a folder. She leaned back and took a sip of her red wine and silently willed the mental images away.

You're safe. No one can get into this house.

Ethan and Milo had kitted the cottage out with enough drones and high-grade security tech to turn it into Fort Knox. She'd been a bit surprised that Razor or one of the other Scythe guys hadn't insisted on staying at the house with her.

Spending time alone with him today had been…an experience. She'd laughed and smiled more in two hours than she had in weeks. He was smart, witty, and sexier than sin. Ugh. The big brothers were going to have seizures when they found out she had the hots for Razor.

The doorbell chimed. Jen glanced over at the display panel and saw Victoria standing outside. She made her way to the entryway and typed in the code. "Hey."

"Hey." The quiet response agitated Jen's stomach. She

took a sip of wine. "You want some? It's a new one Ethan found while in California a couple weeks ago."

"I'm good." Victoria walked in and sat in the armchair across from where Jen had been. She set a folder down on the coffee table, near Jen's laptop. "I think you know why I'm here."

"It could be a few reasons." Jen placed her half-empty glass down. "Hit me with it, sis."

She loved having sisters. Marisol was the quiet, constant, and loving presence—the one Jen could turn to for a hug or reassurance. Victoria was the confident, kickass, and protective one who'd listen to Jen without judgment and make her worries go away without the backlash of guilt she always felt with Ethan and Milo.

Her brothers never intended for her to feel that backlash, but they'd gone through so much to keep her safe when they were younger. She never wanted to let them down.

Victoria smirked. "Calling me sis won't get you out of this. Why didn't you tell us about these threats?"

"How did you hear?"

"Cholo came into headquarters breathing fire like a freaking dragon all over Field and Patch."

"Damn." He must've heard about the threats from Razor. "You've all been so busy. Honestly, I get so many threats I don't take them seriously."

"These are different, aren't they?" Victoria asked, her voice soft. "They've escalated."

Jen swallowed. "Yeah. The cat made it serious."

Anyone who'd kill a defenseless animal to send a message was a freaking psycho. Silence descended a few moments as her mind relived that morning outside her office. Thank God Bea had been running late because of a doctor's appointment for Ryan.

"You need to tell them," Victoria said.

"You haven't?"

"No." She shook her head. "I wouldn't want you spilling my shit, so I've given you the same respect. But, Jen, this is serious. How many threats do you get? Why haven't you ever mentioned them to us?"

"Because they don't matter. What we do is too important. Ethan and Milo would overreact and try and stop some of what I do. I make an impact because I go full-throttle into a problem and meet it head-on. I can't do my job if I'm being held back."

"I get that. Honestly, I do, but you can't make a difference if you're dead." Victoria pointed at the file. "That's a serious threat. There's nothing tying it to Sam's father, which means it could be any of your former cases or some whack job not even related to the work you've done."

"I know, which is why I agreed to Razor and his guys watching over me for a while. I didn't even argue," Jen said, mentally patting herself on the back for adulting so hard. "Did Anarchy get in touch with you?"

"Oh, yeah. He's a hyperactive little monkey." Victoria chuckled as she headed toward the small kitchen. She grabbed a bottle of water and took a drink. "We've fed what we know into HERA on Sam's family. Hopefully we'll get some hits by morning and can go from there. I'm also running that El Paso gang lead down, too."

"El Paso, huh? I hadn't heard they'd found that much out yet."

"Cholo's been busy." Victoria sat. "So...a protective detail courtesy of the Scythe MC. Wow, girl. I don't know whether to shake your hand or knock some sense into you."

Heat rose in Jen's cheeks. "He's nice."

"That man is smoking hot." Victoria grinned. "You can't deny that."

"Why would I?" She took a sip of her wine. "He asked me out."

"What?" Victoria leaned forward. "Jen, that's not smart. He's supposed to be protecting you, not dating you."

"I know. I know." She held up a hand. "Don't screw up my happy vibe. Do you have any idea how long it's been since a man, any man, had the balls to ask me out? Ethan, Milo, and all the other commandoes scare off every decent man in a ten-mile radius."

"If you're happy, I'm happy." Victoria looked at her. "I asked Edge to dig deeper into Razor's background."

"You shouldn't have done that. He deserves his privacy." He'd already shared more with Jen than she'd expected. "He's told me some stuff about his military record. There's more to him and the others."

"We already suspected that from what we'd dug into before." Victoria took another drink. "Besides, this was layered beneath a bigger request to give them some tech to help them out. A lot of what they do runs parallel to Counterstrike's work. Hell, they want to get into personal security. Anarchy mentioned it a couple of times this afternoon."

"What bigger request? What tech?"

Victoria shrugged. "That's up to The Arsenal. I was hoping for drones for their compound and maybe some database access via HERA. Probably not all of the databases, but enough to help them dig deeper than they can now."

"That'd be cool. Razor mentioned they have a lot of crew who aren't good with automotive stuff. That's why they're hoping to get into security work."

"Well, I'm hoping that if Edge vets them then maybe your stubborn brothers will agree to hire them on as contractors to help with some of our cases." Victoria sighed. "We need more boots on the ground for the protective work. We can't do everything."

"That's smart. You've really done a lot since you've come onboard." She hesitated a moment. "Do you miss the FBI?"

"No. I thought I would, you know?" Victoria squeezed her water bottle. "I mean, I spent so many years working to get there and then..."

Then it all blew up and she decided to leave the federal government life behind. "You're amazing. I don't know if I could've walked away from what I'd always thought I wanted."

"That's the important word. Thought. I thought being an FBI agent was what mattered. Now I know that protecting people and making a real difference is what's important. I do more of that in one day at Counterstrike than I did in months at the FBI."

"Milo's one lucky man."

Victoria stood. "And I'd best get back to the house so he can get lucky."

"Eww. TMI. TMI, Sis." Jen hugged her. "Thank you for letting me talk to them. I promise I will."

"Don't wait too long. Cholo has Field and Patch by the short hairs and they're sweating hard. Those two will crack before the end of the day tomorrow."

"In the morning. I promise," Jen said.

Darkness was a rare commodity on the quiet street outside Jen's bungalow. Unlike the neighborhood near the compound, this one had lampposts in abundance—almost too much so. Oh, and they all had surveillance cameras on them.

Razor leaned back in his vintage '69 Mustang and kept his attention alternating between the house and the computer screen precariously perched on the dashboard. He should've ordered one of the prospects to come along and camp around the rear of the house. Lighting was shit back there for both the Davenport places and security cameras were much less prevalent.

It was gonna be a long night, but he couldn't relax at the compound thinking about Jen and the potential threats. He punched the first number on the display of his phone and waited.

"Where are you?" Frenzy growled.

"Outside Jen's. Surveillance detail." Razor paused as curses sounded on the other end. "Anarchy got me hooked into the surveillance footage in the area. Lighting is good on the street in front of both the Davenport homes, but the back alley is darker than hell in comparison with minimal cameras."

"Which I'm sure their personal security system takes into account. Why don't you go test it out and get your stupid ass shot?"

"Frenzy."

"What part of 'you aren't doing shit alone' didn't you understand? You're our fucking President. Sandman's sole job is to protect you. He's apocalyptic right now, brother. You're lucky I called instead of him."

"It's just for tonight."

"Give me ten." The man hung up. Fuck.

Great. One ass chewing incoming. Razor shoved the thought aside and glanced in the vehicle's side mirror. Tension coiled within him as a body appeared. What the fuck? He grabbed his weapon as the man leaned forward.

Molten fury rolled within the man's gaze. Fuck. Razor forced a breath and rolled his window down a couple inches. He unclicked the locks. "Get in."

Ethan or Milo? Razor shook his head and figured it didn't matter. Two sides of the same overprotective coin. The man folded into the vehicle and closed the door quietly.

"You wanna explain to me what the fuck you're doing outside my sister's place?"

"You're smart enough to know." Razor wasn't sure how much, if anything, he knew about the threats against Jen. He hoped she'd shared by now, but maybe not.

"I wasn't onboard with that escort today. I'm sure as hell not okay with this, whatever it is." Ah. Milo then.

"Understandable, but I'm not leaving." Razor motioned toward the laptop images. "Front of the house is solid surveillance wise for three blocks both directions. What's up with the back, though?"

"Fucking HOA. Only minimal lighting is allowed in alleyways between residences, something about the style and make of the majority of homes here and the locations of the master bedrooms or some shit." Milo shook his head and made a frustrated sound. "Blackout curtains aren't in their egotistical brains, apparently."

"I'll get a prospect to camp out in the alleyway at night then."

"You want to fill me in on what this is?" Milo asked again.

"Talk to your sister."

"Damn," the man muttered. He grabbed the laptop and clicked a few times. "How bad?"

"Read the police report." Razor didn't censure the accusation from his voice. Why hadn't either of the brothers known she'd filed one? The man tensed. "I get being busy but, in my crew, family's always priority."

"Fuck you." Milo shoved the laptop toward Razor. He pulled out his cellphone and clicked a couple times. "Get your ass outside. There's a situation."

Razor wasn't sure the HOA would approve of a circa-midnight conversation on the quiet street, but he didn't offer an opinion. It was about time the two busy men focused on their sister instead of their work. He glanced at the laptop and whistled low. New surveillance areas from the back alley now filled smaller screens along the side.

And more images from the front also appeared—likely from the cameras he'd noted on all those lampposts. So, not city cameras. Counterstrike ones. Nice.

"Those are slick," he commented.

Milo chuckled. "And nearly impossible to spot, even in broad daylight. We used regular cameras on this street since the HOA know they're there. The Arsenal helped us kit out the weak spots in the neighborhood with the more undetectable models."

Thank fuck.

A tap sounded on Razor's window. He set the laptop down and folded out of the vehicle. Milo walked around and crossed his arms.

"What are you doing here?" Ethan asked.

"Apparently the escort has been extended," Milo countered. "Either that or our local MC president here is a stalker."

"Jen was supposed to talk to you both," Razor said. "Speak with her in the morning."

"Let's fast forward past that argument and get to the why," Milo said. "Little sis keeps shit locked down tighter than we do."

"Like I said, read the police report that was filed a few days ago."

"What police report?" Ethan took a step toward Razor. He grabbed his cellphone and shot off a text.

Headlights flashed as a black Camaro parked three cars

down. Razor grunted as Frenzy approached. At least he wasn't outnumbered now.

The man flashed a smirk as he crossed his arms. "Figured you'd get caught skulking out here. Maybe we should move this conversation inside?"

"No," Razor said. "We're cutting through this bullshit so I can focus on surveillance. There are some threats against Jen. I don't know why she hasn't shared."

"Fuck," Milo muttered.

"She wasn't taking them seriously because threats are apparently common," Frenzy said. "But the dead cat outside her office rattled her enough to phone the cops and file a report. Not sure why that fancy system of yours didn't pick up on it."

Ethan glared down at his phone. Footsteps sounded from the sidewalk across the street. A tall brunette approached. Victoria Davenport.

"Let me guess. My gorgeous hubby saw you lurking outside and came to find out why." The woman shook her head. She wrapped her arm around Milo. "You should've woken me up. I would've told you about the report."

"You knew?"

"Found out earlier today. Anarchy was hellbent to get his hands on it for Razor and asked for my help." The woman sighed and wiped her hand across her face. "Cholo ripped Field and Patch both new assholes for HERA not flagging us about it."

"Why didn't it?" Ethan asked.

"Whoever entered the details into the APD system misspelled Jen's first and last name. Field and Patch didn't enter some stream of code into the program HERA is running for us that takes typos into account." Victoria shrugged. "That's the gist of what I understood from an annoyed Zoey when they called her in a panic."

Zoey was one of The Arsenal's back-office operatives and tended to be Counterstrike's primary contact, from what Razor understood. He grunted. At least that problem was sorted.

"And the dead cat?" Milo asked.

"No leads on who's behind it," Frenzy said. "Locals aren't looking into it."

"Why didn't she say anything?" Ethan asked.

"She promised to talk to you in the morning," Victoria said. "She thinks we're too busy and didn't want to worry us."

"Fuck." Milo ran his hand through Victoria's hair and hugged her closer. "We can't keep running on fumes. Twelve active cases is too many on top of the day-to-day shit."

"I have an idea neither of you will probably like, but we'll talk through it later this morning." Victoria patted Milo's chest. "Let's get back to bed before someone calls the cops thinking we're burglars."

"You and your crew are on protective detail for Jen," Ethan guessed.

"I talked her into it," Razor said. He glanced over at her house. "For a little while, at least. Frenzy has a schedule worked so we can cover her, Sam and his grandparents, and our other problem."

"We owe you," Milo said.

"No." Frenzy smirked. "Boss man and your sis worked out an agreement. We cover her, she helps us with a few of our legal issues."

"No way." Ethan shook his head. "She's not getting mixed up with your crew."

"Stop." Victoria swatted Ethan's arm. "Edge vetted the entire MC. So did your buddy Tex. Your sister is perfectly capable of negotiating her time. Ease off on the overprotective big brother vibe. It's not cool."

Razor froze. He hadn't realized Tex had vouched for them with The Arsenal, too. The crazy fucker hadn't mentioned it.

"That conversation will wait until daylight," Frenzy said.

"You two head out. Both houses are covered for the night. We'll figure everything out once Jen's awake." Milo wrapped an arm around Victoria's waist. "Thanks for having her back."

CHAPTER 8

Jen trudged into the back door of her brothers' house as if it were an execution chamber. She hated letting them down and, as much as she'd love to argue otherwise, she had. Not telling them about the threats had been stupid and unprofessional.

The sooner they all got on the same proverbial page in that regard, the better. There was too much going on to continue hovering over the same ground.

"Morning," Milo greeted from the kitchen. He chopped vegetables in quick, precise movements. "Have a seat. I'm fixing omelets."

"On a Friday?"

"Why not?"

"Because that's a weekend food. You're too busy to do weekday breakfast, much less omelets."

"Shit changes." Milo shrugged as he set a cup of coffee down in front of her at the table. He leaned forward and kissed her forehead.

What the heck? Had an alien stolen her brother?

"Good morning," Marisol greeted as she made her way

into the kitchen. She rubbed her rounded belly. "The baby is craving bacon. Lots and lots of bacon."

Milo chuckled. "I've got you."

Ethan wandered in half-dressed, a shirt swung over his shoulder. He kissed his wife and stroked her belly. His happy expression shifted when his gaze moved to Jen. Faint lines appeared near his eyes.

Victoria wandered in and sat next to Jen. "Hey, did you sleep okay?"

"Someone should have," Milo muttered.

Uh oh. Jen studied everyone in the room. "What did I miss?"

"I have no idea," Marisol said. "I slept like the dead thanks to Ethan's magical massage."

"Lalalalala." Jen plugged her ears. "Danger. Danger. Incoming TMI!"

Victoria laughed and shook her head at Jen's antics. No one else did, though. She studied both her brothers and noted their worried expressions. She sighed deeply and took a sip of coffee.

"How did you find out?" Jen asked.

"Not from HERA flagging the police reports since they misspelled your first and last names," Ethan growled as he sat.

"How is that even possible?" She shook her head. "I'm okay, you know. There's nothing for you to worry about."

"That's not your call to make," Milo said. "You should've come to us. The fact you didn't feel like you could because we're too busy is an issue we'll be solving."

"Look, the work we do pisses people off. So, I crack a few more eggs than the average attorney when I shake things up. It goes with the territory." She feigned a nonchalant shrug and took another sip of coffee.

She loved her brothers and didn't want them worried. They had enough on their plates as it was. "'I'm sorry I didn't tell you. I honestly wasn't worried until the whole dead cat thing."

"It sounds like you've got everything handled for now. We heard about the arrangement you have with the Scythes," Ethan said. "A couple of them were here overnight watching your place."

"Even though we told them to go home," Milo growled. "Stubborn bastards."

Jen tightened. They were? "Sorry, I didn't know they'd start immediately. That seems like a waste of resources, though. We've got lots of surveillance in this area. Right?"

"We do, but they didn't have full access to all of it," Milo said. "They will starting today. Victoria mentioned having an idea to help us handle this work overload."

The woman smirked at Jen. "It evolved while I was speaking with Jen yesterday. Hear me out before you two jump in. I promise it's solid."

"Okay," Ethan said.

Milo growled. "I never like what you say when it starts with that."

"The protection details for the open cases are kicking our asses." Victoria crossed her arms and glared at her husband. "We can't rely solely on the HERA drones to keep our clients safe, which means we're wasting valuable man-hours watching over them rather than investigating their problems or helping someone else out."

"Which is why we're hiring new people and training them," Ethan said.

"New and training are the key words there," Jen added. "You're having problems finding good personnel."

"No shit," Milo mumbled.

Victoria slammed a folder down on the kitchen table.

"What if I said I could get your twenty-two operatives fully vetted and trained immediately?"

"I'd ask why the fuck you haven't mentioned this before," Ethan said.

"Language," Mari whispered. "Her first word shouldn't be fuck."

Jen chuckled. She couldn't wait to be an aunt. She already had a ton of onesies and adorable outfits bought.

"What's the catch?" Milo asked.

"They're Scythes," Victoria said. "Edge vetted the entire club. They all passed."

"That's not a good plan." Ethan leaned forward. "I appreciate the idea, but we can't employ operatives who are more loyal to someone else outside their work."

"That's a crock of shit," Jen said. "Everyone's more loyal to someone else outside their work. Anyone married. Anyone with kids. You get the point."

"This is different," Milo argued.

"No. It's really not." Jen shook her head. "Razor mentioned they want to start a personal security company. Counterstrike could easily contract that company to provide services to our clients. We can shroud the entire thing in enough legalese to choke a horse. It would work and free your operatives up to do the investigative and intake work."

"Okay, so it might work," Ethan said. "I know Edge vetted them all, but most of their records indicate they aren't team players. That's a problem."

"You're smart enough to read between the lines." Victoria shoved the folder across the table. "If you don't trust The Arsenal crew, then get your friend Tex to verify everything. Again. He's already told you more than once that they are all solid. It's worth a shot. We can't keep up this grueling pace. Someone will get sloppy and possibly hurt. Or worse. Hell, look at what happened with Jen. Field and Patch have both been pulling twenty-hour days. Maybe if they weren't so tired they would've caught the flag issue in HERA."

Milo brought plates piled with omelets to the table and set them down. Everyone took one and settled into eating. She knew the conversation was a difficult one for her brothers. They were as passionate with their work as she was with hers.

She wiped her mouth and looked at them both. "We swore to do everything in our power to help people when we started Counterstrike. We've done so much more than we could have initially hoped, but we're stagnating. We signed on to help The Arsenal without hesitation. How is this any different?"

Ethan rumbled his annoyance as he shoveled more food into his mouth. Marisol shook her head. "It's not. She's right. If they are trained, I don't see why they couldn't handle the lower-level work. It's a smart plan."

"Trigger and the other guys are gonna be down here tomorrow and Sunday to train our new people. Ethan's already invited Razor to bring some of his guys over. Use this weekend to vet them yourself. See what your buddies up north think about them," Victoria said. "Neutral third party."

Ethan and Milo locked gazes across the table. Jen sensed the unspoken conversation they held with one another. Their ability to communicate without words had always enthralled her.

"You brought Mingo and Cholo into Counterstrike. They have a whole crew of their own," Jen commented. "They aren't much different than the Scythes. Neither is Nitro and a couple of your other operatives."

"You think they're ready to start this security company?" Ethan asked.

"They will be when I'm through." Jen smirked. "It's worth a shot. They're protecting me and Sam and his grandparents right now. Oh, and that other woman, whoever she is. Use these assignments as a test."

"That along with their vetting with Trigger and his team should prove whether or not it's a good idea," Milo admitted. "Fuck knows we need the help."

"Okay. We'll see what happens this weekend," Ethan said. "In the meantime, we want to know everything found out about Sam's father and grandparents."

Victoria nodded. "Razor and Sandman are meeting us at headquarters. I'm bringing Jen with me."

She wanted to see Sam before the day got hectic, but she knew distance was necessary right now. He needed time to get to know his grandparents. Bea had promised to drop by the safe house and check on him a couple times today.

Ethan's cell chimed with an incoming text. Jen glanced up as his eyebrows furrowed. "Huh. We've all been invited to a picnic at the Scythe compound Saturday afternoon. For Sam."

"They said they were doing one." And they'd followed through. Her brothers' matching expressions made her chuckle. "They made him an honorary Scythe. The picnic is to introduce him to everyone."

"He's moving to New York," Victoria said softly.

Jen's stomach tightened. She still wasn't okay with his grandparents moving him to a new city. A new home. How much change was too much for a young child?

"You've done good by him, sis. There's only so much we can do before we have to let go," Milo commented.

"I know. It'll be easier to let go once I know the grandparents are cleared. Razor was right. There's something fishy about them." She took a final sip of her coffee and stood. "Ready to get this day started?"

Victoria gathered all the plates, but Marisol swatted her hands away. "Go. I've got this."

"Your appointment's at two, right?" Ethan asked as he kissed Marisol's cheek.

"Yeah. I'll meet you there." She rubbed her back. "I'm ready for our baby girl to come out already."

Jen grinned. The nursery was finished last month, and the storage area was stocked with enough diapers and supplies for several months. To say the couple had nested was an understatement. They'd eventually move to a home of their own but having everyone together felt right.

She, Ethan, and Milo had only had each other for too long. Letting go of the bond they'd forged in their shared hell would be difficult. Maybe that's why neither of her brothers had pushed to move out from the house they'd shared since returning from the service.

Jen was glad they hadn't. She couldn't imagine not having them live next door.

* * *

"Razor!" Sam held out his arms and vaulted forward.

Razor grunted with the impact and hoisted the boy up. Laughter and squeals filled the small living room as he tickled Sam. His gaze swept to the grandparents, who stood near the hallway with matching grim expressions. "How's it going?"

"Okay." The boy's voice lowered. "I was in time out for talking too much and not eating my veggies."

"Veggies aren't my favorite either, but I don't mind them with cheese." Razor set the boy down. "Mr. and Mrs. Gentry. I just wanted to stop by and make sure you had everything you needed."

"Your time is best spent handling the situation that prevents us from taking Samuel home where he belongs," Mrs. Gentry said. "Your friend stopped by earlier and told us about the picnic. While we appreciate the gesture, I'm not sure that's the type of environment a young boy should be exposed to."

"It's a picnic," Razor said, keeping his voice calm despite his rising frustration. Environment? "There'll be lots of things for kids his age. Several in my club have families and kids Sam's age. He'll have fun, something he's likely been missing for a while."

The Gentrys looked at one another. Mr. Gentry cleared his throat. "Well, that sounds perfect. We'd love to go. Does that sound fun, Samuel?"

"Yes!"

"Great." Razor noted the man's wrinkled clothing. Dark circles marred the area beneath his eyes.

So far Anarchy hadn't found anything abnormal about the couple. Mr. Gentry was indeed a CFO of a hedge fund group, but information about the group was vague. He and Razor would be meeting with Counterstrike in a couple hours at their headquarters. Hopefully HERA found more information.

Until then, Razor would trust his gut. It'd kept him alive in the sandbox. "This might be improper, but I'd like to speak with you about possibly investing some funds I have, sir. I've been sitting on a chunk of money for too long. I know I need to invest it properly."

"Of course. I'd love to help you." The man adjusted his shirt. "Naturally, we don't typically accept just anyone as a client, but given the circumstances I'm sure we can come to an arrangement. How much are you looking to invest?"

Several Scythes had pooled the hush money they'd received from the government. They'd never come to an agreement on what to do with the money, though. Anarchy had mentioned HERA could trace monetary transactions with ease, though. So why not do that to dive deeper into Gentry?

"Fifty thousand to start," he said. "I'm sure that's small potatoes for you, but I'd like to start off small and add to it later, if that's possible."

"Certainly." The man smiled wide. "Many of my clients do exactly that. You can't be too cautious these days."

"I must admit I'm impressed a young man such as yourself has that much to invest," Mrs. Gentry said.

"I've always been a saver. I have quite a bit more than that to work with once I've found the right fit. I'd rather trust someone I know. Probably sounds crazy, but given your tie to Sam, I think that person might be you."

A gleam danced in Mr. Gentry's gaze. "Excellent. I'll put together some information for you and we can discuss it at the picnic if you'd like."

"That'd be perfect. A couple of my friends might be interested as well," Razor added.

"Great. I'll make a few copies then." The man motioned toward the dining room. "I think I'll hop right on that. It'll take a bit of time for my people to get everything together."

"Of course." Razor waited until Mr. and Mrs. Gentry disappeared into the dining room area. He crouched in front of Sam. "You okay?"

"Yeah." He curled his lips inward. "They're weird."

"They're old. Old people are always a bit weird." Razor pulled out the disposable cell. "This is for you. Hit my picture to call me. Any time. Sandman's picture is there, too. Did he tell you the secret about this place?"

Razor kept his voice low. Sam shook his head.

"There are cameras inside this house. They hear and see everything," Razor whispered. "Don't tell your grandparents, but we wanted to make sure you were okay since we can't be here ourselves. Someone is just outside at all times, though."

Sam nodded. “Grandma’s mean.”

“Has she hurt you?”

“No, but she yells a lot and says weird stuff I don’t understand.” Sam scrunched up his nose. “And she smells funny.”

Razor wasn’t sure how much of it was a young kid not knowing what grandparents were like or how much was a potential threat. He hugged the boy. “You aren’t alone. I’ll see you soon, okay? Sandman and Jumper are coming by later today to visit with you.”

“Yay!” The boy tucked the small phone into his pocket. “She won’t let me wear my cut in the house.”

“You’ll get to wear it tomorrow.” Razor made mental note to have a few extras in case he showed up without it. “Talk to you later.”

He exited the house before he lost patience with the older couple. They likely meant well. He pulled out his cell and called Sandman.

“He good?”

“I’m not sure. He mentioned the old lady was mean and he was in time out for not eating his veggies. Not sure how much of it is a little kid not understanding grandparents or something else.”

The man sighed. “You know I grew up in a strict home. It’s an adjustment.”

“Yeah.” He paused. “I hope that’s all it is for the kid’s sake. Did you get the meet with the El Paso crew arranged?”

“Tonight. Anarchy will give you the details later. I made a few calls. I’m having a chat with an MC in the El Paso area in an hour. Hopefully we’ll learn more about this crew.”

“Good. We can vet the MC and offer an alliance if they pass,” Razor said.

“That’s what I was thinking. Anarchy is gonna run them through HERA.” The man laughed. “He’d run a grocery list through that system just to play with it.”

CHAPTER 9

Razor was three blocks from Counterstrike when his cell chimed. He ignored the call. Three loud beeps sounded moments later.

Fuck.

An S.O.S.

He pulled over and read the message.

Prospect found package on sidewalk just outside Counterstrike surveillance. Addressed to Jen.

Frenzy had sent a picture.

Forward this to Cholo. See if they've got equipment to scan the package. Or an APD resource that can. Give me the prospect's location.

On it. An address followed.

Whoever was threatening Jen was smart enough to stay off Counterstrike surveillance, which meant they knew where the cameras were. Not. Good.

Razor drove to the prospect's location and parked nearby. He scanned the surroundings and noted a few city cameras within the area. Hopefully they could pull images from them and finally get a name.

"Prez." The prospect motioned toward the package. "I figured it wasn't smart to open or touch it."

"Good call. Walk one block each direction and take pictures of any city cameras nearby. I saw two to the north. There's likely more. Go into the local shops across the street and ask if they have surveillance. If they do, sweet talk them into letting you view it. Screen record anything relevant with your phone."

"Yes, Prez." The young prospect darted off.

If the target knew where Counterstrike cameras were, then Razor had to trap him another way. He sent a text to Frenzy. **Set up a perimeter surveillance on Jen's home, office, and Counterstrike. Two blocks all directions with binoculars. Below radar. No bikes or cuts. Use ghost members.**

Frenzy sent a thumbs up emoji. Then added, **It's like you were in the military and good at this shit.**

Fucker.

I'll have to pull a couple of the ghosts from the shop's night schedule.

Do it. No one outside us knows about this.

You think it's an inside job.

I think this asshole pissed off the wrong crew and knows too much. Later.

Razor glared at the package. No return address. Nothing more than Jennifer Davenport on the top at all. The brown cardboard was sealed together with duct tape.

"Shit." Cholo's curse signaled his arrival. The man stared at the package, then glanced down the street both directions. "Who found this?"

"Prospect. He's sweeping local business for surveillance footage. There are a couple city ones nearby that may have picked up something," Razor said.

"Good call on the local shops. If they have a system, it

likely wouldn't be one online, so we couldn't hack into it." Cholo ran his hand through his hair. "A friend of the Davenports runs a private forensics lab. She's on her way. Not sure if she can pull anything from this, but it's a start. I'll wait for her. You go and fill everyone else in."

Razor left his bike parked where it was since getting any closer was a crapshoot. Parking was a serious pain in the ass in this part of town. By the time he arrived at Counterstrike's headquarters, he had a tentative hold on his anger.

He followed one of the Davenport twins into a conference room and slammed the door behind him. Victoria and Jen sat at the table with the other twin and two tall but lean men he hadn't met yet. He suspected they were Field and Patch, but no introductions were offered.

"Cholo's waiting with the package," Razor said. "He mentioned a friend of yours with a lab."

"Jessica. She owns a private forensics lab, Second Trace. She's solid," Victoria said. "She knows this is a high priority. We need to figure out who this is."

"Agreed." Jen leaned forward and massaged her temples.

"The prospect is working to get any available security footage from the local businesses across the street from the package," Razor said.

"We could've hacked in," one of the unknown men said.

"Not if they aren't online," Razor shot back. The door opened. Anarchy slid in and sat down. Frenzy followed.

"This is Anarchy, Treasurer and resident Scythe geek," Razor motioned. "And Frenzy, my Vice President."

"Oh, right. I'm Field," the blond said. "This is Patch. We're Counterstrike's geeks, along with Victoria."

"Who has access to your camera locations?" Razor asked.

"Why?" Victoria asked. She massaged the back of the twin beside her. Right. So that was Milo.

"Because someone knew enough about them to place a

dead cat on Jen's office steps and a package for her on a sidewalk outside Counterstrike without being caught on them," Razor said.

"We don't have a leak," Ethan said. "But that is strange."

"The three of us, Sandman, and Jumper are the only ones in my crew privy to any Counterstrike intel right now," Razor said. "I'm not saying it's someone on the inside. It could be someone with knowledge on the outside."

"Like who?" Milo asked.

"Permits," Jen whispered. "We cut through most of the paperwork, but we still had to provide the city with information on where we intended to place cameras."

"Right," Patch said. "So we need a list of who would have that information as well as all their family and friends."

"What was in the package?" Field asked.

"It hasn't been opened yet," Ethan said. "Cholo went to the lab. He'll let us know once they have any information."

"We're accessing the city cameras you mentioned to Cholo," Victoria said. "Good call on the local businesses, too."

Razor didn't want praise. He wanted some answers. Too much shit was swirling around the bowl without exiting.

"We'll need to extend our camera reach," Milo said. "Adding a few unknown cameras farther down the streets would help."

"And it'd send up a red flag that we know anything that could trap the bastard," Razor said. "I've got this covered."

"Okay," Ethan said. He leaned back in his chair. "What's your plan?"

"Classified."

"Bullshit!" Milo stood. "This asshole is after my sister. Nothing's classified."

He glanced over at Frenzy. The man shook his head.

"What was that about?" Victoria asked, having obviously caught the gesture.

"Too many cooks in this kitchen," Frenzy said. "We have a plan, one only Razor and I are privy to at this point. We'll read a few of you in, but not everyone in this room needs to know." He pointed and Field and Patch. "You two are out if Victoria is in. And so are you, Anarchy."

The latter didn't balk. He nodded and stood. "I'll grab some coffee. Come on, Field and Patch. This isn't a hill you want to die on. Frenzy and Razor don't fuck around. They'll bleed us out rather than risk anything they've classified. We'll sort through what HERA found out about Sam's family and be ready for the next discussion point."

Both men looked at Ethan, who nodded. Tension filled the atmosphere as the three men left.

"I'm not sure whether to admire your balls of steel or kick your ass," Milo said.

"He's right," Victoria said. "Until we find out how whoever this is knows so much, we contain what we can."

"The permits angle is smart," Razor said, his attention on Jen. "I hadn't considered that. It's likely our leak source, but I want to trap the bastard actually doing this, not whoever he got the data from."

"What's the plan?" Jen asked.

Razor sat beside Frenzy. "To explain that, we'll need to fill you in on things few know about the Scythes. I trust whatever we share will remain between us."

"Of course," Victoria said.

"We have more members than are registered," Frenzy said. "Some of our crew prefer to be as off the radar as possible. We'll provide their information so Edge can vet them, of course, but they live and work in the shadows. Most of the Scythes don't even know they exist."

"Why?" Jen asked.

"They each have their own reasons. Some of them were more ghost than soldier in the military. You live that life long enough and you lose your way back to normal," Razor said. "They operate in the periphery, rarely interacting with most of the club. They drift in and out during our functions. Frenzy, Sandman, and I hold a separate church, or meeting, with them after the main one."

"So your plan involves these ghost members," Ethan said. "Why?"

"Because we need someone watching potential target locations who won't be seen. We need operatives who aren't known threats. If someone is smart enough to know where the cameras are, they likely know every person at Counterstrike and have spotted enough of the Scythe crew to recognize them," Frenzy said.

"It's not like you try to be conspicuous," Milo said. "Your motorcycles and cuts scream your presence from blocks away."

"That's intentional," Razor said. "It's a warning we will fuck with anyone who messes with whoever we're protecting. But that strategy isn't going to catch whoever this asshole is."

"Which is why Razor activated our unknown members. Some work in the shops at night or on weekends. A few do their own thing for revenue right now," Frenzy said. "I've pulled some of them. They'll be establishing surveillance around Counterstrike headquarters, Jen's office, and her home."

"How many?"

"Three per location in twelve-hour shifts," Frenzy answered quickly. "So, eighteen. We have seven more we'd prefer not to potentially burn."

"Christ," Ethan cursed. "How the fuck do you keep that many below radar?"

"Very carefully," Razor said. "Most ran black ops before

they were burned or tapped out. They're all good operatives. The best."

"And you're okay with Edge vetting them?" Victoria asked.

"We can sign whatever confidentially agreement you want," Jen offered quickly. "I'll draft one up for us and The Arsenal."

"That's not necessary. They trust me to have their six." And he trusted the Davenports to have theirs. "We've got the operatives, but we could use some help with the tech. Their work is only as good as the equipment they use."

The request hung within the room a moment. Razor bit back the embarrassment of having to ask for help with equipment, but he wasn't too proud to admit Counterstrike and The Arsenal had far better resources than he did. If it kept his crew safe, he'd bite the bullet and ask for what they needed.

"I'm afraid that's not our call to make," Ethan said. "Our agreement with The Arsenal limits the use of what tech they've gifted us to our operatives only. But Victoria and Jen have suggested an arrangement between Counterstrike and the Scythes that we can expedite and approach The Arsenal with."

Razor tightened.

"What arrangement?" Frenzy asked. He glowered at Razor.

"You mentioned wanting to start a personal security company," Jen said. "Victoria suggested I help you create that and Counterstrike will then hire your company to provide protection support to our clients."

"Employees would have to be vetted by The Arsenal, of course," Milo said. "But it'd free our operatives up to do the investigative work and help additional clients we're currently having to turn away."

That'd be...

Shit. They'd start their company with a guaranteed client base and a known income stream. Talk about a leg up. "We'll have to discuss it with the other officers and the crew members who wanted to work for the company, but that sounds like a good arrangement. We could set up a trial period so we can prove ourselves. I'm sure you have your doubts."

"We do," Ethan admitted. "We doubt everyone not in Counterstrike."

"Ethan invited you and some of your crew to participate in the training we're doing tomorrow," Milo said. "That'll be the best way to prove yourselves quickly. We'll be asking Trigger and his Delta team for their opinion on you. They're a neutral third party."

Right. Neutral. If they were active Delta, they'd have opinions about Razor and the Scythes before even meeting them. Then again, maybe not.

"Most of our crew is leery of active military," Frenzy said. "They've been burned by too many."

"That's understandable," Ethan said. "Trigger and his crew are solid, though."

"Tex vouched for you two," Milo said. "I spoke with him again early this morning when Victoria explained their idea. Give him a call if you're leery of Trigger and his team. He'll vouch for them."

Frenzy tightened beside Razor. Tex had singlehandedly saved both of their lives. If he hadn't gotten involved, they would've both been killed in the sandbox.

"He didn't share any details," Milo added. "But he said there's zero doubt you and your crew could all handle whatever we throw your way."

"Tex wouldn't ever share details," Razor said. "He's asked

permission to clear most of our names more than a few times."

"Why haven't you agreed?" Jen asked.

"It's not his fight," Frenzy answered. "And none of us care what a file says. We all know the truth. Anyone who can't see past redaction and bureaucracy isn't worth our time."

"Tex might respect that decision because he's been where we all were. He understands brotherhood," Ethan said. "But we should probably warn you that The Arsenal will likely wade in if you start working with us."

"From what I've heard about Edge, I doubt she'd wade in. She'll respect our choice just like Tex has." Razor crossed his arms.

Milo chuckled. "Quillery and Edge might understand and respect it, but that hellion they work with, Zoey, is a case of grenades without the pins. There's no way she'll back down from that fight."

"I wouldn't either if I were her," Victoria said. "She was NSA and got burned when she exposed a dirty CIA team. She would've been killed if it weren't for The Arsenal. People done wrong by the government is personal to her."

"We'll talk with everyone involved later today," Frenzy said. "We appreciate the opportunity. What your group is doing is the sort of work we've all wanted to be a part of since getting out." He stood. "I'll go grab the others so we can move on."

Jen sipped her water and ignored the tension headache making its presence known. What was in the box? She kept glancing over at Ethan, who maintained a constant vigil with his texting app.

"Are you okay?" The husky-toned inquiry cast awareness through her entire body as Razor sat beside her.

She nodded. "Yes. Thanks to you. You've got a knack for strategizing."

"It comes in handy on occasion." He took her hand. "He's not going to hurt you. I promise."

She was more worried about everyone else than herself. "I was hoping to see Sam today, but maybe it's better if I stay away."

"I saw him this morning," Razor said. "He's looking forward to the picnic. I had to strong-arm his grandparents, but they'll be there. We'll make sure of it."

"Should we postpone that? Is it safe?"

"I'm sure your brothers will probably have a few ideas on how to make it even more secure, but the compound is safe."

Given how many former commandos there'd be present, Jen didn't doubt Razor's statement. Milo's cell chimed with an incoming text. He glared at the screen a few minutes. Tension coiled within his body.

Her gaze followed the phone as her other brother took it. Same reaction.

"Tell me," she said.

"I think…"

"Tell me." Voice tight, she took a deep breath. Whatever was in that box wasn't good.

"A heart. Jessica says it's from an animal, likely a cow. Your name was carved into it." Milo's jaw twitched.

"Fuck." Razor pounded his fist on the table.

"Cholo asked permission to temporarily install a few drones at the compound for the picnic," Ethan said, inserting himself into the private conversation.

She glared at her brother as Razor replied. "That's appreciated. Anarchy can coordinate that with him. I told him to invite all of you. That includes Trigger and his team."

Ethan nodded. "I'm sure they'll enjoy the break from the training. We won't bring any of the trainees, though. It'll just be those of us you've been working with and the Delta team."

Jen's mind reeled when she thought about what all Razor had just shared. He had a huge freaking team of ghost commandos. At least, that's what she'd read between the lines. She'd known the Scythe MC was pretty big, but that was before he'd shared they had people off the books.

She wasn't sure what Ethan and Milo thought of that. While she understood the why behind it, she suspected more than a few people would consider the move shady.

She didn't, though. She admired Razor and the others for protecting their friends.

Brotherhood.

It'd saved both of her brothers and their friends while they were serving and afterward. She couldn't help but wonder what'd happened to Razor. Tex had saved his life.

Her gut twisted whenever she thought of him in a life-threatening situation. She liked the way he treated everyone around him and admired the way he interacted with those he led. They weren't just club members. He treated them like family.

Brothers.

"Okay, everyone's back. Let's get started," Milo said. His gaze narrowed when it settled on Razor, who remained seated beside her. "What have we learned about Sam's grandparents?"

"Not as much as we'd hoped," Victoria said. "Their databases aren't online in any capacity and attempts to access their system haven't been successful so far."

"How would you access their system?" Razor asked.

"Viruses. It's a worm, really, since it doesn't require interaction from the recipient, but we'll call it a virus since everyone's more familiar with that term," Field said. "That's what

Zoey suggested. She has quite a few that install and embed themselves in all emails, accounts, and transactional records and span outward. The problem is Mr. Gentry and whoever else he works with don't appear to have much of an electronic presence."

"Gentry Enterprises is old school," Victoria said. "Which is shady these days. Most financial organizations have to be online in some capacity now."

"We have gotten into their personal bank account," Patch said. "Nothing stands out. Most of their bills are paid via check. They rarely eat out. Very few memberships."

"So they're old, boring people who rarely go out," Milo surmised.

"That's what we're finding indicates," Victoria said. "They've lived in New York City most of their lives. They transplanted there thirty-four years ago from Buffalo, where they married. Both were previously married. Mrs. Gentry's first husband died in a car accident. Mr. Gentry's former wife divorced him then moved to England, where her family is from. We're working on establishing contact with her."

"So our suspicions could simply be based on them trying to come across as better off than they are," Field said.

Razor leaned back in his chair. A slight smirk appeared on his face.

Frenzy chuckled. "I know that look. What have you done, boss?"

Everyone's attention shifted to Razor. He looked around. "I may have expressed my interest in investing in their hedge fund, or whatever it is. I told him I had fifty thousand to start, and might consider investing a lot more later on if it works out well."

"Why did you do that?" Milo asked.

"My gut," he answered quickly.

"Fuck. His gut is never wrong. That means there's a problem," Frenzy said. "How'd he react?"

"Typical response. They normally wouldn't consider just anyone off the street, but given our connection with their grandson, he's open to it. He's drawing up information for us to review at the picnic tomorrow. I mentioned I might have a few friends who are also interested." He pulled out a card and shoved it toward Victoria. "This is what he gave me for contact information. If we could come up with a reason to email him the paperwork back rather than signing copies at the picnic, would that work to get the virus installed?"

"Definitely," Patch answered quickly. "And we could trace any monetary transactions through their accounts and spread from there. Zoey's virus will even access all the emails he's sent and received, then move to those individual's email accounts."

"They've taken down a lot of very, very bad people using this, and it's never failed," Victoria said. "As for the father, we haven't had any luck locating any additional accounts."

"Which means we have nothing tying him to hiring anyone to stalk Jen," Ethan said. "And he hasn't moved from his rental home since the custody hearing."

"Nor has he made any phone calls or accessed any email accounts we know of," Field said. "We need eyes inside that rental."

"Which we can't do because of our ties to the pending criminal investigation," Milo said. He glanced at Razor. "Jen and I are both testifying about our discussions with Sam's mother before her murder."

"How is Jen representing her son not a conflict of interest then?" Frenzy asked.

"Anyone who meets with us signs paperwork that makes them and their children clients after their initial intake interview," Jen said. "It also gives me permission to offer testimony and reports concerning their safety and their children's in the event something happens to them."

"I didn't realize you'd spoken with her," Razor said. Concern reflected in his gaze. "I assumed you took him on as a client after she was killed. That must be tough."

"It is," she admitted. "She only met with us once, three days before she was killed." Her heart ached at the admission. She hadn't processed the loss yet. "We begged her to let us remove her immediately."

"That's not on us," Milo said gently. "She wanted to give him another chance."

Yeah, and that chance had gotten her killed.

"So, Counterstrike can't bug the rental because it could cause potential problems," Razor said as he glanced over at Frenzy, who chuckled.

"Whatever you're thinking, please don't say it," Victoria said.

"Though, hypothetically, if you were to need to take a piss and make a left at the end of the hall instead of the right, you might stumble into an equipment storage area," Field said.

"Goddammit, Field." Ethan shook his head. "Forget you heard that. We aren't that desperate yet. Besides, that equipment could eventually be tracked to us if it's found."

"Aren't we?" Milo asked. "If he's the bastard who's after Jen, we need to know. If he isn't, we definitely need to know."

"Razor's plan is solid," Ethan said. "We move forward with that, then go from there if we don't get any leads."

"Right, the mysterious plan boss man won't let anyone except a few know about," Anarchy said. "Those are always the most fun, but this is one of the first times I'm not in on it. Which sucks. Huge donkey balls, boss."

"You'll survive," Razor commented.

"One final discussion point," Milo said. "We know you're meeting with the El Paso crew that's rolled into the area.

Cholo will be there and will represent us. Make sure he has the info. If you need backup, let us know."

El Paso crew? Wait. Was that tied to the woman they were helping? The one who was with the South Siders?

"Training starts at six in the morning," Field said. "I'll text you the location. It'd help if you can give us the list of who's coming out with you."

"I'll get the info to you once we've decided," Frenzy said. "And I'll send the other list we spoke of earlier to Victoria, if that works."

"Actually, Razor should send that directly to Edge," Milo said. "We don't need to see that info. The fewer who do, the better."

Shock rolled through Jen. She'd expected her brothers to scour every inch of data they could about the Scythes. Why would they extract themselves from vetting the ghost operatives?

"That's surprising," Frenzy commented.

"We'd do the same thing you have," Ethan said. "We won't disrespect that by forcing our way into knowing anything more than you've already shared. We trust Edge to make the call."

"Thank you," Razor said. His cell phone chimed.

"That's Edge's contact info," Victoria said. "I wouldn't share it with anyone."

"One more thing." Razor looked over at Field and Patch. "Is anyone watching the interior surveillance from Sam's safe house?"

"No." Patch glanced up from his laptop. "Should we?"

"Sam mentioned his grandmother saying stuff he didn't understand," Razor said. "There's been some discipline issues as well. We might learn more about the Gentrys if we watch the footage. I can have a couple of prospects go through it if you'll forward it to Anarchy."

"Exactly how many of those prospects do you have?" Victoria asked. "I'm thinking we need some. They seem to be everywhere."

"Four. No, five." Frenzy sighed. "They do grunt work well and rarely bitch about it. It's like bootcamp for mental fortitude. They either have what we want or they don't."

"That'd be a huge help," Ethan said. "We wanted to keep an eye on the interior and hopefully gather some intel, but with everything else going on, we haven't."

"Consider it done," Razor said.

"Bea could probably listen to some of it," Jen said.

"I have something else I'd prefer to have her work on if she's available," Milo said. "For a different case. Two, actually."

Jen nodded.

Everyone stood and headed out of the conference room. She took her time standing. Anticipation quickened her pulse when Razor took a step closer.

"Are you coming to the training tomorrow?" He stroked her arm.

"I usually don't," she said, "but I might. I'm a bit curious to see how you do against my brothers and their Delta friends."

He grinned. "I'll try and not disappoint you, beauty."

CHAPTER 10

Nightfall encased the area around the compound. It'd taken three hours to get all the security drones Cholo and two other Counterstrike operatives had brought put into place. Anarchy was in heaven even though he'd been told either Counterstrike or The Arsenal would use the drones if a threat occurred.

Razor sat atop the picnic table behind the compound and drank a beer. He hadn't gotten as much accomplished as he'd hoped, but enough got done to set his mind at ease.

Frenzy and Sandman approached. Neither sat. Razor looked at Frenzy first. "Everything in position?"

The man nodded. Good. One worry ticked off. He'd seen the list of the eighteen men Frenzy selected for the surveillance and knew they were the best. If anyone messed with Jen tonight, they'd be in a world of hurt.

Fuck. He didn't want to screw with the potential gang threat tonight. There was a fine line between keeping the peace and ruling over everyone. Some days he felt as though the Scythes danced on the wrong side of that line.

"You make the call yet?" Sandman asked.

"What call?" Razor took another sip of beer.

"Stupid isn't a good look on you," Frenzy commented. "The sooner you make the call, the quicker we can get everything into place. It's the right move."

Ah. That call. He glanced down at the phone beside him. He had more than that call to make, though. He'd opted to send the list of their unrecorded members to Edge via email an hour ago rather than calling first.

He picked up his phone and punched in the number he didn't dare leave in the contacts. Too many people would do anything to have it.

Tex picked up on the second ring. "This is a surprise. Long time no hear from. How is everyone?"

"Good. Settling in." Razor put him on speaker. "Frenzy and Sandman are here with me."

"I've gotten a few interesting calls from Ethan's crew about you. Them and Edge at The Arsenal," Tex said.

"Sorry about that, but thanks for speaking to them," Sandman said.

"I'm glad you're stepping up to help them out. They're a solid crew with too much work. You'll work well together."

"That's the hope." Razor paused. "I'm afraid I need help with something else, on the down low."

"Sure."

"I need interior surveillance equipment. Bugs would work, but cameras would be better," Razor said. "Undetectable and untraceable to anyone."

"Does this have anything to do with a certain boy you're helping them with?"

"Some questions shouldn't be asked," Frenzy said. "This can't be tied to Counterstrike in any way."

"Understood." Tex sighed. "Let me make a few calls, but I

already know where you need to get that tech from. So, I'll likely be in touch with a location to meet them tonight."

"Thanks. We've got a meet to do, but this takes priority."

"We'll catch up soon," Tex said.

"Sounds good." Razor paused a moment. "One more thing."

"Yeah?"

"They want us to train with a Delta crew they're bringing in tomorrow. Trigger and his team. A few of us are hesitant to be around currently active. Your thoughts on them?"

"Those boys see through bullshit. They judge with their own eyes and see more than almost anyone I know," Tex said. "They're solid."

"Good to hear, man. Thanks again," Razor said. He clicked off.

"Wanna bet that tech is coming from The Arsenal?" Sandman asked.

"Not taking a fool's bet," Frenzy said.

He'd accept tech from Satan himself if it kept Jen safe. And getting eyes and ears on Sam's dad was a high priority. He'd hoped to take her for that drive in the hill country this weekend, but it was looking more and more impossible.

Soon.

"You ready to go?" Sandman asked.

"As ready as I'll be." Razor tossed his mostly full beer into the trash and headed to his Mustang, which Sandman would drive.

Riding in a car wasn't as against his nature as it was for some people in an MC. Tonight it was more strategic than anything, though. Frenzy and Jumper would do most of the talking. If the assholes from the El Paso crew called them out on it, then Razor would know they were more knowledgeable about local gangs and crews than expected.

If not…well, it wouldn't matter. Any of his crew could lead. They'd all been trained by the best military in the world to do precisely that. Lead. Make critical decisions without hesitation.

"How did the chat with the El Paso MC go?" Razor asked as Sandman pulled out of the compound.

"Good. They're clean, according to them. Anarchy is running them, though. This crew we're meeting with is bad news. El Fury. Not an original name, but defines their MO. They scorch neighborhoods in bullets and wreak havoc wherever they land."

"Any idea why they'd want to roll into Austin?"

"The challenge. Word's spread farther than we'd expected. Everyone's heard about the effort to clean up the streets here and sideline typical gang bullshit," Sandman said. "They think they're tough enough to take the area."

"Power play."

"Yep."

They fell into a comfortable silence as they made the drive to a small town east of Austin. The desolate stretch of land afforded everyone a bit of breathing room. Razor had sent enough crew ahead of time to ensure security was in their control. He studied the mugshots and photographs Anarchy had gathered so far.

"Not sure why you're studying all those. No way they're stupid enough to have their leaders show up to this shit," Jumper said.

"You never know." Razor shoved the cell into his pocket as Sandman pulled to a stop near a cluster of vehicles.

Cholo and his brother faced off against five strangers. Not a promising start for the meeting. Razor exited the vehicle, but made sure to follow Sandman, who moved to get in front of Frenzy and Jumper. All four stood beside Cholo and Mingo.

"I thought we said no more than four," Frenzy said. "If you can't count, we have a problem before the meeting even starts."

"You have six." A man sneered as another spat on the ground. "No one tells me what the fuck to do. The quicker you learn that the longer you'll live."

"These two aren't with us." Jumper pointed to Cholo and his brother. "The other crews decided you weren't worth meeting."

"They'll regret that. This area is mine. El Fury owns your asses now." The short man took two steps forward and glared up at Jumper. "You must be Razor. You look more like Loser to me."

Razor clenched his fists as the man stared Jumper down. They'd met with a lot of gangs since getting out of the service, an unwanted byproduct of having the MC. Most operated with more savvy and smarts than most would expect. This one clearly didn't. Either that or the short idiot was trying to earn his street cred through this move. Not smart. Downright suicidal.

"They're carrying," Cholo said. "That's against the rules, too."

Good thing they'd all come armed then. Razor wondered if they'd hidden people amongst the sporadic foliage. Probably. Not that it'd matter. They were in the crosshairs of the best snipers the Scythes had.

"Austin and all the surrounding areas are under our protection. No new gangs. No drugs. No bullshit," Jumper said. "Everyone in this area agreed and we will enforce that."

"Right. You and what army? We're four hundred strong, fucker. You'll bleed out before you can beg for a chance to be part of our crew."

Who did this asshole think he was?

Razor studied the other men congregated behind the

loudmouth. None of them offered any names, but he spotted the three he wanted. He didn't know who the pipsqueak was, but he didn't matter.

The real leader and his top two were the farthest away. Arms crossed. Watching. Waiting. He waited until Frenzy glanced his direction and flashed the signs for who was really in charge, not that the man needed the help. He'd memorized the faces as well.

"Why don't you shut up before I lose my patience and let your leader speak for himself?" Frenzy took three steps forward and shoved the short man back. He stared the El Fury leader down. "Or do you let all your men disrespect crews? Hell, I'd shoot any man in my crew who said no one told him what to do."

The man in the middle, aka Trench, shrugged. "This turf was his idea. He thinks he's the big man but lacks the balls to back that up. He'll pay for his disrespect. I punish my crew privately."

"His idea is a bad one," Cholo said. "You should've done your homework. Four hundred won't even make us break a sweat."

"And who are you speaking for?"

"My crew and any others not here," Cholo said.

"And the Scythes side with him," Frenzy said. "As do all of our affiliate chapters."

"What the fuck does that mean?" one of the others asked.

Mingo laughed. "Man, you should've really done some homework. You dealt with MCs before, right? I know you've got one in your area."

"They do," Frenzy said. "And they're with us, along with quite a few other MCs in the state. We aren't a typical club, but we garner the respect and fear of others because they know what we're capable of. They steer clear of trouble and will back our plays to maintain peace."

"Why would they do that?" Trench asked.

"Because we don't involve ourselves in drug running or weapons or any of the other money making endeavors they're in," Jumper said. "They stay far away from us, and we mind our own business."

"In return for that, they ride when we call," Frenzy said.

"How many?" Trench asked.

"Your little friend here can't count that high," Jumper answered with a sneer. "A smart leader never gives numbers. Show, don't tell."

"Are you saying I'm not smart?" Anger mottled Trench's words.

Fuck. This was going south. Short fuses weren't ever a good characteristic for a gang leader.

All five of the men drew their weapons. Frenzy sighed and pulled his.

"Well, that was stupid," Cholo commented. "Advice. Don't ever draw down on the Scythes. That's begging for a body bag."

"You're outnumbered," the short man said. He whistled. Ten more El Fury members appeared from behind bushes to the left and right.

"That was almost too easy," Sandman said with an evil chuckle.

"What does that mean?" Trench asked. His gaze darted around the area. Red dots appeared on all the El Fury members' torsos. Several of their gazes widened.

Razor took a few steps forward. "Lesson one: know your enemy. Scythe MC members are all former military, which means they know how to use the weapons they wield. Lesson two: know your surroundings. You think ten extra weapons is enough in the country? Here's a hint. You aren't on a city block in El Paso."

"And who are you?" Trench asked.

Razor didn't bother answering. They'd wasted enough time with the bullshit meeting already. "You have three minutes to leave this area and an hour to clear out of our turf. If you ever step foot in it again, we will hunt every single one of you down like a rabid animal. You won't like how that ends."

One of the men cursed.

"Two minutes," Frenzy said.

"What's it gonna be, Trench?" Razor looked at the gang leader, whose eyes had widened when he heard his name. "Yeah, we know who all of you are. We know where you live. Who you fuck. Who you want to fuck. We know where your families shop. Where your kids play. We even know who your women are banging 'cause they can't stand your touch. That's just what we learned for this meet and greet. Piss us off by not leaving and we'll really start digging."

"Time's up. What's it gonna be?" Frenzy asked. "I personally hope you stay. It's been boring for too long. I need some new teeth for my collection."

The short man gulped. Eyes wide, he took another few steps back.

Cholo and Mingo both laughed.

Yeah, these fuckers blew in like a tornado and were barely a small gust of wind. All bark, no bite to back it up. None of the shit Razor and the others had said should've rattled them. A real threat would've come loaded with ammunition—knowledge about their enemy's operations. Names. Addresses.

These pricks had nothing but a shotty plan.

"Like I said, this was his idea," Trench said. "He'll be dealt with. Austin and surrounding areas are off limits. I'll make sure everyone knows."

"Good. You do that," Razor said. "You should thank Cholo

for keeping the South Siders away tonight. They wanted your blood for messing with one of theirs."

"What are you talking about?" Trench asked. The short man tried to run but was grabbed. "What the fuck did you do?"

"He tried to force the leader's cousin to join your crew," Razor said. "That didn't go over too well, especially since she'd chosen to leave the South Siders for her man, one tied to a group in Houston. So, see. Now you're on their radar as well."

"He also threatened a matriarch here—one protected by every crew in the area. No one fucks with familia, ese," Mingo said. "We should put a bullet in your brain for that alone."

"Fuck." Trench shot the short man in the head. He glared at his second-in-command. "Get him loaded. We're out of here."

"Told you this was a bad idea," one of the other men said.

Trench and the higher ups piled into a vehicle, but three of the El Fury members hung behind. Anger mottled their features. Razor raised an eyebrow and locked gazes with them.

"You disrespected us!" The man raised his gun.

Gunfire echoed in the area as the man fell to the ground, along with the other two. Trench and his second-in-command exited the vehicle. Shock registered on their faces.

Red dots danced along their torsos once again. Trench cursed as he put his hands up.

"He drew on us," Frenzy said, his tone casual. "You want to make the same mistake?"

"You aren't alone." Trench glanced back at the multiple red dots on his chest. Clearly he hadn't noticed the dots the first time they'd appeared.

"That's lesson three," Razor said. "Always control the situation. Store your trash and leave our area. *I* am Razor, by the way, and you'd better pray you never see me again."

The El Fury members worked quickly to haul the dead men into the trunks of their vehicles. Razor waited until they were almost done to add fuel to their inferno.

"Oh, by the way, Trench." Razor waited until the man's gaze locked with his. "You're on a ninety-day probation starting today. We'll be watching everything you and your crew do. If you so much as twitch the wrong way, you won't see the next dawn."

The man nodded and got into the car. The vehicles sped off, kicking up dry dirt in a storm of dusty fury. Jumper laughed.

Cholo shook his head. "Probation? Really?"

Razor shrugged. "We will be watching."

"Teeth?" Mingo asked. "Seriously?"

"Sounded good at the time," Frenzy said.

"You fuckers terrify me," Cholo said. "Are we done here?"

"Yeah," Razor said. "We're done. Talk it out with Homer and get Lupita sorted. We can have someone escort her to Houston if that's where she wants to be."

"I'll handle that," the man said. "You've done your part." He motioned toward a vehicle pulling up. "That's for you."

Razor grunted and turned toward the unknown SUV. Two tall, muscular men exited. Tattoos covered their arms. Both walked with a confident swagger and had dark hair and the same dark eyes. Brothers, maybe. Definitely relatives.

Neither Cholo nor Mingo attempted conversation as they piled into their car and left. Jumper, Frenzy, and Sandman tightened their proximity to Razor.

Both men halted. The one on the left chuckled.

"That's cute," he said. "I'm Raul, from The Arsenal. This is my brother Dom. We heard you needed some tech. We were in the area for a personal matter and got the call. Tex figured you wouldn't want to wait."

"And you carry that kind of tech around all the time?" Frenzy asked.

"Our fearless brainiacs insist," Raul said. He glanced at the bloody ground. "You handled that well. I almost believed eighty percent of what you said."

Razor chuckled. "I take it you saw? How?"

"A drone," Dom said as Raul removed a duffel bag from the SUV. "We were curious. If you need backup getting that data, let me know. I have people I can call. Cholo's got a few connections, but I have more. They'd shoot their own mother rather than piss me off."

Razor hadn't expected someone like Dom to be tied up with The Arsenal. He carried himself much like Cholo and Mingo. Street trained, not military. Interesting.

"We appreciate it," Sandman said, "but we're covered."

Raul held out two small cases. "That's enough for two large houses, both audio and video. They're small and wide-angled. Undetectable frequency, no metal. Specially designed, so untraceable."

Frenzy whistled. "You sure you don't mind us using this? We'll try and gather them all back, but I can't make any promises."

"Edge said her friend Tex vouched that it was important. They're yours. We've got plenty where that came from," Raul said. "You need help installing them?"

"No. We've got someone who'll get them in once we get a plan on how," Razor said. "The house is never left empty. He's up for the challenge, though."

"Fuck something up. Electrical. Plumbing. Anything that'll encompass the whole house would work." Raul shrugged. "Air conditioning is an easy one."

"Dead rat in the ventilation system," Dom suggested.

Sandman grinned. "You'd fit right in with us. We were thinking along the same lines."

"Good luck. Those will operate with HERA, by the way. Instructions are inside."

"I'll get Anarchy to review all that. We aren't Counterstrike, so we don't have access to HERA," Razor said.

"You will for that," Raul said, motioning to the cases. "Edge mentioned that specifically. I know your crew has locked this area down for gang activity tight. Respect for that, man. I don't know what's going on now, but Edge was very specific you had permission to run those through HERA. You'll want to take her up on that. The system will automatically transcribe everything said in real time."

"Fuck, boss. You give this to Anarchy, and we'll never see him again," Jumper said.

Razor glanced at the cases. "If they transcribe automatically, why isn't Counterstrike doing that with their safehouses? That would've saved a lot of time. We've got eyes on a family right now and have crew members listening to hours of audio."

"Their safehouses were kitted out with tech specific to protection only," Raul said. "They weren't down with invading the privacy of those they were protecting. Plus, these are new tech Counterstrike doesn't have yet. We didn't even know we had these until a few days ago."

Razor grinned. For the first time since the trouble started, he really felt like they'd turned a corner on figuring out some of Jen's problems. "We owe y'all one for this."

"We don't work like that, man." Raul motioned toward where the shots came from. "Though, I wouldn't mind meeting whoever took those shots one day."

"I'll make sure they know," Frenzy replied.

Razor waited until the two men left. He handed the cases

over to Frenzy. "I want these in by tomorrow night at the latest. If he's got problems, let me know."

Frenzy nodded and headed toward his motorcycle. Razor glanced at his watch. Ten p.m. He'd get five, maybe six hours of sleep before training began, but at least one problem was cleared, and another was in process.

CHAPTER 11

Jen startled awake. A hand landed across her mouth, stifling the scream rising within her throat when a man hovered over her.

"Don't scream. I'm a friend of Razor's. Get your phone. We've gotta get out of here," the man said.

Jen had been around her brothers long enough to know when to listen and keep her mouth shut. Intensity resonated within the man's muscular body as he stood beside her bed, weapon drawn.

Gunfire sounded from outside. No, way louder than a gun. An explosion? Fear clawed her insides and scrambled her pulse as she vaulted off the bed, snagged her phone, and nodded that she was ready. She followed him out into the narrow hallway and paused to slip on a pair of sneakers.

He headed toward the back door and motioned her toward a motorcycle parked in the alley. Floodlights filled her brothers' yard.

"My brothers live next door," she whispered.

"Someone else is extracting them," the man said. "You're my charge." He straddled his bike. The loud roar fractured the silence. Wait. Silence. Wasn't there gunfire earlier? "Get on."

This wasn't how she'd envisioned her first motorcycle ride going, but she wasn't going to argue the point. A ride was a ride. She climbed onto the back of the stranger's bike and hoped her brothers, Marisol, and Victoria were okay. Everything in her screamed they wait until she knew for sure, but she had to trust this man because Razor did.

Even a second of hesitation could be a problem. Gunfire sounded from behind them. She stifled a scream when the motorcycle surged forward. More gunfire sounded. Something whizzed by her head and hovered.

A drone.

Shit. That was one of The Arsenal drones from the main house.

The man driving like a bat out of hell cursed and drew his weapon. He aimed at the drone.

"Don't!" she shouted over the loud engine. "That's a friendly. A drone from The Arsenal. It'll help us." She didn't know if he even knew who The Arsenal was, but something she said or her firm tone must've gotten through because he didn't shoot at it.

Another appeared in front of the motorcycle. A bright light appeared from it, pointing right.

"Follow it! Someone's mapped out an exit." She trusted those drones. Whoever was manning it would help them out of whatever the heck was going on. She squeezed the man tighter and willed her breathing to slow.

They angled right, following the drone. Then the motorcycle banked a hard left into a narrow alleyway. The drone darted past their attempt at combatting its plan and continued forward. It shown a light in their faces. The man continued, unfazed by the drone.

Oh boy. The badass who'd driven her away had pissed off whoever was behind that drone. Not. Good. He accelerated.

Loud thumps sounded from behind them. Jen turned her head and stifled her scream when she saw a small car following.

"Hang on!" the man shouted. Jen squeezed his waist tighter and screamed when the motorcycle went airborne. What the hell? A ramp?

Her bones rattled their anger when the bike landed. The man pushed a button on a black box and slowed. A high-pitched whizzing sound echoed from behind them.

Boom.

The thunderous sound was followed by a huge ball of fire. Jen blinked as smoke filled her eyes. The car was in flames. Holy shit. Holy shit. Holy.

The commando had not only had an exit path planned out but had also armed it with freaking bombs. *Deep breath, Jen. He's a friendly.* She really hoped he knew Razor. What if he didn't? Why hadn't she had a secret code his crew would use? Ugh.

She screamed as the motorcycle surged forward once again. The drone must've accepted he was in control because it fell back behind them while the other one remained near her head.

She forced a deep breath and assessed herself. No injuries. Yet.

Cold air brushed across her exposed skin. Fleeing her home in the dead of night while wearing a pair of thin pajama shorts and a chemise wasn't smart. Mental note: wear real clothes while sleeping for the next week.

The motorcycle stopped a few minutes later. Jen looked around the narrow alleyway behind a convenience store. The man got off and headed toward a black muscle car of some kind.

He motioned toward the passenger's side. "Get in."

Right. Now probably still wasn't the time to ask questions. *Follow orders without hesitation.* How many times had Ethan and Milo drilled that into her head? Tons.

The drones both flitted into the vehicle when she opened the door. The man cursed as he started up the car. She belted herself in and expended a breath. Now what?

He shoved his cell phone into a holder on the dashboard and punched a button as the car powered onto the nearby road. He blew through a red light and made a hard left. 1:04 a.m. shone on the dashboard's clock.

"Talk to me," a voice ordered through the phone.

"Package secure. Two unknown fuckers are in the backseat. Friends of yours?"

"Yeah. Arsenal drones." The voice paused. "Jen? You okay?"

Frenzy. Thank God. Someone she knew. "I-I think so. What happened? Where are my brothers? Victoria? Marisol! She's about to have a baby." Okay, not about. She still had a couple months to go.

"Hopefully not tonight," Frenzy commented. "Shadow?"

Okay, she had a name for the phantom operative. Shadow. It totally suited his dark, growly personality.

"She was my charge. They're Grim's." Shadow glanced over at Jen. "Sampson will need backup. Two targets DOA. One in custody. Explosive ordnance."

"Fuck."

"They were outside the security system's range when Sampson spotted one target aiming an RPG at the house. Red alert went out."

An RPG? As in a freaking rocket propelled grenade? What the heck?

Silence descended for a few beats. Jen licked her dry lips and added, "Don't forget about the boom in the alley."

"Yeah, we've already heard about the boom in the alley," Frenzy said, amusement evident in his tone. "You surprised whoever was running the drones at The Arsenal. I'm thinking that doesn't happen too often."

The fact Frenzy wasn't at all surprised told Jen he'd expected something like that from Shadow. Damn. Ethan and Milo had seriously underestimated the Scythes.

"You told us to bring our A game, boss," Shadow said.

"Any other surprises in the area we should know about?"

"That'll depend on how clean Grim's exit is," Shadow said. "I'm inbound. ETA ten minutes."

"Make it less. Razor's chewing through his last strand of patience, man."

"Fuck." Shadow hit the end call button and glanced over at Jen. "You Razor's?"

"Uhm, I don't think so." But her body heated at the idea of being his woman. Tingles ignited along her skin.

He chuckled. "You are."

"So, you must be one of his ghost crew then." Jen nodded her acceptance and wrapped her arms around herself. "Thanks for getting me out."

"Took a fuck load longer than I wanted to break that security."

"I'm kind of surprised the drones didn't dart you," she muttered. "They're supposed to."

"Oh, they tried." Shadow made another turn. "I moved faster than they probably expected. A hazard of the job."

"Right." She glanced back at the drones, which still hovered in the backseat. "I think those are loaded with some really bad stuff, just so you know."

"Noted," he said, amusement evident in his voice. "I'll have you to Razor soon."

Jen remembered the gunfire. "You aren't hurt, are you?"

"No." He glanced over. "Are you?"

Streetlights finally shone enough for her to study the man's features. Dark blond hair hung in disarray around his rugged jawline. He was handsome in a mean cut way. Tall, like Razor, and muscular. But leaner than Razor or Frenzy.

Her phone! "Shit. I lost my phone somewhere."

Shadow sighed and punched the button on his phone.

"Yeah?" Frenzy asked.

"She lost her phone. Have a prospect follow my route and find it. I'd start by the inferno and backtrack from there. Don't let them touch any boxes or crates with a red and black X on them unless you want to field test their bomb disposal skills." Shadow's gaze swept down her slowly. "You might want to grab some clothes for her."

"What the fuck?" Razor's voice exploded on the other end of the line.

Shadow chuckled and ended the call.

"That probably wasn't smart," Jen advised.

"Nope, but it was almost more fun than that ride we took," he said with a laugh.

"I wouldn't mention that to Razor either. He was supposed to be my first ride." Okay, that didn't come out the way she meant. Heat crawled up her face.

Shadow chuckled. "Definitely Razor's. This is gonna be fun. It's about time Prez found a good woman."

"You don't even know me."

"I know you never hesitated tonight. You did what I said. If you'd been a few seconds slower that RPG could've blown us both up. We couldn't assume Sampson had that fucker sorted. So, yeah, I know all I need to about you, lady." Shadow grinned. "Welcome to the Scythes. I've heard of trial by fire, but this is the first RPG introduction."

Someone had tried to blow her up. The statement started a ripple of fear that iced her insides. A tremble settled in her bones. Her ears rang. Eyes burning, she tried to force a deep breath.

"Hang on. We're almost there."

* * *

Razor paced the entry to the compound. Frenzy and Sandman hauled him back whenever he went too far into the yard. Crazy fuckers were itching for a beat down.

Where was Shadow?

"Calm down," Frenzy said. "Sort your shit before she gets here."

"Grim just phoned," Anarchy said from inside the compound. "They're five minutes out."

Thank fuck.

No injuries, except the assholes who'd gone after Jen. An RPG. Some crazy fuck had almost blown her and her house up. "Tell me we know who's behind this."

"Not yet, but we've got one alive for questioning," Sandman said. "Sampson's bringing him in. Jumper's heading the cleanup team with the local PD. We'll probably need one of the Davenports to smooth that over."

"Already handled," Anarchy shouted. "Edge is online. The Arsenal is working it."

Headlights appeared in the distance. He vaulted forward and waited as Shadow's Charger rolled to a stop. The man exited quickly, as if sensing the thunderstorm waging within Razor.

"She's in shock," he said as he ran toward the passenger's side. Razor cut him off and opened the door.

Jen's wide eyes latched onto him. He noted her pale face as she surged into his arms.

"Fuck." He kissed her head. "You're okay, beauty. I've got

you." She trembled in his arms. "Someone get me a blanket. Why the fuck isn't she dressed?"

"No time," Shadow said.

Sandman tossed Razor a blanket. He wrapped it around Jen and drew her into his arms. He carried her into the compound but fought back the urge to take her to his bedroom. She'd want to see her family.

"Your brothers and their wives are safe. They'll be here any minute," he whispered into her ear.

"Thank you." She rested her head against his chest. He sat down on the sofa.

"Someone get her some water," he ordered. He stroked her cheek. "Stay with me. You're safe. Everyone's safe."

"Incoming," one of the prospects shouted from outside.

Razor kept his attention on Jen, rocking back and forth. She stroked his arm.

Milo and Victoria entered first, holding each other's hands. Ethan came in carrying Marisol.

"Put me down before you get a hernia," Marisol said.

"Hush," Ethan mumbled as he headed toward the sofa. He sat beside Razor. His concerned gaze slid over Jen. "Sis?"

"I'm okay," she whispered.

"She's in shock," Frenzy said. He handed a blanket to Ethan, who wrapped it around his wife.

"What happened?" Victoria asked. "If you have any chocolate, that'd probably be good for them to nibble on."

"On it," Jumper said. The man had a sweet tooth and always kept the kitchen stocked with chocolate. Thank fuck.

Milo sat on the other side of Ethan and dragged Victoria into his lap. The woman swatted his chest but curled into him.

"It was like World War III," Marisol said.

"I just want to know who was on them tonight," Anarchy

said. "The security alarms I had activated for HERA went off seconds before the freaking explosions and gunfire started."

"Jen's house?" Razor asked.

"Fucker got his shot off, but Sampson intercepted fast enough to prevent a direct strike. Front of it'll need significant work, though. The yard is a hole. Fire department is there and containing the fallout," Frenzy said.

"The HOA will love that one," Milo muttered. Victoria chuckled.

"Who was on them?" Anarchy asked. "I never saw the schedule. Hell, I didn't even know anyone was assigned to them."

Razor glanced over at Sandman. The man motioned toward the private meeting room. "Let's talk in here. Jumper, stay on with Edge and see what we can do to help."

Razor stood with Jen in his arms and carried her into the conference room. No way in hell was he leaving her alone or turning her over to someone else. Milo entered with Victoria. Both looked back into the other room.

"Ethan's sitting this one out," Milo said. "I'll fill him in later."

"Boss, we should bring Jumper in here. We'll need to speak with Edge to get an update," Frenzy said.

"Call him in." Razor settled Jen in a seat. "Do you want another blanket?"

Razor dreaded the conversation they were about to have. It was long overdue and one that'd test the friendship they'd formed with Anarchy. The man should've known about the ghosts when the MC formed, but they'd all made a judgment call. Leaving him out of the loop had been a necessary decision, even if it was a shit call.

"I'm fine, but some clothes would be good when there's a chance?"

Milo's gaze swept to his sister. "Why's she in that?"

"Probably because there wasn't time for a wardrobe change," Victoria said. "We only had time because Grim literally screamed 'Incoming! Get your asses up and out here!'"

"The RPG was aimed at Jen's house, so there was even less time," Frenzy added. "The fact she got out is a miracle."

Razor winced. "None of them are good with people."

"They got the job done," Milo said. "Ours had the vehicle on and ready to go by the time we got downstairs. Less than three minutes from entry to exit. Impressive."

"That's two minutes more than it took with Jen," Sandman said as he sat. "That man moves fast."

"No shit," Jen whispered. "Whoever was running those drones probably wants to kick his ass. They tried to tell him where to go with lights and he was not having it. Then we went airborne and boom. That explosion nearly gave me a heart attack."

"Airborne?" Victoria asked.

"Explosion?" Milo shouted.

"There were some complications. Someone gave chase. Shadow was prepared," Frenzy said. "We need to find out what other traps he has out there."

"He's probably already en route to handle them," Sandman said. "He left as soon as Jen was inside."

"I didn't even get to say thank you," Jen said.

"I'll make sure you get a chance later," Razor whispered. He ran a hand through her messy hair, then glanced around the room as Anarchy entered with his laptop. The door thudded shut.

"Jumper's tapping out of this meet so he can field problems from the scene if needed. More of our crew is riding out there. Okay, so," the man said. "Who the hell was on them tonight?"

"Remember that line item on our monthly budgets I promised to explain one day?" Sandman asked.

"Yeah."

"That's who was on them tonight," Razor said. "We have some Scythe members who are under the radar."

"Way, way under," Frenzy added. "You know a few of them. Shadow was on Jen."

"Holy shit. Okay. That makes sense," Anarchy said. "You should have told me."

Razor blinked and sighed in relief. He was taking the news better than expected. Hopefully he'd take the rest as well.

"Wait. You said under radar when you told us," Milo said. "I didn't realize that meant your own crew doesn't know about them."

"Only Frenzy, Sandman, and I," Razor admitted. "And now Anarchy. We'll tell Jumper later."

Shock resonated on both twins' faces as they looked at one another. Yeah, they'd gotten the subtext of the admission —he'd trusted them with the unknowns before his own crew.

"What happened?" Victoria asked.

"Get Edge on first," Frenzy said. "We'll need an update anyway and I'm not repeating myself."

The phone rang.

"Everyone okay?" a male voice asked.

"You aren't Edge," Frenzy said.

"No, I'm Jesse Mason. She's on the phone with the APD Chief of Police and I think the governor or some other government person. Not sure. Is everyone okay?"

"Yes," Razor said. "This is Razor. Frenzy, Sandman, Anarchy, Jen, Milo, and Victoria are in the room. Thanks for the assist tonight."

"We didn't do as much as we could have. Things went south before we even knew there was a problem," Jesse said. "Your men reacted fast and handled it very well. Who was with Jen?"

"Shadow," Frenzy said. "Jen mentioned he probably pissed one of you off."

"No. We were just trying to figure out what his plan was. You should've had coms."

"That would've helped," Sandman said. "From what little Grim, Shadow, and Sampson have shared, Sampson caught a target aiming an RPG toward Jen's house. He neutralized him and alerted the other two to extract their charges while he handled the other two threats."

"The fire has been put out. Whatever he did prevented the structure from being directly hit," Jesse said. "It would've been a lot worse if your men hadn't been as good as they are."

No shit.

"Two targets are DOA. The other is at a secondary location awaiting questioning," Frenzy said.

"HERA's facial recognition scans identified all three as mercenaries," a woman said. "This is Edge, by the way. Zoey is working on hacking their system to try and find out who hired them via any electronic trail or the DarkWeb."

"So we still don't know who's behind this," Milo said. "Any movement from Sam's father?"

"None," Razor said. "That problem is in process, though."

Milo tightened. "What does that mean?"

"That means we're putting a pin in that until you, Ethan, and Victoria aren't in the room," Edge said. "That's between Scythe and The Arsenal. Counterstrike is not part of that."

"Understood," Victoria said. "What's the plan going forward?"

"Training should probably be cancelled," Milo said.

"And the picnic," Sandman added.

Fuck. Razor hated disappointing Sam. The kid had been through enough. His gut twisted at the thought of cancelling their activities. "Sounds like retreating to me. We don't run from a problem. We face it head on."

"Agreed," Frenzy said.

"Someone just tried to blow up my sister's house," Milo said. "They aren't getting another shot at hurting her because we kept moving on like it didn't happen."

"Thoughts, Razor?" Edge asked.

The inquiry sounded more like a challenge than a real question. He took a deep breath and gave his honest answer. "They fucked up tonight. They didn't expect the trap we sprung. We didn't catch the real psycho behind this, but we'll get answers soon. Until we do, we spring another trap."

"Meaning?" Sandman asked.

"Meaning we use the training and, if necessary, the picnic to lull our target into thinking we're either stupid or falsely confident," Frenzy answered.

"Right." Razor looked at Frenzy. "We should modify the schedule for our ghosts. Have them double down on the training location and the picnic, which should be easier with Jen's house not on the radar."

"That's crazy," Anarchy said.

"No," Edge said. "It's the smart play."

"Agreed," Jesse said. "That's what we'd do, even though it goes against the grain of keeping those you care about safe."

"With Scythes and Counterstrike operatives onsite at the picnic, we'd have over seventy trained onsite," Razor said. "That wouldn't be the smart target."

"Neither would the training," Milo countered.

"We're missing a critical piece of the puzzle," Edge said. "Someone's after something and I can't help but think everything is somehow tied together."

"Or that is a false assumption and we're missing a critical piece of the puzzle," Jesse replied.

"Agreed," Frenzy said. "We just can't figure out what, how, or why."

"We'll be closer tomorrow," Razor said. "We can send the

virus and fill in some missing pieces on the Gentrys. We'll have answers from the mercenary by then."

"Virus?" another female voice sounded.

"Zoey?" Anarchy asked.

"Yeah?"

"Anarchy here. Razor's convinced Gentry to let him invest some money in the hedge fund. He thought we could use one of your viruses to root around in their offline systems and trace it through the banks and emails." The man paused. "I started putting it together."

"Good. Send it to me. I'll look it over and make any changes," Zoey said. "That's a good plan. HERA will shred through intel quick once the email is sent. I'll take point with Anarchy on that. When is it going down?"

"Tomorrow at the picnic," Razor said. "Fifty thousand is all I offered, but I mentioned a few more might be interested."

"Good. Let's get at least two more. The how much doesn't matter. They might send money to more than one location if there are multiple deposits at the same time."

"A few of us will be crashing your training tomorrow," Jesse said. "Though, you might not see us."

Frenzy chuckled. "Careful. We might take that as a challenge."

"Are you sure you have time for that?" Milo asked.

"We'll make time," Edge said. "Which of this list is on the sidebar mission?"

Razor tightened. Fuck. This wasn't how Anarchy should find out. "Knight with a K."

Anarchy paled. "What? He...he died. I stood over his casket."

"So did two of the bastards who almost put a bullet in his brain," Frenzy said. "You were still locked in with them for six months afterward. He couldn't risk you knowing the truth."

Anarchy swallowed. "And after I was out?"

"We're watched," Frenzy said. "You know we are. You're the one who tells us whenever those satellites hover over the compound. We couldn't risk mentioning him. Shit, it's a risk just saying his name aloud in this meeting."

"You were tight with him. We couldn't risk them not seeing you in mourning," Razor said. "It was a shit call, man. I'm not gonna lie. This has eaten at all three of us since we made that play."

"But we didn't have a choice," Sandman added.

"I get it." Anarchy nodded. "You still should've told me afterward."

"Sorry, man. You know we would have," Sandman said.

"That's on me," Razor said. "I made the call. If you're pissed with anyone, take it out on me." That's what leaders did—fall on the sword for their brothers.

"I get it. I do. Just sucks not to know," Anarchy said. "I'll get some scramblers for this room."

"No need," Edge said. "We'll bring some equipment with us."

Thank fuck. Razor sighed his relief. They'd needed to kit a secured room in the compound for a long time, but finding good enough tech was damned near impossible. Not having one had ground their investigations into things to a halt because they couldn't risk discussing it.

"We can pay you for the tech," Razor said. "We just didn't have a resource to get it from and didn't want to link ourselves to Tex by asking him for it."

"No payment necessary," Jesse replied. "And we understand why you didn't ask Tex. You didn't want him linked to the Scythes and fall on someone's radar."

"Several someones," Frenzy muttered.

"Okay, that's enough for tonight. We'll circle back tomorrow," Edge said. "Razor, is your crew point on the interrogation?"

"No," Milo said.

"Yes," Razor answered. He looked at Milo from across the table. "We can go further than you're willing to go. He's ours."

"I'll go anywhere to protect my family."

"You don't have to. This is ours," Frenzy said. "Counterstrike keeps their hands clean."

"He's right," Victoria whispered.

"Text me the address he's at," Edge ordered. "And the time. I'll send someone to assist in case help is needed. People tend to talk quickly when he enters a room."

"Or piss themselves," Zoey commented. "If he doesn't show up before you start, mention The Judge and see what happens."

"Fuck," Anarchy whispered. "He's not real. He's a legend."

"Oh, he's very real," Zoey said.

"We won't be sending Jud. Gage is going," Edge said.

"Wait. Why? This is so a Jud thing," the woman argued.

"Jud is needed elsewhere," Jesse said. "We'll talk about it later."

Razor glanced at his watch. Four a.m. "Any chance of delaying the training by a few hours?"

"Already done," Milo said. "Ten a.m. start. I gave them the compound's address since they're still coming in early. I hope that's not a problem."

"Not at all," Sandman said. "I'll get everyone settled into rooms. They aren't anything fancy, but the beds are clean and decent."

"We appreciate it," Victoria said. "Are you sure there's room?"

"Yeah. Most of my crew will likely spread out around the

perimeter and bunk down. They get jumpy when shit goes down," Razor said.

Everyone stood to disperse. He kept his attention on Jen as she rose from the chair. The blanket fell open around her chest. The thin material did little to hide her gorgeous body.

"Come on, let's get you to a room so you can sleep." He guided her down the hall and to the room nearest his. Dickish move, maybe, but he wanted her close in case she had a problem.

She entered slowly and turned a full circle. She clutched the blanket closer.

"Hey," he whispered. He cupped her face and waited until she looked up. "Talk to me."

CHAPTER 12

"Talk to me."

Jen couldn't process everything that'd happened. She fought in a courtroom, not on the streets. This was so far over her head she was drowning.

One step at a time.

"I'm overwhelmed," she admitted.

"Pretty sure we all are. You're safe. I won't let anyone hurt you." He cupped her face. "You need to crawl into bed and get some rest. We'll figure everything out in the morning."

Sleep was the last thing she wanted. Awareness arced between them as she wrapped her hands around his middle and rested her head on his chest. "I know this is weird because we don't know one another that well, but will you stay with me? I…I don't want to be alone yet. My mind's not going to calm down."

Razor ran his hands through her hair and rested his other hand on her lower back. "I'd love nothing more than to crawl into bed with you, but that's a terrible idea for several reasons."

She glanced up at him, so drawn into his intense obsidian

gaze she forgot to speak. Getting lost in the moment with Razor seemed like the perfect escape, one she desperately needed.

He traced his thumb along her cheek. “Fuck. Don’t look at me like that. I’m trying to be the man you deserve right now.”

“Then stop denying what we both want,” she whispered. “Or am I reading too much into this? It’s been a long time since I’ve been this drawn to someone.”

He groaned and claimed her mouth. Heat spread through her as the kiss intensified. He tasted of peppermint and tobacco and commanded the moment with the same savage confidence he always possessed.

Jen surrendered to the onslaught of sensations as he nipped her lower lip, then licked the small bite of pain away. Then his tongue swept into her mouth and the carnal need ignited. She moved her hands beneath his T-shirt and scored her nails across his warm skin in a silent plea for more.

“Fuck, you taste better than I imagined.” He kissed along her jaw, pausing near her earlobe. He nipped it, then continued trailing his mouth down her neck. “I have no business dirtying you up. You deserve better than me.”

“Shut up,” she growled. “Don’t you dare say that.” She yanked his T-shirt over his head and ran her hands down his bare chest. She admired the flex of his abdominals beneath her touch as she kissed the Scythe tattoo on his chest. A skeleton wearing military fatigues holding a sickle. Blood droplets dripped from the weapon and trailed down his torso in a long line. She touched each set of initials inked into his skin, all held within dog tags. “It’s beautiful and sad all at the same time.”

“My brothers who didn’t make it home.” He touched the tattoo. “I’ll tell you the story, but not tonight.”

He tugged on her hair until she looked up. His molten

gaze made her pulse quicken as he claimed her mouth. He caressed down her arm, then over to her waist.

Then up her side until his fingertips grazed her nipple from beneath her chemise. He cupped her breast and squeezed, firmly enough to make her writhe forward. The edge of the bed pressed against the backs of her knees.

She grasped his belt and undid it. Their tongues dueled in an all-out battle for dominance—one she knew she wouldn't win. She didn't want to win. Anticipation burned within her, a fiery need that spread through her as she unbuttoned his jeans and shoved downward.

Razor severed the kiss and pulled away. A protest rumbled from her throat. "Kills me to say this, Jen, but we aren't doing this tonight."

"Why the hell not?"

"Because you deserve more than a hard fuck and that's what this would be right now. We're both exhausted and too wired from what went down earlier." He stroked her cheek and kissed her mouth softly. "Get in bed. We'll sleep. Tomorrow night you're mine."

"I should make you sign a contract swearing that," she grumbled as she turned and crawled into the bed. "You'll stay with me?"

Indecision flashed across his face as he looked down at her. He glanced at the closed door, then back to the bed. "Fuck, this is a bad idea."

"It's not."

Razor leaned down and removed his boots. She fought the need to run her fingers through his thick hair and watched as he removed his jeans. The boxer briefs did little to hide his arousal. Stifling a moan, she stared at the prominent bulge.

"Keep looking at me like that and we'll have a problem," he warned.

"I'm a great problem solver." She smiled as he crawled into the bed beside her. Shifting to her side to face him, she reached out and dragged him closer. "This is what I need, Razor. You here with me, holding me. Making me forget about everything."

He sprawled onto his back and pulled her against him. She settled a leg across his and draped her arm over his torso. Head on his chest, she willed herself to behave. This was enough for tonight.

"I never asked if you had a girlfriend or someone special," she whispered.

"I wouldn't be kissing you and wanting to fuck you if I did." He played with her hair and sighed loudly. "There hasn't been anyone in a long time. I'm clean and haven't ever gone ungloved with anyone."

She traced the blood droplets down his body. "Neither have I. I'm on the pill and I'm clean."

"Fuck," he muttered.

"What are you thinking?" She glanced up at him.

"About being in you bare, feeling you clenching my dick as you come." He touched her chin. She peered into his gaze. "I want to fill you with my cum and cover you with it. Mark you as mine."

Damn. The caveman style possessiveness within his declaration should either terrify or piss her off, but she couldn't help but want that. No one she'd dated had ever been like that with her. She wanted Razor to be that man, the one who would forget the niceties her billionaire heiress life decreed. Her gaze moved downward to his hard cock. She traced his abdominals and angled downward, but he captured her wrist before she made it past his belly button.

"Don't. I'm hanging on by a thread, temptress. I'm not fucking you in the compound where everyone will hear your screams. Those are mine." He threaded his fingers through her hair again.

"You play with my hair a lot."

"It's gorgeous," he whispered. He reached over with his other hand and turned off the small lamp.

Jen closed her eyes and focused on his heartbeat beneath her ear. The gentle glide of his fingers through her hair lulled her to sleep.

* * *

Knight took a sip of his water and watched the target house. The last light had turned off an hour ago, but entry right now would be suicidal since at least ten armed combatants were inside.

Fuck.

Frenzy had explained the importance of getting the tech in place ASAP. He hated waiting for a soft entry when it meant hours of delay.

His cellphone rang. He glanced at the caller ID. Unknown caller.

Yeah, not happening tonight. He never answered unknown calls.

It rang again. Persistent fucker, huh. He glanced down. "Answer me, Knight."

What the fuck?

He clicked answer but remained silent.

"Knight, I'm Edge. From The Arsenal," a woman said. "I'm a friend of Razor's."

"Okay. How did you get this number? Better yet, how did you do the caller ID thing?"

"We can talk about that later. I see you're outside the target house."

“How the fuck do you know that?” He looked through the mirrors but didn’t see anyone on the vacant street.

“Later. Shadow should be at your location in a couple of minutes. He’s going to have a couple of drones with him that will help you get into the house while everyone’s sleeping.”

“There are ten armed combatants in there,” he said. “I’m good, but not that good, even if Shadow assists. We need a silent, soft entry so they don’t know we’re there.”

“Thus the drones. You get a way to get them inside, and I’ll make sure everyone sleeps for a solid two hours without waking. You’ll need a gas mask.”

Who the hell was she? What she offered was too good to believe. No way was he trusting a stranger, even if she did supposedly know Razor. That shit burned him bad once. Damned near got him killed.

“Lady, I don’t know you.”

“No, but I’ve looked into your file. The real one,” Edge said. “I’ll take those bastards down myself if you trust me to help you with this.”

Knight tightened. Now she was entering crazy land. No one could touch those assholes. “That’s not possible.”

“It is. They’ll all go down by the day after tomorrow,” she said. “I never fail on a mission, and you are my mission now, Knight.”

What. The. Fuck? Fine, he’d play her crazy mental game. He already knew how it’d end up—him living half a life, off the radar, while his brothers rotted beneath the ground. And the assholes responsible still doing their twisted shit. “Why? Why do this for a dead man walking?”

“Because it’s the right thing to do and The Arsenal never leaves a man behind,” she said. “You and Anarchy were on a team with one of my operatives two years ago. He’s new here, but he’s still one of ours. Which means you are, too.”

Two years. That’d mean… “Fuck. Who? I didn’t think

anyone else got out." Someone else got out. Fuck. They needed to be protected, even if they'd been in the dark. Knight hadn't shared what he'd discovered with anyone.

"Bishop. He thought he was the only one until half an hour ago," Edge said. "The reunion will have to wait."

Shock stilled his breath a few moments. This shit was not happening. A tap on his car window drew his attention. Shadow stood two feet away.

"Shadow's here," Knight said. Was he really trusting a stranger right now?

"Good. Hang up and use the com in the black case. I'll stay on while you get this done. Shadow can help you put everything in place."

He exited the car. Shadow's gaze narrowed. "You good, man?"

"Fuck no. Weirdest shit just happened."

"Tell me about it. That was me a couple hours ago," the man said. He set the black case down on the car. He opened it and popped one of the coms into his ear. "For what it's worth, I spoke with Anarchy and Frenzy. Edge is with The Arsenal and they're solid. Whatever they say, they can back up without hesitation. Anarchy talks like she's the operation's messiah. She's never failed a mission."

Shit. Knight took the other com. Edge's voice sounded immediately into the com.

"Okay, guys. Let's get this done quick. My daughter, Jessie, will be up soon and I'd like to pretend to get some sleep. We'll need an open window or some space large enough for the two drones to fly into."

Knight admired her to-the-point orders. The zero bullshit persona was what he needed right now because his brain was still processing the bombs of hope she'd dropped earlier. Was she for real? Could they help get his name cleared? Give him back the dignity and trust he'd lost?

Nothing will bring back the men slaughtered because of you.

He focused on what she'd said. "Front door," Knight said quickly. "Security system is shit. Give me two minutes."

He and Shadow made their way to the side of the house. Knight popped the panel and got to work. It took sixty seconds to bypass the alarm. Overgrown hedges in the front of the house hid their progression to the front door.

Shadow picked the lock while Knight used a magnetic device to disengage the bolt. One minute later, the front door opened soundlessly.

Shadow opened the larger case he'd been carrying and pushed a button on two drones. They rose and disappeared inside.

"You'll want to put those gas masks on now," Edge advised.

Knight and Shadow put on the masks and entered the house. A gas of some sort hung in the air. Four men sprawled on the floor. The TV played a baseball game. What the hell?

He set the case he'd been carrying down and got to work. The sooner he got everything in place, the better. Shadow dragged the sprawled men to the sofas and chairs.

Smart. They'd think they fell asleep.

Silence sounded through the com, but Knight suspected Edge watched everything he did since a drone remained at his side as he worked. Frenzy had been clear to hit every room from multiple angles for full coverage. The cameras were sophisticated equipment he hadn't seen before.

"I'm activating as you put them into position," Edge said. "They're already recording and transcribing. Anarchy will have full access once he wakes up."

"Perfect."

It took forty-five minutes for him and Shadow to wire the entire house and position everyone onto a bed, sofa, or chair. They exited via the front door, which they relocked.

He went around the side of the house and reactivated the security alarm.

His pulse rattled hard by the time they were back to his car. "We're out."

Shadow crouched down and secured the drones into their cases. "I'll get these back to the Davenport home and into position, Edge. Thanks for the assist."

"Glad to do it. I'll be in contact with you both soon." The promise buried within the words struck Knight hard. Shadow visibly shuddered beside him. He didn't know the man's story. No one who ghosted within the Scythes ever shared. They all had their reasons, ones they either weren't ready to share or couldn't.

Knight removed the com and stared at Shadow. "What the fuck just happened?"

"Razor just hooked the Scythes to Counterstrike and The Arsenal," Shadow said. "The latter's taking an interest in us. Brace yourself, brother. Our wait is over."

"Fuck." Knight leaned on his car. "Fuck."

He wanted to believe what Edge had said, but he couldn't let the hope take root, not if them wading in could get them killed. Too many had already died because of him.

"Get some rest. Shit's going down tomorrow. They'll need us both sharp."

* * *

Jen stretched and glared at the clock near the bed. Three hours of sleep wasn't much, but it'd have to do because today would be a long, packed day. She opened her eyes and visually feasted on the washboard abdominals near her head.

Mmm. She could get used to waking up like this. Too bad he would probably nix any morning fun of the carnal variety. While she appreciated him not wanting to do anything where people could hear them, she had never been embarrassed by her sexuality.

To play or not to play? So many options for the latter. She feigned sleep for a few seconds, then rolled over and away from Razor. Slowly opening the nightstand drawer beside her, she froze. Holy heck. Whose room was this? The sheer volume of sexy play paraphernalia astounded and grossed her out in equal proportions. She'd never, ever use half this stuff, but hmm…the cuffs could come in handy.

After all, she wanted to play and Razor wanted to be a gentleman. Nope. Not today. They'd almost died last night. Correction. She'd almost died. She definitely deserved a bit of relaxation, and she knew precisely what she wanted.

Her pulse quickened in anticipation as she set the restraints near the pillow. Razor was so handsome. His face softened in sleep, making him sexier than ever. The slightest movement would wake him up. After all, he was a highly trained operative. Was she really going to do this?

A hand gripped her hip, then she was flipped over onto her back. Amusement danced in Razor's eyes as he peered down at her. "Good morning, beauty. Whatever you were planning, don't."

"Hmm. Me thinks you doth protest too much." She wound her arms around him and leaned her head upward until their mouths touched. "And good morning. It would've been a better start if you'd given me a couple minutes to get my nerve up."

"What were you planning?"

"Nothing I'll tell you. There's always tomorrow morning," she teased. A groan escaped her when he kissed her neck. "Don't you dare get me turned on and stop."

He chuckled as he caressed from her waist in an upward trajectory. "I'd love to start the morning off by sliding into you and feeling your sweet pussy grip my dick, but half the compound would hear us. That's not happening."

Her body heated at the thought. A glint shone in his gaze when he held up the cuffs. She feigned nonchalance when he lifted them up and arced his eyebrows. "I thought they could be fun."

"I love that you're playful in bed, but for the record, you'll never need to keep me there. I'm always up for whatever you want to do." He tossed the cuffs onto the nightstand. "Though, I'd prefer you in them over me."

He claimed her mouth with a carnal kiss that left her breathless. Her nipples hardened as she arced up and writhed against him. "Then let's play."

"Tonight," he promised. He rested his forehead against hers. "How are you doing?"

"Okay, though I wouldn't complain about another couple hours of sleep," she admitted. "You?"

"Great. It's been a long time since I've had a gorgeous woman wrapped around me all night." He feathered soft kisses along her lips. "I can't even remember the last time I slept with someone."

"Not sure I want to hear about your conquests," she whispered. "Though, I get what you're saying. It's been a while for me, too."

Razor stilled, his gaze turned intense. "You're more than a casual fuck to me, Jen. I don't know what this is between us, but I know it's important enough to handle with care."

"Tonight you're mine," she declared. "You promised me last night, and I'm holding you to it."

"We'll see how today goes." He caressed her cheek. "We aren't rushing this."

Jen wanted to scream her frustration, but she appreciated being more than a conquest. Someone he wanted to get to know first. "I didn't have sex until freshman year in college.

It lasted all of two minutes. I didn't understand what the big deal about sex was until the next semester when I met Harrison. I thought we had a connection, but he apparently wanted to educate the entire school, so that didn't last very long." Ack! Verbal diarrhea. Eject. Eject.

"Should I track him down and kick his ass?"

"Nope. My dorm mate and I took care of him," Jen said with an evil grin. "She was pre-med."

"Oh boy. Pre-med and pre-law. I bet you two got into some trouble." He kissed her mouth, deepening the contact until she felt it throughout her body in heated tingles. Tonight couldn't come fast enough. "I was fourteen. She was nineteen."

"Damn. Go you." Jen chuckled. "A bad boy, even back then."

"She was a...I guess the polite term is a club groupie. Popping my cherry was her birthday gift to me, via Gramps. She'd tried the year before, but I saw her tits, blew my load about five seconds later, and ran away." Razor chuckled. "In my desperate attempt to escape my shame, I tripped over a bunch of crap, including one of those old-fashioned razors Gramps had laying around. It sliced up my calf. Six stitches and a couple hours later, I had my road name. Razor."

Laughter tumbled from Jen. She couldn't imagine Razor afraid of anything, much less a woman wanting to have sex with him. "Tell me that's not true. Oh. My. God. Wait! Does everyone in your club know?"

"No." He grinned. "Only Frenzy and Sandman. And now you."

Wow. Jen's heart thudded hard. He'd given her a secret, a big one. "She must've really been in love with you to turn around and try again the next birthday."

"I was the president's grandkid. Back then everyone assumed I'd take the reins when Gramps decided to turn the mantle over." Razor lay back on the bed and drew her against him. "Then I decided I wanted something different and told him I wanted to join the military. I'd just graduated high school. Fuck, he was pissed. Didn't talk to me for over a year."

"Damn." Jen hated hearing that. "Did you reconcile?"

"Yeah. I got back home a couple years after enlisting and we spent my entire leave riding with the club. That became our thing. I'd come home and we'd ride. We'd spend hours on the road. No conversation. Just the fresh air and the freedom of the open highway." He sighed. "We had that for five years before he passed."

"And your parents?" Jen asked.

"Dad did some crazy shit and got caught after killing a couple of locals in a bar fight," Razor said. "Mom wasn't ever about the MC life, so she cut us all loose after that. I was ten."

She couldn't imagine a mom abandoning her child. Jen's stomach tightened. Her own mom had endured so much to try and protect Jen and her brothers. "That's her loss. Do you ever see him?"

"No. Gramps always taught me to surround myself with the type of person I wanted to be. That wasn't dad." He sighed. "He didn't last long inside, died when I was thirteen."

"No siblings?"

"None. I sometimes wish I'd had some, but growing up in the club, I had so many I considered family. I think that's why I wanted to be military so bad. I knew it'd be a brotherhood. I'd heard Gramps talk about it often enough." He stroked her hair and stared up at the ceiling. "Then everything went to shit."

Jen tightened. She didn't want to ask, but the curiosity rode her hard. What had happened?

"My spec ops team was given a mission to take out a local tribe leader. Intel was spotty at best and command wouldn't listen when we expressed our concern," Razor said. His voice lowered. "We went in, but everything went to shit quick. We figured out the target was supported by a different branch of our government. Killing our own wasn't something we were prepared to do. Command ordered us to continue. I refused. When we got back to base, I was hauled into custody. Charges kept changing, but the gist was I was branded a traitor. Somewhere between leaving and returning, all proof of the initial orders was gone."

"Damn. How is that even possible?" Jen's mind buzzed with ideas on how to help him uncover the truth, but she quickly came to the conclusion there wasn't much she could do in the military arena. Her legal reach only went so far.

"I have no idea. There's more to it, but that's the gist of how I was tossed out on my ass." He touched her shoulder. "One day I'll get the proof, if it still exists."

"I bet Mary, Vi, and Zoey could help." Or they'd know who could.

"I'm sure, but I won't ask. Not until the rest of the Scythes we can clear are taken care of. I'm okay with who I am. I know the truth. Those I care about either accept that, or they don't." He peered into her eyes. "I hope you understand."

He was putting his brothers first. "I do. I know you're a good man, Razor. Even if I don't know you're real name yet." She grinned.

"Banner Nilon, named after my Gramps." He chuckled. "Razor is better."

"I don't know. Banner's pretty sexy, too," she whispered. She stroked his stubbled jaw. "Thank you for telling me."

"I want you to know everything about me. This won't work if I keep things from you. I feel like I already know so much about you, but I know there's more to discover. I'm looking forward to that."

"Me, too." She smiled. "Too bad we can't stay in bed all day."

He growled and kissed her. Pleasure ignited along her skin. She moaned. He severed the kiss and whacked her butt. "Time to get up and eat. I'm betting we have intel to get through before training starts."

Ugh. Jen wanted to hide out and forget about the troubles awaiting them. But they wouldn't go away, which meant she needed to adult hard today. Too many people were risking their lives to get answers. She wouldn't let them down.

* * *

Razor walked into the compound and through to the room they held church in and froze. A faint buzzing noise struck his senses first, followed by a wall of screens along the back wall. A high-tech looking glass table with black edging sat where the scarred table once was.

What the fuck?

He hadn't realized he'd spoken aloud until everyone in the room laughed.

"Sorry, Prez," Anarchy said, in a tone that indicated he was definitely not sorry. "They showed up a couple hours after everyone crashed and got to work."

And who were they? His gaze scanned the room and halted on a blonde, a brunette, and a woman with purple and pink hair. The three looked up from their laptops, which were set beside Anarchy's on the table.

"Meet Edge, Quillery, and Zero D, the brains behind The Arsenal and my new best friends." Anarchy rubbed his hands together. "So, what world-changing thing do you want me to do first, Prez? I have the keys to the kingdom."

"Hold up there, bucko. You're provisional," the purple-haired woman said. "I'm Zoey. Edge is Mary, and Quillery is

Vi. I know your club goes by road names or call signs or whatever else you bad boy commandos call it, but we go by our given names more often than not."

"Sit," Edge said, in a tone that made him mentally vow to never, ever call her Mary. That name didn't give the woman justice, not after the shit she'd done for Knight and Shadow in the early morning hours after someone tried to kill Jen with an RPG. "We'll get started in a minute. There are a couple of people missing."

"Started with what?" Razor sat.

The door opened. Jen slid in, followed by both of her brothers and Victoria.

"Good to see you, but you two," Vi said as she motioned to Ethan and Milo, "should go outside and have coffee. There are donuts. Eat, drink, and be merry with Trigger and his team. This shouldn't take long, but you can't be in here."

"Why the hell not?" one of the twins asked.

"Milo, we discussed this," Victoria said. "Come on. Donuts sound perfect. Let us know when we can come back in."

"Will do," Zoey said. "So, who's on this vagabond team you put together while sleep deprived?"

"Jud as team lead," Mary started.

"Oh boy. This will get interesting really quick," Zoey cut in.

Edge glared. Vi took a sip of her coffee. The latter continued. "Kristof, Spade, and Mia. Drink your coffee, Mary. We've got this. Jud was way too excited to assist with this."

"So, we have a team with two assassins, an underworld spook so dark we still don't know what all she's done, and an operative who has no boundaries? Yep, this'll get weird real quick. Why don't we have an ordnance expert?" Zoey asked.

"Because two of those four can handle ordnance," Vi said. The door opened. "And this is off book. *Really* far off book."

Razor froze when Knight walked in, followed by Shadow, and Grim. Dom and Raul sauntered in and shut the door. "Will someone please tell me what is going on in my clubhouse?"

"Right. This is a promise being paid out," Edge said. She cut her gaze to Dom and Raul. "Where is he?"

A knock sounded at the door. The two men moved and opened it. A tall man with pale gray eyes and dark hair entered. His gaze swept the room, pausing on Anarchy, then on Knight.

Bishop. Razor's breath swooshed from his lungs as the three men ran at one another and hugged. Emotion choked the atmosphere within the room. He leaned over to where Jen had sat beside him. "Good morning."

Red rose in her cheeks. "Good morning."

His dick hardened as though the husky whisper was wrapped around him. Fuck, her mouth was a registered weapon. The way she'd... *Control yourself, man. Focus.* "How are you feeling?"

"Good. Very good." She sipped her coffee. "You?"

He hadn't felt this good in years, if ever. Although he wanted to do nothing more than drag her to his bed and spend the day there with her, he knew whatever was about to happen would be intense. The Arsenal had commandeered the compound and was about to rain hell down on someone if his suspicions were correct.

Knight had called him shortly after Jen had fallen asleep. The conversation had been quick, but rife with emotion—mainly confusion and hope. Tons of fucking hope from a man who'd had none for years since almost his entire team was killed. No. Slaughtered.

"This is a black-in-black mission, entirely off book," Edge said. "I know you three have a lot of catching up to do, but it'll have to wait. Our window just opened. Sit."

The three men sat. Knight rested his forearms on the new table. "You must be Edge. Thanks for last night. I'm surprised you're here so quick. This isn't about what you promised a few hours ago, is it?"

"It is," Edge replied. "We don't mess around with situations like this. The quicker we respond, the better. You've waited long enough to breathe free air. When we tracked these assholes down and found them within driving distance of our compound, we acted."

The Arsenal compound was only three and a half hours from here, which meant the assholes who'd done Knight wrong were within a day's drive max. Fuck. All this time. If they'd known, Razor could have…

Could have what? Gotten himself more on radar? No. The Scythes didn't have the clout they needed in this arena. But Edge and her Arsenal crew did, and they hadn't hesitated to set a wrong right.

The woman donned a headset. Vi and Zoey did the same. The screens at the front of the room flickered, as did the surface of the table. What the heck?

Jen chuckled. "Fancy."

No shit. Razor remained silent as the three women did something on their computers. Voices sounded through speakers he hadn't noticed in the corners of the room.

"Everyone's in position," a voice sounded through the com. An image flickered on the table's surface when the man spoke. Jud, aka The Judge. Anarchy had mentioned him being a phantom, the bogey man whose name alone terrified anyone with an active braincell because he was one of the most lethal assassins in existence.

"Remember the objective," Edge said. "We're sending a message. Blast it far and wide."

"Understood." A woman's image popped up on the screen.

Mia. "Anyone want to tell me why there's a bar in the middle of nowhere serving liquor at dawn?"

"Because anything goes down there. Focus," Zoey ordered.

Surveillance images showed a brunette's progression into a small bar. Someone sang onstage, but he didn't recognize the language. Where the hell were they?

Before he could ask, more footage from a secondary location appeared. Two men made their way into a small house. Early morning shadows cloaked the area around them, but the video was crystal clear. Razor watched as they made their way to a back bedroom. They descended on the bed's inhabitant.

A man's screams sounded through the speakers, then stopped when one of the operatives held a knife to his throat.

"There are two ways you can die tonight, Gus. Quick or very slow." Jud's image lit up on the table, indicating he was the speaker. Razor appreciated whoever had made it easy for him to follow along.

"Whatever you're being paid, I'll double it."

Razor tightened when the promise thundered through the line. How would Edge and the team act? Gus wasn't just anyone. He had the political connections to follow through with his promise, even if he was a sack of shit. He may have "retired" from military service, but his high ranking kept him in the loop more than most anyone would realize—a fact Tex had shared a few times.

"My honor isn't for sale, especially to a prick like you who sold out his own men when they stumbled across your sick, perverted bullshit," Jud said.

Knight tightened at Razor's right side. He fisted his hands and kept his gaze locked on the screen. This was the bastard who'd destroyed Knight's reputation and then tried to kill him. If it hadn't been for Tex, he would've been in that coffin two and a half years ago.

Knight had survived the explosion, but barely. Razor had seen the man's scars, wounds he hid from everyone but a trusted few. He'd had the foresight to call Tex despite the pain. The former SEAL had gotten him out and somewhere safe.

Then he'd called Razor.

Razor set a hand on his shoulder and squeezed.

"Tell me the names of everyone involved in your pedophile ring and I'll kill you quick," Jud said.

Pedophile ring. Was that what Knight had stumbled across? The man had never offered details, and Razor hadn't pried. Anger rolled through him. Why hadn't he asked?

"We already know about Tynes and Gimbal," the second man said. Razor glanced at the table's surface. Spade. "We know there are more." A scream echoed through the room as Spade broke Gus's arm.

"Bone breaks won't make sick shits like him talk." Jud's maniacal grin flashed on the screen as he ran the knife down the man's chest. At first Razor didn't think he'd cut him, then he saw the blood. "Shallow, cut down, then across. One section at a time. Too deep and he'd bleed out."

"What's he doing?" Anarchy asked.

"I think we're getting a lesson in how to skin an asshole, Jud style," Zoey quipped. "Ugh. Maybe donuts weren't a good idea."

"Switch back to Mia," Edge ordered. "We don't need to watch Jud to know he'll get the answers we need. HERA's recording."

"Thank you." Zoey pushed a couple of keys and only Mia's feed showed. She sat at a table sipping a drink. Two men bookended her, their lustful gazes locked on her low cut and snug dress.

"Tell me, have you always been pedophiles, or did you work your way into it?"

"W-what?" the one on the left asked as he paled.

The man on the outside of the booth tried to slide away, but Mia grabbed him by the neck and slammed his face onto the table. "Going somewhere? I was just getting started."

"Who are you?"

"Justice." She held up a vile. "Here's how this'll go, boys. Give me the names of all the people involved in what happened to Gus's team and I let you drink this. It'll be a painless death, one you don't deserve, but I'm in a good mood right now. I suggest you accept my kind offer."

"You're crazy," the man on the left said.

"Probably." She pulled out her cell. "Option two is this." She clicked the screen and held the phone out so both men could see it.

Whatever they saw made them both pale. The one on the woman's right almost puked.

"Don't be stupid like Gus, or you'll meet The Judge tonight. So, which will it be?" The woman smiled sweetly at them both. She lifted her drink and took a sip. "A nice painless drink with Justice after you spill your guts, or would you prefer The Judge to spill them for you?"

Silence descended as the two men looked at one another.

"I'm hoping for the latter. Really, the man is genius with his craft," she commented. "I'm creative, but he's truly inspired with sick shits like you, especially when he's in a foul mood. And, just to say, getting dragged out of his bed in the middle of the night to deal with you has made him very, very irritated."

Mia patted both of the men on their backs as a dark-haired man sat opposite them in the booth. He shoved a pad of paper and a pen toward them.

"Write every name down," the man ordered. Kristof.

One of the men reached for the pen and paper. "I-I was just the money man. I never touched any of them. I swear."

"Right. Sure," Mia said. "Less talking, more writing. The Judge looks like he's ready for another test subject. Be smart, boys." She glanced at Kristof. "Want to have breakfast after this? I'm starving but can't decide between a nice, thick and bloody steak or eggs with ketchup. I didn't even know ketchup on eggs was a thing until one of the women mentioned it."

Kristof shuddered. "No. No eggs with ketchup. That's just..."

"Don't judge a pregnant woman. They get whatever they want," Mia advised. "Steak it is. Though, finding somewhere that'll serve it this early will be a problem."

Kristof chuckled. The amusement echoed in the room as Zoey added her laughter.

"Damn. She is nuts," Zoey said.

"She's smart. She's using their fear and feeding it by imposing a normalcy," Edge said. "They thought they were untouchable. She's showing them they are nothing more than a chore before her day truly begins."

"I don't ever want to cross anyone on that crew," Frenzy commented.

Neither did Razor. Vi grinned and shook her head. "You'd better not be wearing those clothes when you get home, Jud."

"Like I'd be that messy," he chided over the com.

Razor's attention shifted back to Mia and the two men as one of them spoke. "You can't do this. We're—"

"We know exactly who you are," Kristof said. "And we don't care. Hand over your phone."

Mia grabbed it off the table and tossed it to Kristof. He glanced at the list the other man was making, then down at the phone. When the man pushed the paper toward him, he nodded and tapped the screen several times after he inserted something into it at the base.

A ring sounded on the speakers.

"Gimbal. Do we have another one already?" a man's voice sounded.

"Idiot," another said. "Not on the phone."

"They're secured," the first man argued.

A third and fourth started asking questions to who they assumed was Gimbal.

"Gentleman, your friends Gus, Gimbal, and Tynes are about to meet a very painful and agonizing end. You have six hours to turn yourself into the contact I'm about to send. If you don't…" Kristof paused. "I'm really hoping you don't."

"Who is this?" one of the men asked. "You don't want to fuck with us."

"Oh, but I do. I really, really do," Kristof replied. A chime sounded. "Oh. Perfect. Here's a little insight into your future if you opt for ignoring my warning." He tapped a few buttons on the phone. "Six hours, gentlemen."

He clicked off and glanced at Mia, who shrugged. "They're stupid. They'll probably run, then we can hunt again." She poured the liquid into each man's drink and stirred them both with a straw. "Is that all the names?"

Both men nodded.

"Excellent," Mia praised. "You both made the right decision. Now, drink up. Quickly. I've already wasted enough time with this. Oooh. What about pancakes instead?"

Kristof shook his head. "Whatever you want, *Justice*."

Silence enveloped the room a few minutes as Mia and Kristof sat with the two men. She patted them both on the cheek as she slid out of the booth. "I'd say have a nice afterlife, but we all know where you're going. You deserve far worse than this."

Kristof offered his arm as she moved to his side. She

smiled up at him. They made their way out of the small bar and toward a black car.

"They're clear," Vi said a few moments later. "Team one. Status?"

"It's done," Spade said. "Message delivered." An image flashed across the screen.

"Holy shit," Jen whispered into the thickening silence.

Carnage. No. Artistry in blood. The image was distinctive —a knight above one word. Checkmate.

Razor wasn't sure who the message was to, but he doubted it'd be missed. How would Edge cover this up?

She wouldn't. She wanted this message to get out to whoever they still hunted.

For Knight, Bishop, and Anarchy. His brothers. These strangers had done this for his crew.

"Good work. Check your six and get home. This never happened," Edge said. "Did we get everything HERA needed?"

"And then some," Vi said. "Bank info was on the phone. Jud got the rest."

"Tear it all down," Edge ordered. "You know what to do with the funds."

Knight tightened. "Respect for what you just did, but I don't want a penny of it."

"We figured you wouldn't," Zoey said. "We'll have a chat later today. You three and me. I have an idea what we can do with it. If you say yes, I'll make it happen."

"Tell us now," Anarchy said. "No more secrets from my brothers."

"Gus kept files. Pictures of the victims," Vi said. "We locate their families and send the funds to them. It won't undo the damage done, but it'll give them what they might need to start a new life."

"New identities. Homes," Zoey said. "We'll make it happen."

"Why?"

"This is what we do." The woman glanced up from her screen. "Or part of it. We make assholes pay for their crimes and empower the survivors. We turn the tables and walk away. Wash away what we did like it never happened."

"But the message," Razor said.

"We aren't done hunting," Edge said. "One more is out there. It'll take time to cut him off at the knees, but we will. Then we'll end him."

"No one outside this room will know," Vi said. "For their own good. Especially Counterstrike."

Her gaze landed on Jen. Razor wished they hadn't let her in the room. "Why is Jen here?"

"I'm your attorney, and as of now, theirs should they ever need me. Street justice isn't always okay with me, but I know them and they wouldn't do this unless the crimes were so heinous and the perpetrators so embedded within the red tape they'd never face true justice if they were exposed."

"They wouldn't," Edge said. "These are the tough calls that are sometimes necessary. Everyone in this room understands that." She looked at Knight, Bishop, and Anarchy. "You're in the light now. Well, in two days. It'll take that long for Tex to work his magic after their unfortunate demises are discovered."

"He shouldn't be part of this," Razor said.

"It was his call," Edge said. "You've safeguarded him well, Razor, but he's chosen to help because these men betrayed their team. They slaughtered your brothers in arms, and they will never see real justice."

They wouldn't. None of the assholes who'd screwed over his brothers would. Most of the situations weren't nearly this extreme. All Razor needed for most of them was evidence. Proof.

"In case you missed the memo, we're wrapped up in your shit tight now," Zoey said. "We're wading in. Either help us or stay out of our way."

"We'll help," Knight said. "Whatever you need. Whenever. Even if it isn't our shit. Thank you."

Emotion filled the man's words.

Bishop cleared his throat. "Never thought I'd get this justice. I figured I'd do what I could at The Arsenal to help others find theirs."

"No one fucks with our family," Vi said. "You are part of that family, Bishop. Which means so are the rest of you through him. There's nothing we won't do for our crew."

"As long as he doesn't piss Nolan off too bad," Zoey quipped. She looked around when Vi swatted the back of her head. "What? He's grumpy right now. Bishop's the noob on the team. He's gotta know this stuff."

"We'll handle the rest," Vi said. "You guys have a picnic to coordinate."

"And some Deltas and commandos to impress," Razor said with a grin. "I'll try and be gentle."

"Please don't," Zoey said. "I promise they won't be."

* * *

Razor sealed the door shut behind him and took in the new meeting room. They'd all taken half an hour to get breakfast—not that many had actually eaten after witnessing the mission. Knight and Bishop were still chatting in a corner near the kitchen.

"New soundproofing," Anarchy said between sips of coffee. "One of The Arsenal's operatives drove it up an hour ago."

The Scythes had a safe meeting area now. He glanced over at the women huddled at the front of the table. "Thanks for that."

"Any time," Edge said. "We haven't heard anything about the man you detained."

Neither had he. Razor pulled out his cell and set it on the table. He scrolled through the contacts until he found Purge's name. The man was more psycho than most everyone Razor knew, but he was damned good at getting answers when no one else could.

"Prez." The man's voice sliced through the room's silence when Razor tapped the speaker button. "Our new friend has been light on the sharing, but he's coming around. They've been working out of Eagle Pass and Del Rio the past couple of years, doing mostly wet work for hire. I'm getting details on that, but our bud Brad Taylor doesn't have much on who hired them to go after Jen. They were paid a hundred large up front with the promise of another hundred after it was done."

Razor grunted and swept his gaze to Frenzy and Sandman, who'd both sat on the other side of the table from The Arsenal women. Anarchy nodded as he typed on his laptop. Zoey whispered in his ear and pointed at the screen.

"Something's not adding up," Purge said.

"Talk it out," Edge ordered.

"They were contacted six weeks ago." The statement thundered through the room. Ethan and Milo both cursed and shoved themselves from the wall they'd been leaning against. "We've got another active target if that's true."

Translation—Sam's father wasn't behind Jen's threats. Fuck. "Get everything you can about their operation. Anarchy and his new friends might be able to pull more from their computers or other shit."

"And Brad?" The underlying question within the inquiry

tightened Razor's gut. There wouldn't be any question at all if this was solely a Scythe mission.

Razor cut his gaze to Jen's brothers. They both tightened and glanced at Edge, whose attention was on Razor. She held up four fingers. "Sit on him for a few more hours. I'll have a decision by then."

He clicked off and ran his hands through his hair. Fuck. What now? "Get a team together from those not involved in last night's shit. Get to Jen's office and round up her files. You'll probably need to take her or her assistant with you."

"Hazard and Bea can meet them there," one of the twins offered. "Most of Jen's work should be online as well. She can give access to whoever needs it."

"That'll work," Sandman replied. "Anarchy and Edge can be point on the online stuff. We'll have the office files within two hours."

"Homer's cousin is in Houston," Frenzy said. "The turnover went off without any problems. Homer's square. Mingo is shadowing his crew, just in case."

At least there was one thing off their plate. Razor grunted his approval. "We're missing something important. Why just her and not the two of you?"

"Fuck if we know," one of the twins replied.

"Then let's ask her." Zoey exited the room and returned a few minutes later with Jen.

Razor's body reacted to Jen's presence like a livewire. She moved toward him and didn't stop until her arms wound around him. "Hey, beauty. We need to chat."

"Zoey said some things weren't adding up. How can I help?"

"What work are you doing outside of Counterstrike?" Edge asked. "You are the target. Not your brothers. We need to figure out why."

"We're sending some people to your office to gather files.

Hazard and Bea are meeting them there," Sandman said. "Anarchy and Edge need access to your online files."

"Of course." She rattled off a user ID and password. The brainiacs started typing on their laptops. "As for what I do outside of Counterstrike, it hasn't been much. A few restraining orders and a couple of lawsuits. All the details are in the miscellaneous folder."

"The order came down six weeks ago if what we've found out is right." Razor touched her hair. "What started back then?"

Her eyes widened. "Damn. That makes sense. I should have thought about that. But it doesn't make sense. I mean, he's in jail."

"Who?" One of her brothers growled the question.

"Calm down, Milo," Ethan said. "We're gonna figure this out. Give her a minute to process."

"It doesn't make sense, but it does," Jen whispered.

"What? Give us details so we can help you talk it out," Zoey ordered.

"Mahoney," Jen said. Razor tightened. "He was arrested as part of the Guerillo operation, though."

"Why are you thinking he's behind this?" Razor asked.

Jen glanced over at Edge and Zoey. "He was a partner at the law firm dragged into Guerillo's plans. Mahoney was his attorney. He made a deal with the feds to testify against the leaders in Guerillo's cartel in exchange for immunity and witness protection. He got off too easy."

"What did you do?" Milo asked.

"I found out who all was victimized by his scheme and filed a lawsuit on their behalf." Jen chewed on her lower lip. "It was settled out of court, but I got the bulk of his finances. But, again, he's in federal custody."

"That doesn't mean he's not behind it," Edge said. "Either him or someone who was working for him."

"Fuck, that makes sense. Guerillo used the city cameras to follow Hazard's and Bea's movements," Ethan said.

"And whoever's been threatening Jen has been doing the same," Frenzy said. "What happened with the list of people with access to those cameras?"

"Victoria and I narrowed the potential threats down to three, but without anyone to link them to on the other end, that thread was halted," Anarchy said. "We can continue it now and see if any of them are connected to Mahoney."

"Or anyone Mahoney is connected to," Zoey said. "I'll show you how to expand the net."

"I don't remember you mentioning that lawsuit to us," Ethan said.

"Honestly, I spent a few days getting everything together and filed it." Jen shrugged. "I moved on to active Counterstrike cases after that because we were covered over."

"Fuck, we should have suspected him immediately when we heard about these threats." Milo slammed his fist against the wall.

"You've been slammed. We'll help get Counterstrike organized so this doesn't happen in the future, but things fall through the cracks all the time no matter how organized you are," Edge said. "All you can do is remember no fire ever goes out completely. There's always an ember still burning."

"I think now's a great time for all you commando types to go train or blow something up," Zoey said. "We have enough intel gathered to dig. Let us do our thing."

Sandman and Frenzy stood. Razor trusted them both to get the files needed from Jen's office. Relief filled him. They were finally getting some fucking answers. He touched Jen's cheek. "You okay?"

"Yeah. I'm just feeling pretty stupid I never considered Mahoney a threat. He's a lawyer. A blowhard." She heaved a deep sigh. "Damn. I was so sure it was Sam's dad."

"Tunnel vision," Zoey muttered. "That's why group think works so well."

Razor understood what the woman was saying, but he didn't want Jen doubting herself. "Look at me, beauty."

Her gorgeous eyes were watery. Fuck. He wanted to kiss away her pain and self-doubt, or whatever other monsters made those tears form. "The work you do is important. You make a lot of enemies, but none of them will ever touch you. Do not ever doubt yourself or the work you do. You keep kicking ass and let us worry about the fallout. This isn't your fight to handle alone."

"He's right," Ethan said as he approached. "We should have realized you'd gone beyond our original scope to help those hurt by Mahoney."

"We should have asked what you were working on," Milo added. "We won't make that mistake again."

Razor recognized the blame the brothers were piling on themselves. He did it often with his crew. "Don't pile the blame onto your backs. Your workload exploded after Guerillo went down. You've recognized the problem and are actively working on it."

"Victoria's done a lot to help organize the operational side of Counterstrike," Edge said. "You need more help in that arena. Specifically, someone to gather information from the legal, operational, and investigative sides and disperse that intel to everyone. That'll prevent this from happening in the future." She put a hand on Anarchy's shoulder. "Field and Patch are good, but they want to be more operational. They won't ever give up the field work. Since you're signing a contract with the Scythes, I'd recommend you consider Anarchy to coordinate that for you."

The man's eyes widened. He paled. Razor grinned. "He'd be perfect for that role. He's bored off his ass."

"No shit," Sandman muttered as he exited the room.

Ethan and Milo looked at one another. The latter nodded. "We'll chat after this is all over."

And after they'd vetted themselves with the Deltas today. Razor offered a chin lift. Clearing his crew was still the priority, but actively helping others would go a long way in keeping the morale of his club up.

* * *

"I never thought I'd get my ass kicked this hard while firing a paintball gun worth more than my house," Sandman said as he went belly down in a ditch beside Razor.

Razor couldn't help but laugh. He'd expected today's "training" to be hard, but he'd underestimated exactly how involved it'd be. Two teams of Scythes were facing off against one Counterstrike team and the Delta team. Four groups total, each vying to capture the flag atop a flagpole in the middle of the battlefield.

The objective seemed easy enough. Add in the assorted landmines and other surprises, though, and the mission was far from simple. Everything was computerized, from the weapons they shot to the "explosions" from the computer run explosive ordnance.

Although Razor would prefer spending today ferreting out the threat against Jen, he couldn't deny training with his men felt good. Shooting guns and blowing shit up went a long way toward calming down and getting his head sorted.

"Three targets in the northeast structure," Frenzy said. "Red team. No clue where the others are. They're all still in play, though."

Red team was Delta, and they were damned good at what they did.

"Four blue are to the south," Jumper said. Blue was the other Scythe crew. "Their other three remaining are to the southwest." Only three had gotten hit so far—not bad considering the competition.

Yellow only had two combatants remaining. Razor almost felt sorry for taking out the two he had, but Ethan and Milo had been clear—no holds barred. They wanted reality, not friendly combat. The Counterstrike operatives making up the yellow team were good, but it was evident they hadn't worked together for long and needed to work on their communication skills.

Razor, Frenzy, Sandman, and Jumper had opted to go in as four rather than add anyone to their group when Anarchy begged to remain on the sidelines and watch the HERA system grade everything.

"Let's head north," Razor said. "We'll cull the red team but look alive. Their other four are out there somewhere, likely on the periphery picking stragglers out. Find them."

The three men exited their makeshift "camp" and made their way through the fallen structures to avoid the open area filled with landmines and other wicked problems they'd prefer to avoid.

"We using these fancy coms now?" Frenzy asked.

"May as well," Sandman replied.

Razor grunted his approval and waited until the other separated. They'd each take a structure and clear it as they made their way toward the target location, which was a quarter klick away. He was impressed with the training setup and wished he could get something similar set up for his crew. This was what he'd loved about being part of a team—the challenge of working together to achieve an objective.

He entered the squat building and slowly made his approach through the narrow hallway. A flash struck his vision. Pressing himself up against the wall, he opted for stealth rather than a trigger-happy response. No one in this challenge should be sloppy and give away their position, which meant that flash was intentional.

He entered the nearest room to his left and breathed a sigh of relief when he noted the secondary exit. Clearing the area quickly, he continued forward via the other door.

"Yellow down," Frenzy said via the com.

A buzzer sounded a few seconds later, indicating one of the other Scythe team had been taken out. Damn. He really needed to train them better. Some weren't at the level Counterstrike would likely expect.

Razor shifted his weapon as he entered a large room. A man adorned with a yellow patch on his left arm squatted behind a couple of crates. While the hiding spot wasn't bad, it left his back exposed to the door Razor had just used. He took the shot, then moved onward to clear the rest of the building.

"Damn." The man stood. His jaw twitched as he offered a quick chin lift.

Razor would have time to chat with him later, but not now. There were still seven active from the Red team, and he was determined to cull that number, even if by only one. It took three minutes to clear the building. His skin pricked as though he was being watched, but he couldn't find anyone.

"Proceed to target," he ordered via the com. "Let's end this. Frenzy, you're primary."

"Understood. I'll grab the flag for us." Razor couldn't help but smirk as he made his way out of the building. If anyone were somehow listening into their coms and shouldn't be, they were about to have a big surprise.

The area around the flagpole was clear, but that didn't surprise him. Anyone lying in wait wouldn't want to be seen until their target was closer. He assessed the high vantage points, then swept his gaze along the thicker brush farther back. Shrubbery rustled, barely a discernible movement. He aimed and fired without hesitation.

Adrenaline surged as he made his way toward the target area. Surprise filled him when he realized two flags flew, not just one. Huh.

Frenzy shot out into the clearing from behind a building. He turned and shot behind him, then continued forward in a lunge that carried his large body behind a vehicle. Yellow paint splattered the metal.

Razor grinned. He followed the shot's trajectory and shot. "Yellow down."

"Final yellow down," Sandman said.

"We've already proven we're all good with the guns," a man said as he appeared behind Razor. "Let's see what we do without them." He tossed his weapon onto the ground and offered a big grin.

Razor tossed his weapon and held up a signal for his team to stand down. He noted the red band around the man's arm, which marked him as a Delta. Fuck yeah. Now this was getting fun.

One by one the seven red team members appeared in the clearing. Each one motioned toward one of Razor's team as the others remained a distance away. The challenge had shifted and become a one-on-one competition. Fine by him.

Jumper went down first. The tall operative who'd taken him down offered a hand to haul him up moments later. Razor shifted his attention to his challenger.

Pain shot along his side with the first strike, followed by a quick blow to his gut a second later. Razor grunted with the impact, but countered with strikes to the man's throat, then his gut. Punch after punch landed, both on him and the Delta. Neither backed down.

Sweat dampened his skin as the fight continued until a

shrill whistle filled the area. Razor kept his attention on the Delta, who grinned.

"Go ahead and look," the man said.

"Nah, I'm good. You go ahead."

The man chuckled.

"Carry on," someone said. "We have the flags but go ahead. I've got five on Trigger."

"No way. Razor will win. I'll take that bet," Sandman said from above him.

Wait, what? Razor darted his gaze toward the pole, where a tall man and Sandman were both standing on a narrow platform near both flags. Each man held one.

Sandman shrugged. "I took the second-place flag, boss. It's only fair since they've got seven remaining."

"You started with four," the man beside Razor said. "Both teams are as they started. It's a draw for first."

Razor couldn't help but smile as he held his hand out. "Razor. You and your team made us sweat more than once."

"As did yours." The man took Razor's hand. Shook. "Trigger. Let's introduce our teams. Tex had a lot to say about you all when he phoned earlier today."

Razor bet Tex shared more than he should have if the man's tone was any indication. "He's a damned good man."

"He is." Trigger clapped Razor on the back. "He said your crew was solid and to ignore the bullshit you've been dumped in. From what we saw today, I believe it. You ever need anything, we're just a call away. Though, we do wander down here more often now. Milo mentioned you might start helping Counterstrike out."

"That'll depend on today. Most of my crew haven't had good facilities to train in for a while. They're rusty." The admission stung, but he wouldn't bullshit anyone—not when people's lives were on the line. If the Scythes took on protecting Counterstrike clients, they'd have to be ready.

"You'll get them there. This is a great setup and will likely get better," Trigger commented as he motioned toward Edge and the other women huddled around a laptop with Counterstrike's geeks. "Those women are fierce."

"They are." His gaze cut to Jen, who stood with the other women. Her laughter lit the area up.

"Let's help gather the gear. We'll help your crew get the picnic organized."

"Everything should be mostly done, but we'd appreciate help with whatever's left." Razor halted. "Apologies in advance for any weirdness you might have with some of the Scythes. Most don't judge someone without getting to know them first, but they're protective of one another and quick to act."

"No explanations necessary. I know a lot of them haven't had the best experiences with active military," Trigger said. "Hopefully today they'll see we aren't all like whoever did them wrong."

Razor hoped so. His gaze cut to Jen as she made her way from the group and headed toward him. Blood surged southward into his dick. Waking up with her this morning had been…

Everything.

Fuck. He wanted to dirty her up, fuck her a hundred different ways, then do it again and again. Women like her didn't fit in someone else's world because they were the ones everyone orbited around. Not because she was pretentious or anything like that. No. She was just that amazing.

Trigger's amusement rumbled from beside him. "I see where your attention's at. I'll see you later."

Razor gave the man a chin lift, then honed in on Jen as she came to a stop in front of him. He set his hands at her waist and dragged her close until she pressed up against him. Her arms wrapped around him quickly, zero hesitation to dirty her pretty pink top with his sweaty, dirt-crusted gear. "You have fun watching us?"

"Yeah. You did good." She ran a fingernail down the memorial tags he always wore and scrunched her nose. "You need a shower. Want me to wash your back?"

"Mmm…I'd rather you focus on something else." He ran his hand through her hair. Tugged. Possessiveness struck him hard when she emitted a soft moan. "You like that."

"I like a lot of things," she whispered back. "I'll have to make a list."

"I'm looking forward to reading it." Then he'd add a few more things to it, starting with her gorgeous mouth wrapped around his cock. "Come on. Let's go see how wet you can get."

CHAPTER 13

Jen grabbed the watermelon from the fridge. Watching Razor and the other Scythes square off against the Deltas had been fun. The newly recruited Counterstrike operatives had done well against the other teams, but they'd been far out of their element against the trained men.

The conversation earlier in the day plagued her, though. Why hadn't she realized Mahoney was a potential threat? Had she truly not realized he was, or had she simply discounted him because he wasn't the type of problem she'd expected?

Footsteps sounded behind her. She glanced over her shoulder as Milo entered the kitchen. Hmm. She'd expected a forced conversation from one of her brothers, but she'd expected Ethan.

"You shouldn't be fucking around with him," Milo said.

Jen sighed. So much for enjoying the day. She'd expected the conversation but was still disappointed. When would her brothers learn to leave her personal life to her? "Razor isn't up for discussion."

"He should be." Milo shut the kitchen door and

approached. His gaze swept the large, open area. "This isn't half bad for a clubhouse."

Nothing about the Scythes' clubhouse was pristine, but every room had soul. From the scarred tables and well-used sofas to the kitchen island, which sported names carved within the wood. Were they members? She traced the Scythe emblem etched within the surface and smiled. Even their skeleton logo had a personality all its own, much like the members.

Revelry echoed from the compound's main room even though the door was closed. "They're good men."

"I know they are. We wouldn't be here if they weren't." Milo touched her back. "Why him?"

"Why not him?" She turned and leaned against the island. Someone would eventually notice she hadn't returned with the watermelon she'd come in to cut up. "If you're going to lecture me like I'm five, at least put yourself to work."

She shifted to face the island and picked up the knife. Hmm. How was watermelon sliced? Shrugging, she got to work.

"Damn it. That's not how you do it." Milo grabbed the knife and muttered. "You've always been useless in the kitchen. Does he know that?"

"I don't think he'll care since I'm not useless in the other rooms, one in particular." She waggled her eyebrows when Milo shot her a disgusted look. If she was getting lectured, she'd make damn sure to make big brother squirm. "He's good for me. He doesn't treat me like a fragile princess."

"Then you aren't looking close enough. A blind man would see he treats you like a queen." Milo continued cutting the watermelon.

"Isn't that a good thing?"

"Depends." Milo plated some of the melon and cut his

gaze to hers. "You deserve someone who'll put you on that throne for the right reason."

Jen tightened at the implication. "He's not using me. He could care less about my bank account."

They'd had this conversation multiple times through the years, whenever anyone new entered their world. Gold diggers came in all varieties and sexes. They'd been more problematic for Ethan and Milo than her, though, mainly because very few dared approach her thanks to them.

"You're a smart woman. Promise me you'll stay that way."

She cocked her head and regarded Milo. "You think he's after something."

"I don't know what to fucking think," he growled. "That's half the problem. Part of me is relieved he inserted himself into your life because he pulled our heads out of our asses. We weren't seeing the troubles circling around you. He did."

Jen reached out and touched his arm. He set the knife down. "Don't. You have always protected me. I'm not that scared little girl crying and hiding in the closet." They rarely talked about those nights they'd survived. Together.

Ethan and Milo had always stood between her and their father. Their mother. "I'm strong because of you and Ethan. You kept me safe back then, and you still do today. But you've armed me with what I need to keep myself safe. You've got a new family starting. I'm not yours to protect any longer."

"You will always be mine to protect." Milo gritted the statement out through clenched teeth. "You're my baby sister."

"And I love you for that." She walked around the island and hugged him. "I promise I'll always come to you if I need help, but you aren't the only one I have to turn to now. That's because of you."

Milo pulled away. "He did good today. Even the Deltas

were impressed."

Razor's team was the only one still fully intact against Trigger's team. Jen didn't understand commando life, but she'd recognized Razor's skill easily enough. He was better than good. Way, way better.

"And the new Counterstrike operatives?"

"We expected them to fail miserably. They're new and haven't worked together. They did better than we predicted. With time and training, they'll be great." Milo plated the rest of the melon. "But you were right. The Scythes will make a good addition to the protection details. Get the paperwork started."

She nodded. She'd already started. "Is everything in place for later? With Sam's grandparents?"

"Yeah. There's enough surveillance set up in this compound to hear a gnat fart from a mile away." Milo smirked. "Gotta admit I wouldn't have agreed to half the shit Razor has in that regard if I were him."

"He agreed because they care about Sam."

"He agreed because he cares about you and you care about Sam." Milo kissed her forehead. "I'm not blind, sis. I just want you to keep your eyes open and see you're already in deep with him and his crew. Make sure this is what you want. If not, cut yourself loose now."

Jen swallowed. She was already in deep with Razor, too. The admission hung on the tip of her tongue. Milo suspected as much. He didn't need affirmation. "Love you."

"Love you, too." He took the plate of watermelon. "Let's get out there before they send a search party."

They'd just entered the main area when Mary and Zoey approached. The latter smiled at Milo. "Mind if we steal her a minute?"

"Sure." He kissed Jen's cheek. "See ya later, sis."

Jen tugged on her blouse and regarded the two women.

Determination glinted in their gazes. "What's up?"

"That depends," Mary said. Uh oh. She had that calm voice, the one Ethan said was her Edge persona making its presence known. "We have a plan, one that'll likely piss off your brothers."

"It wouldn't be the first time they got upset. What's the plan for?" She glanced around the filled room. She was a bit surprised they were talking about this in the open. "Should we go somewhere else?"

"No. That'd send up too many red flags. Every Scythe in here has their eyes on you," Zoey said. She waggled her eyebrows. "He's hot, by the way. Razor."

"Zoey," Mary warned.

"What? He is!" Zoey shook her head. "Fine. Here's the thing. Whoever is after you won't ever surface with so many commandos and badasses shadowing your every move. HERA's spit out two potentials: his son or his assistant, whom we believe was the second-in-command for his grandiose plan to form a crew of his own. He'd gotten further with that than the investigators realized."

"HERA found several offshore bank accounts and a nest of email accounts," Mary added. "Mahoney planned to do what Guerillo was doing—extort upper echelon within metropolitan areas. Rather than an army to hold them hostage, though, he was going to blackmail them."

Damn. What an asshole.

"So can we pick the two potentials up and question them? Turn them over to the authorities, along with the evidence?" Jen asked. She really wanted the threat over.

"We could," Zoey said. "But that'd take time, not to mention a few uncomfortable discussions with authorities. We didn't exactly come by Mahoney's name the legit way."

Right. They'd realized his potential involvement because one of the Scythes had interrogated the man and found out the timeline. Damn. She couldn't let Razor's crew get in trouble for helping her. "So what do we do?"

"Catch him in the act," Mary said. "I've spoken with the Deltas. I'm confident you're still being watched closely enough for whomever it is to notice your departure from this compound. If you leave alone and go to your office, he'll likely move in."

Jen gulped. Alone? She was all for doing whatever it took to find the asshole, but that didn't sound safe. "I'm not sure that's a good idea."

"The Delta team will be in position to intercept," Mary explained. "Along with a few of Razor's group—men he wouldn't easily recognize as being a Scythe."

"And will Razor know about this?" She already suspected Ethan and Milo would be kept in the dark, which she was okay with. But keeping it from Razor felt wrong.

"We can get him to intercept you before you leave the compound. It'd be up to you to convince him this is a simple run to the office to grab files Hazard and Bea didn't find." Mary paused. "You can tell him what you want once you're in the vehicle and on the way. City cams are focused on the compound, though. We can't risk him reacting badly if you share what the plan is too soon."

Jen nodded. They were being watched. Revulsion shuddered through her. "My personal notes are in my safe. I keep them separate from the main files, so I really do have stuff I should probably hand over." But could she do this?

Could she live with herself if she didn't? "You think this is the smart play, the way to keep everyone safe. No more RPGs or other dangerous stuff?"

"He's escalated multiple times," Mary said, her voice soft. "Moving from notes to a dead cat, then to an RPG. We neutralized that one mercenary group, but that doesn't mean he won't activate another."

"Damn." She swiped her hands down her jeans. "Did you find others?"

"Yes. We're still chasing down who's on the other side of the emails," Zoey replied. "This is totally up to you. We can come up with another plan if this won't work for you."

"I'll do it." If it kept those she cared about safe, she could definitely do it. "When?"

"Now," Mary said. "The Deltas are already positioning themselves in your building. You won't see them or the Scythes, but they are there."

Wow. "You really don't mess around." She looked around at the clusters of people laughing and talking. Scythes dominated the area, their leather cuts branding them as a brotherhood easily. But most were conversing with Counterstrike or Arsenal personnel like they were one really big and crazy family.

She would not let Mahoney or his flunkies hurt any of them. She took a deep breath. "Let's do this."

* * *

"Razor!"

Razor turned and crouched moments before Sam impacted with him. The boy hugged him tight, then pulled away. "Look! Isn't my cut cool?"

"It is." Dark circles appeared beneath the boy's eyes. Was he not sleeping well? Razor's gaze cut to the grandparents. "Hello. Welcome to our clubhouse. The food will be ready soon. Drinks are under the tree over there, along with a few snacks."

They'd kept the spread simple since the friendships and togetherness were always the priority at Scythe events. Very few of his brothers had found women, but those who had were huddled with their kids and women. He'd told them to keep the kids on a leash until he got a better read on the grandparents.

"Thank you. We're fine," Mrs. Gentry said. She touched Sam's shoulder. "Mind your manners. Remember what we discussed."

"Yes ma'am." Sam's shoulders drooped.

Razor motioned toward the gathered families. "Why don't you let him meet the other kids? We can tend to business now, if that works for you, Mr. Gentry."

"Of course." The man tugged on his wrinkled polo shirt. "Where would you like to do this?"

"Right this way." Razor guided the elderly couple into the clubhouse and toward the meeting room. He'd been assured everything was in place. Sandman, Anarchy, and Frenzy moved into position behind the couple as they entered the meeting room. "Mr. Gentry, these are my friends. They'd like to invest as well."

"Certainly. As I said, we typically don't accept just anyone, but we'll make an exception in this instance." The man sat at the head of the table and set his briefcase down. "The paperwork is very standard for this sort of investment. Feel free to read over it and ask whatever questions you have, but I assure you it's all above board. No reason to worry if you don't understand it all."

Right, because they were jarheads with no brains. Anarchy chuckled beside him as the man doled out folders to each of them.

Razor's gaze swept over the newly overhauled meeting room. The chipped table they'd once used had been replaced with a state-of-the-art touch screen computerized surface that gleamed with a shaded glass framed with black. Large screens were hidden behind a matching wood panel along the back wall.

"Get him to put his cellphone on the table if you can."

Edge's request from an hour ago thundered through his brain as everyone opened their folders and started reading the contents.

"I appreciate you doing this," Razor said. "We've wanted to invest for a while but didn't know how to get started."

"Most people don't." Gentry preened as he leaned back in the chair. "This isn't what I expected for a meeting room. I must admit I had certain...expectations."

"Most people do," Anarchy replied. "Who should I make the check out to? Or do you prefer a wire transfer? I can do it with my phone if you'd prefer."

"Right. Right. A check or wire will work," Gentry replied. He pulled his phone out. "I can deposit the check from my phone. My assistant has been forcing me to get more automated."

"It's a pain in the butt to learn new things," Sandman said. He pulled his checkbook out. "Who do I make it out to?"

"Gentry Enterprises," the man replied quickly. "Normally, we'd discuss specific goals you'd each like to achieve so I could put you into the right portfolio."

"We aren't doing that?" Razor asked.

"Since you're all starting off small, I'll diversify you with a growth strategy to begin. We can go from there." The man's hand trembled when he reached out to take Sandman's check.

Razor held his breath as the man deposited the check via his phone. It'd been on the table for a couple minutes. Was that enough? Would these electronic deposits work? How long would it take?

"If it's okay with you, I'd like to put a hundred thousand of our club's money into an account with you," Anarchy said. "I'm Treasurer. I hate seeing that much money not gaining interest."

"That's smart." The man glanced down at his phone.

"We'd probably best do that by wire. I'm afraid I have daily limits on what I can electronically deposit for checks."

Most bank apps did. Razor nodded his assent when Anarchy glanced at him. They hadn't talked about a fourth investment, so what was the man up to?

He zoned out as he signed the paperwork and let his Treasurer deal with Gentry. There was something in the works above his tech level, and he was okay with letting someone else carry that load as long as they got the answers they sought.

It took half an hour to answer the old man's questions and get the paperwork scanned and emailed to him. Razor thumped the table a couple minutes after the emails had been sent. "You mind calling and verifying receipt? I hate to think about our social security numbers and shit out there. Emails make me nervous."

"Certainly. I'll call right now." The man rose. "If you'll excuse me."

"Of course. You can use my office. First door on the right," Sandman offered.

Office was a generous term for the closet-sized space. Razor waited until Gentry left, before speaking. "What's up with the fourth account?"

"That's Edge and Zoey," Anarchy said, hands raised. "Not even our funds."

Okay then. Good enough. "Will this shit work? He deposited everything by phone. The wire won't go through until Monday, right?"

"The phone got cloned," Anarchy explained. "Whatever call he's making now will put others on the radar for HERA to dive into. Edge and Zoey will chase the trail so we have answers forming before we get a financial trail to follow Monday. Relax, man. We've got this."

"Good." He stood. He hated the idea of Sam with those

two any longer than necessary, but chances were high there was nothing anyone could do for the kid. If they didn't find anything wrong, he'd have to go to New York with grandparents he didn't know.

They'd done what they could for now. The waiting game had begun. Now what?

The list of worries rolled through his brain. Kicking back and having a few beers with his crew sounded like a perfect day, but there was too much hanging on the line for Razor to relax. He made his way outside and hunted down his quarry.

Cholo and Mingo both turned at his approach. The latter offered a greeting. "Figured you'd search us out."

"Have they made headway on the Mahoney angle?"

"Careful, man," Mingo advised. "You're sounding more like the twins by the day. We're debriefing after the picnic. The brains wanted a couple hours to work their magic."

Right. The two brothers looked at one another. Cholo tensed. Something else was going down.

"What am I missing?" Razor asked.

"You'd best go find your woman. A couple of the Arsenal women were chatting with her earlier. Whatever they said was intense." Cholo motioned toward the packed parking lot. "She headed toward the vehicles."

Damn. He headed that direction. It didn't take long to find Jen punching in numbers on an electronic lock. The SUV's doors didn't open. "Need a ride somewhere?"

Jen's eyes widened as she whirled to face him. "Wow. You scared me."

"Sorry." He pulled her into his arms. "What's the matter?"

"Nothing. I just have to run an errand real quick." Her gaze swept the area. The frantic movement tightened Razor's gut. Something was definitely up.

"Talk to me, beauty." He cupped her face.

"I've got to go get some stuff from the office. Bea didn't

know I kept some files in a safe in my office. Mary thinks what we need is in those." Jen motioned toward the vehicle. "My brothers must've changed the code." Though she didn't say the words, he recognized the plea within her gaze. She wanted him to come.

"Come on. I'll take you," he said. "You shouldn't go alone." The fact she'd even tried surprised him. Jen didn't take unnecessary risks.

"Are you sure?"

"There's nowhere I'd rather be than with you. Besides, I think we could both use a break from the crowds." Hesitation flashed across her beautiful face as her gaze cut to where Sam played with Ryan and some of the other kids. "He's good. All the Scythes have orders to keep eyes on him."

"Okay. Thanks." She followed him toward his Mustang. She whistled low when they arrived. "It's not a bike, but it gets me around. Hop in."

"You keep the keys in it?"

"No one out here will mess with my ride." He started it up and waited until she'd latched her seatbelt. "Your office?"

"Yeah. Fourth and Congress."

He knew where her office was but remained quiet as they made their way toward downtown. She fiddled with his radio until she landed on an old rock station. Music filled the vehicle. "I didn't figure you for old rock."

"Ethan listens to it a lot. It's grown on me," she replied. "You must like it. It's one of your saved stations."

"I listen to a lot of stuff." It typically depended on how long he was driving and who was with him. "What are you picking up?"

"I keep my personal notes about cases and my work separate from the main folders. We have all of the latter, but Mary wants my personal notes." She chewed on her lower lip. He battled the urge to lean over and kiss the bruised flesh. "I still can't believe I didn't think about Mahoney."

"There are different types of danger," Razor said. "Sometimes it takes a neutral third party to see the danger. We get too close when we're involved."

"You've probably seen a lot of lurking dangers. I know my brothers have." She hesitated a moment. Her palm ran down her jeans. "I never got to thank Shadow for what he did. Is he going to be at the picnic?"

"No. He and the others don't come around very often," Razor admitted. "Only a handful of us know they exist."

"That must get lonely," she whispered.

"It does, but most of them need the isolation. Too many people sets them off." Razor gripped the steering wheel. "I was like that when I first got back. Sandman, Frenzy, and Anarchy were the only three stupid enough to stay at my side."

"They sound like good friends. When Ethan and Milo left the service, they weren't the same as they were before. They never really talked about what all happened, but I knew they were haunted. Wounded on the inside. It sucked not being able to help them."

"You did. Just being there was enough," Razor replied. He would've given anything to have a sister or any family worth a damn to come back to. "Coming home to no one is harder. Gramps was all I had other than his MC."

"You have a big family now, though." She looked out the window. "They really love you. Sometimes the family we choose is much better than the one we're born into."

He reached over and squeezed her knee. "It is. I saw one of your brothers follow you into the kitchen earlier. Are they giving you shit?" Was that why she was so fidgety?

"Yes, but it's nothing I can't handle. They're overprotective," she said. "They protected me when we were young.

Ethan and Milo always stood between me and Dad. It's a hard habit to break."

He stopped at the red light and touched her cheek. "No one's ever hurting you again. They can stand between you and a threat. I won't ever shove them away, but I'll be there first."

"Only if you let me stand between you and any threat against you." She stroked his hand. "For this to work, it has to go both ways."

His gut tightened. "Do you want to tell me what's really going on?"

"That depends." She licked her lips. "Promise not to go spazzo?"

Razor's jaw ticked. "Something's going down."

"He won't ever come directly for me with so many of you protecting me," Jen said. "Edge and Zoey have the Deltas in my office and around the building, along with some of your crew. The women think we're still being watched and that he'll move in."

Fuck. He gripped the wheel tighter. "You don't have to do this."

"No, but I am because it keeps everyone I care about safer. I don't want another RPG or something even scarier coming at us," she whispered. "We could turn over what we know, but that'd mean explaining how we came to the realization Mahoney's involved."

And that'd expose the Scythe interrogation of the mercenary they'd yet to turn over to authorities. Shit. "Edge could find a way around that."

"This is the smart plan. I can do it. I just need you to trust them to help me." She touched his arm. "Please. I want to do this. I need to do this."

Although he hated the idea of her in danger because of him, he nodded. She was a smart and capable woman who wouldn't want anyone fighting her battles. The light switched to green.

"Did they give you a com?" He glanced over. She pulled her hair back. He spotted the small earpiece. "I'm onboard with this, Edge. She's not going in alone, though."

Jen smiled as she reached into her pocket and pulled out a second com. "They figured you'd refuse to stay in the car. We think it's either Mahoney's son or his assistant. The assistant was supposed to be his second-in-command for the new blackmail network they were forming."

Razor put the com into place. "This plan had better be solid, Edge. Who of my crew did you recruit?" And why the hell hadn't anyone told him?

"We kept you in the dark because of the city cameras trained on your compound," Edge said. "We couldn't risk you reacting badly."

"That's what the new secure room was for," he argued.

"True, but you were using it with the Gentrys at the time and our window was closing. The Deltas are only in town for a little while."

Razor bit back the argument poised on his tongue. He likely would've made the call as well if he wasn't personally involved. "Understood. I'm getting her out of there if things go sideways."

"We wouldn't expect anything else from a badass commando," Zoey said in the com. "We've got this, Prez."

He made the last few blocks to her office in four minutes. Parking was a pain in the ass, but she had a reserved spot in the garage. The sooner they got this done, the better. Hopefully this would work and the asshole threatening her would get caught.

CHAPTER 14

An awkward silence filled the building when they entered. Jen often ventured into her office during after hours, so the stillness was commonplace. Her pulse quickened as they made their way toward the elevator bank. Was someone watching them on the surveillance cameras? Would this work?

Razor touched the small of her back and guided her toward the elevators. He reached out and hit the up-arrow button. "So, you've got a safe in your office. That's smart."

"I value my clients' privacy. Since I choose to sometimes make handwritten notes rather than store them online, it's necessary." Her words sounded stilted. Damn. She sucked at this.

"Deep breath," Zoey said in her ear. "This is just a trip to the office with Razor. Relax. Better yet, hug him. Just be with him."

That she could do. The numbers above the nearest elevator bay decreased, signaling its imminent arrival. She took a step toward Razor and wrapped her arms around him.

"Thank you for coming with me. I hate that I dragged you from the picnic."

He kissed her softly, then moaned. "I love spending time with you however I can get it. I know we talked about a date tonight, but I want a full day. Tomorrow is ours."

"Oh yeah?" Was he serious, or was this part of the act? "Does that mean I don't get you tonight?"

He nipped her earlobe. "You're in my bed tonight. Not at the compound, at my house."

Anticipation shivered through her. The elevator pinged. With an arm around her waist, Razor moved them into the elevator. He steered her into a corner and captured her mouth. She surrendered to the molten heat spreading through her and deepened the kiss.

"Yeesh. It's like all you commandos get a manual for things to make Operations uncomfortable," Zoey muttered. "We can see you."

"Operational silence," Mary said. "He's doing what he should. Acting normal."

"Yeah. Yeah."

Razor severed the kiss and chuckled softly. Hot breath fanned along her ear. "I'm going to have you in this elevator one day. Soon. Then every time you step in here you'll think of me. Us. You'll feel me buried deep inside you whenever you come to work. You'll know what's waiting for you when you get finished with your day."

"Movement on south stairwell," a male voice said in the com.

Jen stilled. Razor's grip on her waist tightened.

"Easy," he whispered. "I'm here."

She ran her hand across his recently shaven jaw. "I was looking forward to whisker burn."

"Oh yeah?" His eyes glimmered with amusement. "I'll enjoy making that happen one day."

The elevator dinged as it arrived on her floor. Her knees wobbled a bit as they made their way into the entryway. Razor moved toward her office on the right of the elevator bay. Jen pulled her key out and halted near the glass door. Her glanced over her shoulder at the stairwell. Would the stalker leap out and attack immediately?

Warmth surrounded her trembling hand. Razor took the key and unlocked the door.

"Movement in lobby, east side," a different voice said.

"First target entering target floor via south stairwell," Zoey said. "Blue team, maintain positions. Red, move in on eastern movement. Green, fan out. Drones have identified two vehicles near potential egresses. Maintain perimeter security."

Clicks sounded in Jen's com. She entered her office's lobby and took a deep breath.

"You need anything else other than the notes from the safe?" Razor asked, his voice calm. Confident.

"No, I don't think so." She entered her office and focused on the objective. Get the notes. Act normal. Trust everyone to do their part.

She slid the door to her office closet open and stifled a yelp when she saw a man looming in the corner. He held up a finger to his mouth in a "be quiet" move. Shadow. Her heart thundered hard in her chest. Why the hell had no one warned her he'd be there? Narrowing her gaze at the Scythe, she focused on unlocking her safe.

Silence sounded from the area behind her. Why wasn't Razor talking? "You want to pick anything up before we head back to the compound? Do we need anything for the picnic?"

Fear crawled through her when no response came. She grabbed the thick file with her notes and turned. A man stood behind Razor, but the gun he held against Razor's head became her focal point. Anger surged, vying with the terror. Why hadn't anyone stopped him?

"Stay calm," Mary said. "The situation is contained. Get him talking."

Contained? The asshole had a gun pointed at Razor's head. How was that contained? "Who the hell are you? What do you want?"

The young man smirked. "Bret Mahoney Junior. You and I are overdue for a long talk, bitch. You've ruined everything."

"Your dad's at fault, not me." Jen tossed the folder onto the nearby chair and reached behind her to partially close the closet door. Was Shadow hidden well enough? Was she in the way? Was he the containment? "Why are you doing this?"

"You know why!" The man's hand trembled as he pointed the weapon at her. "Fucking bitch. Getting Dad arrested wasn't enough. You just had to take every penny we had."

"You're the one who's been threatening me," Jen said. The confession would go a long way to making this problem go away. "I was only doing my job. The people your father victimized deserve justice. Compensation."

"Fuck them!" He shoved the gun against Razor's throat. "You're gonna pay for what you did to us."

"What are you doing?" The question thundered from behind Bret as a large man entered, weapon drawn. "This isn't what we agreed to."

"Fuck you, man." Bret glared at the other man as he pointed his weapon at Jen. "You're so worried about keeping the network going that you don't give a shit about making this bitch pay."

"Both targets in play," Mary said on the com. "Green team, scour the perimeter. Lee Jones would not come alone. We're missing combatants."

So Lee Jones was Mahoney's second-in-command. Her

gaze slid over the tall man with light blond hair slicked back. What the hell was she supposed to do now?

"You're in on this together. The threats against me." She shook her head. "Those were stupid, you know. If you hadn't dropped off the dead cat, I never would've realized there was a problem. Why take the chance?"

Lee's jaw twitched. "This idiot is so focused on making you suffer he's forgotten what matters. His dad was clear. We keep the network going. It'll get him out."

"Nothing can get him out," Razor said. "The feds have him locked down tight. He's going to rot in prison where he belongs."

"Shut the fuck up!" Bret slammed the butt of his gun toward Razor's head.

But Razor crouched and punched the man in the gut. He moved so fast she could barely track what was happening. He grabbed the gun and aimed it at Bret, who was now on the floor and holding his stomach.

"Idiot!" Lee spat the word as he reached out and grabbed Jen's hair. She kicked out, aiming for his balls, but hit his upper thigh instead. The man grunted but didn't fall like she'd hoped. Fear clawed up her throat when she looked at the weapon now trained on her. "Drop the weapon or she dies."

Her pulse beat hard as she looked at Razor. He'd yet to comply, and she hoped he wouldn't.

"Drop the weapon, or you die." The growled order came from behind Jen, but she didn't startle. She knew that voice. Shadow.

Movement behind Razor drew her attention as Trigger, Brain, and Lefty moved into the room, weapons trained on Lee.

"It's over, Lee," Trigger said. "Drop the weapon and get on your knees. Hands behind your head."

"Idiot! I told you it was a trap, but you wouldn't listen." Lee tossed the weapon and glared at Trigger. "You've made a grave mistake. You won't leave the building alive. Unlike Junior, I plan."

"Four targets down east of building," a voice said.

Thank God. Jen squeezed her eyes shut as Lefty and Brain secured Bret and Lee. It was over.

"HERA just spit out two security guards working in the building," Zoey said. "I've tracked one to the floor beneath Jen's office and the other in the west stairwell just about to enter the lobby."

"Doc and I are on the one near Jen's office," a man said in the com. "Lucky, you and Oz take the lobby."

"Roger."

"Status, Green team?" Mary asked.

"Grim's scouring cell phones. We have a secondary threat incoming, a block away. We'll engage."

"Roger, Sampson," Zoey replied. "I'll assist with the drones."

One of the drones hovered near Trigger's head as he lowered his weapon. His gaze swept her, then focused on Razor. "You good?"

"Yeah." Razor's jaw twitched. "That was too close. Why was that asshole not taken out before he got in here?"

"Because we now have evidence proving his involvement," Jen said.

"He had a gun pointed at you!" Razor pulled her into his arms. "Fuck. Never again, beauty. Never again."

Jen leaned into his embrace and kissed his throat. "I'm okay. It's over. We're all okay."

"FBI agents should arrive in ten minutes," Mary said. "HERA is scouring cell phones the green team cloned. Red and blue teams, clone your secured targets' phones."

"On it," Brain said as he pulled phones off Lee and Bret.

Confirmation of the other Deltas doing the same sounded in Jen's ear, but she didn't pay attention to the chatter afterward.

Her gaze swept to Shadow, who stood on the other side of the room, as far away from the three Deltas as he could get. "Thank you, Shadow. For everything."

He offered a chin lift as he folded his arms in front of his chest. "If we're good, Edge, I'd like to squirt before the feds arrive."

"Go," Mary replied. "I'll make sure the others get out without incident."

If not, Jen would see to them. It was the least she could do.

"I'd better call Sandman, give him and Frenzy a heads up," Razor said as he pulled away from Jen.

Damn. She should phone Ethan and Milo. They would not be happy.

* * *

Razor wanted nothing more than to spend the next couple of days alone with Jen. Making love to her for hours would go a long way toward calming the beast within him. Fuck. That'd been too close.

His brain didn't even still on the thought of making love to her instead of fucking. He'd fallen for her weeks ago and wouldn't deny it to himself or her. Not after today.

The Mustang growled as he pulled into the compound. Scythes hovered around Ethan and Milo. Both men glared as Razor parked.

"They aren't happy. Let me handle this," Jen said.

"We need that to happen inside and away from Sam and his grandparents," Razor said. "Hopefully we'll have answers on whatever the fuck they're up to soon so we're done with all the shit."

"Then I want that hill country drive you promised me." She leaned over and kissed him.

Pleasure ran through him. She didn't shy away from touching or kissing him when others watched. Fuck. He'd never expected a woman as good as her to give him that. "I don't deserve you, but I'm sure as fuck too deep to walk away."

"Don't you dare." She touched his face. "I'm too deep to take that blow. All that matters is what you and I want. Everyone else will either understand or I'll kick their asses."

Razor chuckled. "I'll help. Come on, let's get your brothers calmed." Then he'd have to do the same with his crew.

Jen remained at his side, arm around his waist as they made their way toward the group. Ethan and Milo dragged her into a tight hug. Although he couldn't hear what the two men said, the tension in their stances spoke volumes.

"Prez," Jumper said. "You square?"

"Yeah." He glanced over at where the Gentrys stood with Sam and some of the kids. "Let's move this inside."

No one argued as everyone filed in behind him. Jen shuffled forward until she stood beside him. The unease in his gut loosened when she smiled up at him and took his hand. Fuck. He'd fight the world to keep her safe.

Everyone sat around the table. Shock stilled him a few seconds when Jen plopped down on his lap and wrapped an arm around his shoulder. His little warrior was making a statement—one he was more than okay with. He folded one arm around her back and rested the other on her jean-clad thigh.

"I think it goes without saying that Ethan and I are pissed this shit went down without us involved." Milo paced the area near the door. His gaze swept to Razor and Jen. "Glad you're okay, sis. But this shit never happens again."

"Agreed," Razor said. Fuck. He'd almost gone nuclear when that second asshole aimed his weapon at her. He focused on the Delta team as they joined the huddle. "Thanks."

"Any time," Trigger said. "Did we get everyone, Edge?"

"There are a couple HERA tracked down that weren't there," the woman replied quickly. "Feds already have them in custody. Zoey's going to get with Tex and run through the data again to make sure we didn't miss anyone, but we're confident it's over."

"Mahoney Senior is in federal custody, enrolled in witness protection," Vi said. "This entire mess is on them. They didn't tighten his leash. We've turned over evidence HERA obtained that he's been corresponding with his son via a burner phone. By not involving Counterstrike as heavily in today's mission, we've kept you clean so you can make a brief statement concerning the previous threats against Jen without being detracted from your work." The woman's gaze cut to Ethan and Milo. "That's what matters. Your work is too important to be derailed by red tape."

"The recruits you hired when Bea's problems happened are good. They're ready for field work and work well with Travis," Edge said. "I know you're contracting some of the Scythes for protective details, but they could do more, assuming they'd want field work. It's something for you all to consider going forward."

"Agreed," Victoria said. "Thanks, Mary." She looped her arm around Milo's waist. "It's over. That's what matters."

"We still have Sam to worry about," Jen said. "Tell me we have answers."

"Oh we have answers that spewed out more questions that we've also answered," Anarchy said. "They're running a modified Ponzi scheme. New money pays out old promises, but only partially. That's kept the scheme running longer than they normally do."

Damn. Ponzi schemes relied on new investments to feed the older layers. "How many victims?"

"HERA's still pulling names," Zoey replied. "We'll turn everything we've obtained over to the FBI. The Arsenal has an ongoing contract with them, so the evidence should be admissible, especially since this group has been flagged in their system."

"They're broke," Edge said. She motioned toward the display on the largest screen. "Ponzi schemes normally tank at some point, usually when the volume of new investors can't keep up with the need for payouts to the older layers. This modified version was smarter in that they actually did invest some of the money they took, but those investments haven't done well in the recent economy."

"Email communications indicated some of the older layers were demanding their assets be returned to them," Zoey said. "That's when Gentry Holdings first hit the FBI radar."

"That was last year," Anarchy said. "They saved their asses and got off the feds' radar, but did so by crawling into bed with an organized crime family based out of Miami."

"Tell me they weren't that stupid," Razor said.

"They were," Zoey sing-songed. "So stupid. They used some of the dirty money given to them to payout on the older layers. It kept their scheme afloat, but now they've stolen from a very, very bad group."

"Why want Sam?" Jen shook her head. "I'm still missing why they want him. They scraped their daughter off. Why risk getting their grandson?"

Edge chewed on her lower lip. "I'm with you. That still

doesn't make sense, but we've found no intel surrounding Sam."

"Sometimes idiots are just idiots," Zoey said. "Maybe he's the latest marketing gimmick. They take in the terrified grandkid and garner enough attention from a target demographic to get traction. New investors. Or maybe they're just nuts."

Anarchy nodded his head. "She's right. Hopefully we can get that answer from them, but we might never find out."

Razor knew Jen wanted an answer. He ran his hand down her hair. "Cuts to the bone we might not find out the why, but you've done right by Sam. They won't be taking him. Focus on that."

"Fuck," Ethan cursed. "That means Sam goes back into the system."

"I wish there were other family members. He deserves better than this, but at least we have some good foster families who are Counterstrike vetted," Jen said. "He'll be okay. Happy."

Edge's lips thinned. She crossed her arms and glanced at Anarchy, who rubbed the back of his neck and sighed heavily. Razor raised his eyebrows. "Tell me."

It was Sandman who spoke, though. "Sam needs a family—a real one not in it for the paycheck. I'm sure those families are solid, but they've got no direct ties to the roots he wants."

Milo's jaw twitched. "I'm not blind. That kid has latched on tight to your crew, Razor. It's the first taste of real family he's had, except for the mom he saw murdered. He needs extensive therapy. One of those families can give him that."

"So can we," Sandman replied. "We have two Scythes who are married with solid families. Both are licensed by the state as fosters. Either of them would take him in. More importantly, they'd adopt. He wears our cut. He's brotherhood.

That might not mean much to you, Davenport, but it does to him."

Quake and Tater both had solid families. They'd married while in service and both their wives had stood strong at their side when shit went down. Both men were a beacon within the Scythes for what the single members wanted. Loving wives. Kids. Yeah, they'd do good by Sam because he'd be loved. Both families would go all in to heal Sam's soul.

"Yeah, but he's only had that for a few days," Ethan argued. "We can't decide his future based on a few days."

Razor looked down at the beautiful woman beside him. She relaxed against his side. "You're quiet. You know him better than anyone standing here. What do you think?"

"He's been dealt a really shitty hand more than once," she said. "Mrs. Woods would need to vet them, but I think he'd be happier with a Scythe family. That'd give him a much larger family, both Scythe and Counterstrike."

Razor agreed but didn't offer an opinion. He was biased. He'd been raised within a club. He knew the underlying value of the love brotherhood offered. No one's opinion really mattered because it should be Sam's choice, not that a kid his age fully knew how to form one. At least, that's what the court-appointed advocates would likely think.

Ethan studied Razor from across the huddle. Intensity resonated in the man's gaze. "Your thoughts, Razor?"

"I was raised in my grandpa's club. I'm biased."

"You've got insight they don't, Prez," Anarchy commented.

"He's right," Milo replied. Arms crossed, he smirked. "I assume you're pro-Scythe for placement."

"I am. We'll be a part of his life no matter where he lands. Can they give him a better homelife than the other foster families?" Razor shrugged. "That'll depend on what people consider important. There's more to life than an ivy league education. Quake and Tater can't provide monetary riches, but they'd give him what matters. Love. Family."

"The others would do that, too," Ethan commented.

"Yeah, but he'd be a foster," Jen said, her voice soft. "None of them want to adopt. They'd never look at him differently than they do their own children, but those around them aren't the same. That divide would be there at his school. Kids can be mean."

"Do they even want a long-term placement?" Anarchy asked.

"I don't honestly know." Jen bit her lower lip. "Everything's been short-term so far."

"Then we all know how this should go, assuming Sam and Mrs. Woods agree." Victoria looked up at Milo. "Hazard and Bea should stay with Sam. They can help Quake and Tate keep him occupied while the arrests take place. He shouldn't see that."

"So that's going down today?" Trigger asked. Amusement glimmered in the man's eyes. "You all don't mess around."

"It'll take a few days to gather all the evidence the FBI will want," Edge admitted. "But there are a couple of outstanding warrants for both Gentrys. They can be pulled in for those."

Translation—Sam would not leave this compound with his grandparents. That was a win Razor would take. Everything else would work out because none of the people around him would accept anything else, and fuck knew he wouldn't.

CHAPTER 15

It'd been a long, exhausting day but Jen was grateful for everything that'd happened—except maybe the assholes who'd trained weapons on her and Razor. While she was glad Anarchy and The Arsenal brains had figured out what Sam's grandparents were up to, she was still unsettled.

Why had they fought so hard to get Sam?

The picnic was ending as darkness settled over the Scythe compound. It'd been a long, long, tension-filled day. Most everyone gathered suffered from the same sleep deprivation she did, but revelry still echoed around her. Sam ran around playing with Bea's son, Ryan, and the other kids.

"He's happy," Razor whispered against her ear.

A shiver ran down her body, which heated at his nearness. Amusement rolled from him in a sexy chuckle. She leaned her back against his front. "I can't help the reaction I have to you."

"I love the way your body reacts to mine," he said. "I can't wait to feel you come around my cock. Again and again."

"Unless you're going to drag me into the compound and follow through with that promise, behave." She squeezed the arm he'd wrapped around her waist. "Tonight isn't going to happen, is it?"

"Afraid not." Regret filled his voice. "Tomorrow you're mine. A long ride into the hill country will do us both good. We've got a cabin up there if you're game."

A night alone in the hill country with Razor? Yep, she was all in. "I can't wait."

A man with salt and pepper hair kissed a pretty blonde as they left the children playing and headed toward Jen and Razor. Love shone in their faces when they looked at one another. This was one of the couples Sandman had mentioned earlier. These were Sam's potential future parents.

"How will this work between Quake and Tater? I mean, if they both want Sam, won't that create a problem?" She'd worried about that ever since Sandman mentioned the two couples.

"That's not how we operate," Razor said. "They've already talked it out, while we were chowing down. Sandman had a word. If Mrs. Woods is onboard, Tater and Mandy will be the placement. They've got two boys around Sam's age, and a little girl."

It sounded like a perfect environment for Sam. Two brothers and a little sister. Instafamily. The couple paused a couple feet from Jen and Razor. The man offered Razor a chin lift. "Prez. Jen. This is my wife, Mandy. I'm Tater. We wanted to introduce ourselves and see if you had any questions."

"I probably have a million of them, but honestly, I'm exhausted. We all are. I've seen how happy Sam is playing with your sons and the others." Jen motioned toward the play area where Sam was chasing a soccer ball. "That's all the proof I need."

And it was. Scythes hovered in a semi-circle near the

kids. Sandman and Frenzy both cheered when Sam kicked the ball into a net. More revelry boomed in the area as the other Scythes joined in. The kids on Sam's team drew him into a group hug. Their laughter and joy spread through the area like a shockwave washing away the past few weeks.

Tears burned her eyes. "This is the right call."

"It is," Razor whispered against her ear.

"He's a beautiful and bright boy," Mandy said with a smile. "He's already anxious to see our oldest son's car collection. Mark just turned eight last week. Neil is six. Our youngest, Anna, is two. We left her with my parents. Both of our parents live in Austin, as do my two brothers and their families. He'll have a large family outside of the Scythes."

Nervousness filled the woman's voice. Jen stepped away from Razor and took the woman's hand. "It's a pleasure to meet you. Please don't be nervous. I already know you're great parents. I see that in the joy your kids shine with. You're good people. I know Sam will be happy with you, and I'll fight whatever battle necessary to ensure he stays with you. Mrs. Woods is a great social worker. She'll see how good you are for him."

Tater kissed Mandy's cheek and squeezed her shoulder. "Our boys are already looking forward to a campout in the backyard with Ryan and Quake's son. He's five. We don't have a lot of money, but he'll have everything he needs and more love than he can imagine."

"Money can't buy happiness or love. I know that more than anyone," Jen said. She'd learned that the hard way, watching her father drag them down that treacherous road. "Your family has grown today because you're part of the Counterstrike family now as far as I'm concerned. We will always have your backs. I will always have your back."

"Thank you." Mandy patted Tater's chest. "He mentioned the security company the Scythes are starting. I'm so glad he's going to start doing more work that he loves. We both admire what Counterstrike does. I'd love to help out however I can. I'm an office manager with a small marketing firm right now, so if there's anything at all I can do to help, please let me know."

Office manager. Perfect. "Honestly, I'd love to introduce you to Victoria and my brothers. We're drowning in administrative work right now. Victoria's done a lot since she started working with us, but we need help. Lots of it. An office manager is exactly what we need so she can remain focused on the teams."

Tater smiled. "Mandy is a force to be reckoned with when she's working. She won't shy away from a challenge. She can stand up to anyone. Hell, she's knocked more than a few of my Scythe brothers into line."

"She has." Razor chuckled. "Anarchy used to tremble when she entered the compound when he first took on the Treasurer position."

"He did not. That man never trembles." Mandy winked at Jen. "But, I did knock him into shape and teach him the proper way to handle the Scythe books. So, yes. I have no problems with alpha personalities or growly badasses. I'm betting there's not much difference between Counterstrike's operatives and my crew."

"You're right." Jen couldn't wait for Mandy to meet with her brothers.

A high-pitched whistle sounded from near the compound's entryway. Jen glanced that direction as three black SUVs pulled up to a stop. Men and women in black suits exited the vehicles.

"Feds are here," Sandman said from a few feet away as he jogged toward Razor. "Want me to handle it, Prez?"

"No. I've got it, though I suspect they'll want to chat with Edge and Zoey." Razor kissed Jen's mouth. "Later, beauty."

Her gaze swept the exterior of the compound. Her heartbeat quickened. "Wait. Where are the Gentrys?"

"Inside," Sandman said. "Jumper detained them a few minutes ago. We're doing this quick and quiet, for Sam's sake." The man's gaze cut to Tater and Mandy. "You two keep him playing with the kids. We'll let you know when it's over."

The couple nodded and turned to head toward the kids, but Jen's mind was on the Gentrys. They'd figured out what the couple was up to, so why was her brain still unsettled? Why had they wanted Sam so bad?

"I need to talk with them before the feds take them into custody," Jen told Razor.

"Jen..."

"Please. It's important. I know we're missing something important. I can't rest until I get that answer. The feds won't care enough to ask. They'll be focused on the scheme and the dirty money, as they should be." Her gaze moved between Razor and Sandman.

"We'll keep them busy," Sandman said. "You won't have long, so be quick."

"You are not alone with them." Razor clasped her face. "Promise me. You keep Jumper or one of The Arsenal crew with you."

"I promise." She'd already had one gun drawn on her. Going through that again the same day? No thanks.

She headed toward the meeting room. Determination filled her as she looked at the elderly couple. Jumper, Mary, and Zoey all looked up from their laptops when she entered. Mr. and Mrs. Gentry were both handcuffed and sitting at the table.

"I need to speak with these two before the feds," Jen said. Her gaze swept to Jumper. "Alone." She didn't know why, but her gut was telling her whatever answer she got needed to be kept private. She trusted the Scythes, but she was Sam's attorney first and foremost.

"Fuck no. Prez wouldn't agree to that." The man shook his head.

Mary pointed at the two drones aimed at the Gentrys. "They won't move or they'll get knocked out. We can't leave you alone with them, but you can have a few minutes as long as Zoey and I remain in the room."

Jumper sighed as he made his way toward the door. "Make it quick. I'll stand guard outside."

"Thank you." She smiled up at the man.

She waited a few minutes before resting her palms on the table and glaring at the couple. "Why?"

"We demand to speak with our attorney."

"You aren't under arrest yet, idiots," she spat angrily. "Why come all the way down here and drag Sam into your fucked up world? You didn't give a shit about his mom. Why?"

"That's none of your business," Mrs. Gentry said, sniffling. "This is all a huge misunderstanding."

Jen slammed her hand on the table. "Why!"

"Maybe ease off on the table abuse. That costs more than your brothers' house," Zoey muttered. "Okay, little badass. We get it. We missed something."

"We did." Mary started typing away on her laptop.

They'd find answers. Jen knew they would. Think. Think. Think. What could they possibly get by taking Sam? He was young. Maybe it was simply a marketing ploy, but that didn't track. What else could they do with him?

"They're egotistical idiots," Zoey said. "Talk it out. You've dealt with a lot of crazy stuff through Counterstrike. What could they gain by getting custody of Sam?"

"He's our grandson! Of course we want him," Mr. Gentry said.

"We failed to protect our daughter. He's a second chance at doing the right thing," his wife replied. "Please. We aren't bad people. This is all a huge misunderstanding."

"Yeah. Right." Zoey shook her head. "You're money-hungry idiots."

Money-hungry. Jen's gut soured. Too many families opened their homes up for the "easy" paycheck that was a foster child. The Gentrys wouldn't get any money, though. Or would they? "Sam's parents. The house and monetary assets were in both of their names, so those will remain with his father, even if he's rotting in a prison."

"Could they sue him?" Mary asked.

"Possibly." Jen paced. Sam's mom had loved him so much. She wouldn't have wanted this nightmare to unfold for him. Realization dawned on her a few seconds later.

No. They wouldn't.

Angry voices sounded from outside the meeting room. Shit. She was out of time.

"Life insurance," she whispered. "This is about a big payout; one they would've used to run away or keep their scheme going."

"Shit." Zoey nodded. "I'm on it. I'll find it."

"Tell no one." She couldn't risk the fallout. Sam needed her protection. Too many money-hungry trolls would crawl out of the woodwork if she was right. If his mom had bought a hefty life insurance policy on herself, it could possibly have paid out to him. Sure, it would default to her spouse, but if she'd been killed by that spouse?

Yeah, it would definitely go to Sam. Eventually.

But how would her parents have known?

Tradition. The answer thundered through her brain. "You raised her to always think ahead, didn't you? The moment you were notified of her death, you knew there'd be a hefty life insurance payout. The beneficiary would automatically be her husband, but a halfway decent attorney could make that roadblock go away since the bastard murdered her. You rotten assholes."

"You don't understand," Mrs. Gentry whispered.

"You're right. I'll never understand depraved idiots like you." Jen took a step away from the table as the meeting room door opened. Her time was up.

She had the answer she'd needed. Now all she had to do was make sure the answer didn't harm Sam. He'd suffered enough.

* * *

It took just under two hours to answer all the FBI's questions. Exhaustion plagued Razor. It'd been a long fucking day, but it wasn't over.

"It's over," Sandman commented. He held out an unopened beer. "What's got you tweaked?"

"Not sure." The lie slid out easily enough as he cracked the beer open and took a sip. His gaze cut to Jen, who was in the corner with her brothers. She'd spoken with the Gentrys but hadn't shared what she'd found out yet.

"You aren't under the radar with her."

"Didn't intend to be." He glanced at Sandman. "I'm taking her to the cabin tomorrow. No interruptions. She needs a break."

"Good. You need that, too. It's about time you found a good woman." Sandman grinned. "You just had to pick one with an army of skilled operatives at her back."

Razor chuckled. "Gotta keep from getting bored." He couldn't imagine ever getting bored with Jen. Now that the dangers surrounding her were settled—for now—he was looking forward to spending time with her. Getting to know the woman beneath her persona better.

With that thought in mind, he tossed his unfinished beer in the trash and headed toward the huddle. Ignoring the fact she was with her two overprotective brothers and dragging her away would be suicidal, but he'd had enough face time with the two men the past few days.

"Hey." She smiled up at him. "I was just telling them you were kidnapping me tomorrow."

"Sharing my nefarious plans?" He kissed her mouth. "Not sure that's the smart play, beauty."

"You're solid as far as we're concerned," the twin on the left said.

"But if you hurt her, they'll never find your body," the other added.

Jen laughed. "You still can't tell them apart, can you?"

"Nope." He didn't particularly care to if he was entirely honest.

"If you're good, I'll tell you the secret," Jen whispered.

"Did you get what you wanted from the Gentrys before they were hauled off?" Razor asked. Both brothers tensed at the question, but the one nearest him smirked.

"Yeah, Jen. What'd you find out?"

Razor tightened at the dare buried within the gruff question. Something was up. They were testing her.

No.

Him.

"Just a yes or no," Razor said. "I just want to make sure you're okay. That's what matters. I don't give a damn about the details, especially if they're privileged."

"Really?" The other twin leaned back in his chair. "Why not? Don't you care about our sister other than her looks?"

"Milo." Jen glared at him. "Don't."

Razor took her hand. "I do. That's why I'm not asking what I have no business knowing. Everyone's got secrets they've gotta keep, a fact you both know. We didn't survive what we did in the sandpit or whatever other hell we found ourselves in by not playing smart.

"There'll be a lot she can't share with me. It's her job to protect people, same as it is ours. I'll keep her safe so she can do that, but that'll include her knowing I'm there when she needs me—even if it's ranting about a problem in vague terms so she can calm her mind and enjoy life outside of what she does."

"That's a pretty statement," Milo drawled. "It'll get old quick, not knowing what's chewing away at her."

"She can handle her own battles. You both know that. She's always had you to help when needed. Now she'll have me, in whatever way necessary." He caressed her cheek. Her beautiful eyes widened. "I won't ever dig for what I shouldn't because I trust your judgment. But I will always be a sounding board for when shit eats away at you. Whatever you found out locked you down, beauty. I saw it the moment you stepped out of that office. You were in full on battle mode. That's sexy as fuck, but you've gotta know I'm not ever a threat to you or anyone you protect. I'm your shield. Yours and theirs, for however long you want me to be."

"Thank you," she whispered. "I did find something out. I could probably share it, but…"

"But for Sam's sake you want to lock it in the vault and protect him," Ethan said. "I get it, sis. I do. I just wish to hell this wasn't solely on you. He's our client just as much as he is yours."

Which meant she hadn't told them either. Razor noted the tension in both of the brothers. "I get it. Neither of you want her locking down because of what all just happened, but she's damned good at what she does. So are you. If she's not telling anyone, there's a reason. Hell, with how exhausted we all are, I'd be surprised if she could even think through how to navigate whatever she found out."

"That's exactly what I was trying to tell them," she admitted. She looked down at the scarred table. "I need to process it for a while."

"Fair enough," Ethan said.

"Just tell us if it's a potential threat," Milo said.

Jen shook her head. "I-I don't think so. Maybe to Sam. I honestly don't know yet."

Razor let the admission roll around in his brain a bit. "Jumper left the room, but Edge and Zoey remained. That means The Arsenal knows."

"Then we should, too," Milo growled.

"Leave it be," Razor warned. "She's exhausted. I'm taking her home so she can rest. Tomorrow we're having a relaxation day. Give her the space she needs to work through it."

"He's right," Ethan commented. "Sorry, sis. You know we love you. We're here when you're ready."

"Thanks." She licked her lips. "You know they live right next door to me. It's kind of stupid for you to drive me home." She slapped her hands on her face. "Wait. I don't even have a home. It's a mess. Isn't it?"

"Yeah," Milo said, his tone gentle. "It'll take some work to get it sorted, but we will." He pulled out his cell and looked at Razor. "I'll send you an address of a safe house we have in that neighborhood. Travis and a couple of the new operatives packed up some of her stuff and dropped it off there."

Razor's cell chimed with an incoming text. He stood and touched Jen's back. "Come on. Let's get you home before you crash."

Jen hugged both her brothers then smiled at him. He guided her toward the exit. The problem simmering in her head would wait. He'd make damn sure she got the rest and relaxation she needed.

He paused at the locker beside the exit and snagged a

helmet, which he passed to her as they made their way toward his bike.

"I know you're tired. I don't need a ride to the safe house," she said.

He paused at his bike and cupped her face. "I need to get you home. I can't get the image of that bastard's gun pointed at you out of my head. Give me this play."

She touched his jaw and kissed him. Pleasure shot through him as he tasted her. Mint. Arms wrapped around him, she deepened the kiss. Blood shot southward, hardening his dick.

A soft moan escaped her. She writhed against him. As much as he wanted to continue, she deserved better than a make-out session in the compound's parking lot.

"You'll stay with me, right?"

Fuck. Talk about a temptation. "Yeah. Give me five minutes. I'm gonna pack a few things so we can leave from your place in the morning." He took a couple steps backward before he surrendered to the need to kiss her again.

"Thank you," she whispered. "For everything, but especially for what you just said. I couldn't get them to understand."

"You're exhausted," he said. "I'll always have your back."

He headed inside to pack a bag. As hard as being near her without making love to her would be, he'd give her what she needed tonight—rest.

CHAPTER 16

Jen's second motorcycle ride was so much better than the first. Sure, the first had been a heart-pounding flee from a freaking RPG, but this one had been more thrilling. Molded against Razor's hard body…

She ignored the need pulsating within her as she guided Razor toward the bedroom. They both needed sleep more than sex, which sucked because she wanted him.

"Not sure this is a good idea, beauty," he muttered when they entered the bedroom. His gaze swept to the queen-sized bed. "Fuck. It almost killed me sleeping with you against me once."

"I'll behave." Maybe. She drew his T-shirt over his head and ran her hands down his ripped torso. The man's body was lethal to her control. She kissed the helmet of his tattoo and ran her fingers along the scythe. "This ink is hot. Sad, but deep."

Razor ran his hands through her hair, then claimed her mouth. Need pulsated beneath her skin. She relaxed against him, craving the heat. Their tongues dueled, a carnal war she didn't want to win.

She gasped when he severed the kiss and removed her shirt in a speed that defied reason. Then his mouth was on her, trailing a path from her neck downward. He cupped her breasts, sliding his fingers beneath the lacy bra then upward along the straps, which he slid down her arms.

Deft fingers ran down her back and undid the clasp. She writhed forward, craving his touch. He massaged along her arms and kissed her again. She undid his belt, then the button of his jeans as she nipped at his mouth.

He teased her nipples, the sweep of fingers so agonizingly soft she growled her frustration. Amusement rolled from him as he licked her lips. "Patience."

"Don't you dare stop," she warned.

"I'm not stopping until you come on my mouth, beauty. I want your taste on my tongue tonight." He licked and kissed downward. "Fuck. You're gorgeous, sweetheart. I'm gonna dirty you up tonight, mark these tits with my come."

Yes, please.

She unzipped his jeans and slid her hand into his pants. She moaned as she stroked his hardened length. "I want you to fuck me hard, Razor." She squeezed his cock, relishing the moan he emitted.

Anticipation beaded along her skin when Razor stripped her bare. His dark gaze turned molten as it slid down her exposed body. This was what she'd needed. Tonight she wasn't an attorney or a billionaire heiress hiding from the limelight.

She shoved his pants down. He stepped out of them and his boxers. His cock was thick and long. Her pussy clenched.

"You're too good for me," he whispered. He drew her into his arms. "But fuck if I'm letting you go."

"You'd better not. I know a few commandos who'd chase you down." She nipped his shoulder. "I've wanted you since that meeting. The way you looked at me."

"Is that why you kept squirming?" He chuckled. "Sexier than hell. Those sexy skirts of yours make me hard, beauty. They make me want to hike them up and fuck you hard."

She stroked his hard length. "I'm all yours."

Razor tossed her onto the bed and claimed her mouth. They warred with the mouths, stroked and caressed each other. While Jen hadn't ever felt inhibited in the bedroom, she'd never surrendered fully to the carnal need consuming her in a fiery inferno.

Her sucked her nipple, then grazed his teeth along the achy bud. The sensations shot through her and pooled arousal between her legs, where his fingers deftly plunged. She writhed upward, craving more. Desperate to sate the burning need.

By the time he'd touched and tasted his way downward, she was lost within the pleasure. One hand splayed on her lower stomach, he settled between her legs.

"Razor." She threaded her fingers in his thick hair. "Please."

He kissed her mound and plunged his fingers deeper into her. Their gazes locked as he pulled them from her and sucked them. "Fuck. You taste better than I imagined. I could eat you for hours."

God. She wouldn't survive that long. A moan escaped her. He licked along her pussy, teasing her with agonizingly slow forays near where she wanted him the most. His thumb rolled across her clit.

He licked her pussy, alternating between using his tongue and fingers to fuck her while his other hand focused on her clit. Her breath escaped her in soft pants and moans as pleasure assailed her.

She cried out as the sensations erupted through her, the orgasm more intense than she'd ever experienced. Hand in his hair, she clung to him, tightening her thighs around his shoulders.

Sweat dampened her skin by the time she came down from her climax. Razor rested both his hands near her head and kissed her softly.

"You should rest, beauty," he whispered.

"No way. I'll rest after you fuck me." She stroked down his powerful chest. Gripping his cock, she writhed upward. "I want you. Inside me."

"Fuck." He kissed her mouth once more.

She guided his cock into her. He plunged deep, then stilled. "Fuck. You're thick. Give me a minute."

The kiss turned slow, intimate. By the time he moved, her entire body beaded in awareness, heated wherever he touched. He paid homage to her breasts, sucking on her nipples as he fucked her so agonizingly sweet.

"Harder," she whispered. She writhed upward and scored her nails down his back. Their gazes locked. "Fuck me, Razor. Let go."

Arms wrapped around him, she inhaled his scent as he quickened his thrusts, powering into her hard and deep. She gasped, meeting each powerful plunge greedily.

Their movements turned frantic. Carnal. No matter how close they were, she wanted more. Needed to feel him deeper. Lost within the sensations, she clung to him as another wave of pleasure surged within her.

Razor roared his release moments later. He collapsed against her. She closed her eyes and relished the weight of his body against hers. Sweat dampened their skin.

He trailed kisses along her face. Intensity resonated within his gaze when it locked with hers. "Fuck, beauty. You just ruined me for anyone else. That was…everything."

Sated and blissfully relaxed, she touched his face. "It was. Thank you."

"You don't ever need to thank me for anything, especially that. It was my pleasure." He kissed her softly, then shifted them until she was curled against his side. Arm around her, he moaned. "I need to get you cleaned up. Then you can sleep."

"Don't. I want to fall asleep in your arms and filled with you." She smirked at the shocked look on his face. "I like being dirtied up by my biker."

Laughter rumbled from him. They both knew they'd shower soon, but she let the silence settle in the room. It'd been a long rough day, but she loved how it had ended. The chemistry between them was undeniable.

"I want this," he said. "You and me. We can make it work."

"We will," she promised. "What you said earlier, to my brothers. I'm that for you, too. Your safe harbor when shit goes down. I know there are things you won't be able to tell me. With your brotherhood, the things you all went through. But I'm in that battle with you, Razor. Always."

"None of it will be pretty."

"Wars never are. None of you started them, but I'll be damned if we don't end them all and win every last one." She looked up at him. "Do whatever you need to and I'll stand at your side. No matter what. I know Mary and The Arsenal will help you."

He chuckled. "You're right. They're committed to helping, which is great because they're top tier, though I won't ever call that woman by her given name. She's Edge all the way."

"Thank you for telling me." She wasn't sure how to heal the blow he'd taken by doing the right thing. "I wish I could make it go away."

"You do. Just being here, in my world. You show me the good I can still do, even if it's not in a uniform."

"Oh, I don't know. That cut is definitely a uniform."

He chuckled and kissed the top of her head. "Rest, beauty. Tomorrow we ride."

Jen couldn't wait.

* * *

Jen shifted in the booth and glared at the restaurant's other patrons. "They need to stop staring."

They'd slept until almost noon, then headed out on the open road outside of Austin. The farther they'd gotten from the city, the more relaxed she'd felt. At first, she'd worried about being on a motorcycle for that long, but Razor rode as though the vehicle was a part of him. The confidence and calm he'd exuded had melted away any worries she'd had.

"We're strangers. That's what locals do," Razor commented, amusement in his tone. "Besides, you're the most beautiful woman they've likely seen in years. Of course they're gonna stare."

"The women are practically sitting in your lap when they come over here to welcome you to town," she clipped.

And he'd told them all to get lost, that he was spending the day with his woman. Jen couldn't help but smile at that. She liked being branded as his woman. Caveman was sexy on him.

He smirked.

"Don't. I'll fully admit I'm possessive."

"That's sexier than fuck." He kissed her hand.

She took another forkful of pecan pie. "This place has great food. How did you find it?"

"We ride this path a lot when the weather's good. The growl of the bikes, the warm and fresh air. The open road. It calms our minds."

"I can see that." And she could. Wrapped around Razor, she'd enjoyed every mile they'd ridden today, which almost made up for the text she'd gotten from Victoria. "I'm sorry we can't stay at the cabin tonight. Everyone's anxious to turn over the rest of what HERA found on the Gentrys and Mahoney's assholes. Early morning was the only time the feds had open."

And boy was there a lot to turn over. Truckloads of evidence against Sam's grandparents the feds could use, along with unofficial leads on Sam's dad. The latter would be a bit problematic to explain, but Mary assured Jen it wouldn't be a problem.

HERA had identified everyone connected with the Ponzi scheme, along with all the victims. The Arsenal had even found the crime syndicate from Miami and identified all of them. Essentially, they'd done all the legwork for the feds in record time. So, they'd probably forgive the covert way they'd uncovered Greph's shady world—one where he'd gotten in deep with a local gambling ring a few nights before Cindy's death.

That was why they'd fought that day. Why she'd died. Why she'd finally taken the brave step to contact Counter-strike, then doubted that move and decided to give him a chance to clean up his act.

Jen was glad the truth was finally uncovered, but she hated that the woman wouldn't get to see her amazing son grow up.

"We can come up to the cabin whenever you want. It's not going anywhere, and neither am I." Intensity resonated in his gaze. "I never asked how it went with Mrs. Woods yesterday. The feds had me in the corner asking more questions than they should have."

"That's what they do. They dig." She studied him a moment. "Mrs. Woods is going to look into Tater and Mandy, but they've done everything they needed to to be fosters. She said they'd had a couple children before."

"They have. Both older. One was fourteen going on fifty with serious attitude issues." Razor shook his head. "It took our whole crew to contain him at times, but he calmed and got his head sorted."

Jen admired the Scythes for going the distance on a teenager in the system. "Not many would've done that. Teenagers are always hard to place from what little I've seen."

"I'm thinking you've seen a lot."

"I have. Mrs. Woods is good. She'll do right by Sam." And she would. Jen hadn't told anyone what Mary and Zoey had found out. Sam's mom had a one million dollar life insurance policy. Given her husband had murdered her, he wouldn't get a penny of it—which meant it'd go to Sam.

While that was great, it was a huge issue if the boy wasn't happily settled in a home with a family who cared about him instead of the huge paycheck. She'd do what she could to lock the money away in a trust, payable only to him, but she didn't want to make assumptions that everyone was as greedy as some of the assholes she'd handled in the past.

Tater and Mandy were amazing from what she'd seen at the picnic. They'd do right by Sam. "I'm just relieved Sam's in a good home he'll be happy in."

"He's got a big family surrounding him now," Razor said. "Tater texted me earlier. The kid had a rough night. Nightmares. Wet the bed. Mandy wants to get him into a therapist immediately."

The fact they'd already reached out for one was a great sign. They truly cared about Sam. "We have more than a few who are really great with kids. Most work pro bono for Counterstrike clients."

"Money wouldn't be an issue. We aren't rolling in dough, but all of our crew do well at the shops." Razor leaned back in the booth. "But I'll make sure they know. Forward who you think is best for Sam and Mandy will get an appointment for him."

She pulled out her phone and found the list. She forwarded it to Razor's number. Heat rose in her cheeks. "I'm finally using your number."

He chuckled. "It's a shame you haven't ever used it before now."

She shoved her half-finished pie to the side. "I'm thinking I'll be using it a lot from now on."

"Your brothers might not like that."

"Not that either of us care what they like." She did, though. Deep down, she wanted them to see how truly great Razor was.

"I'm willing to prove myself to them, beauty. You're worth whatever it takes." He stroked her chin with his thumb. "And I like how protective they are of you."

She smirked and motioned toward her unfinished pie. "I think we're done here. I'd like to stop off at that outlook again." The beautiful view into the valley below had been perfect. So serene. Jen had fought the urge to contact her realtor and ask her to look into who owned the property. It'd be a perfect getaway.

"Oh?" Razor's eyebrows hiked up. "Liked it that much?"

"Yeah, but I like the idea of getting my real dessert there even better." She ran her foot up his leg. "I want my biker to give me a different kind of ride there."

Razor snagged his wallet and tossed two twenties on the table so fast Jen couldn't help but laugh. Oh yeah, her life with him in it was going to be an adventure. A very sexy, fun one she couldn't wait to enjoy.

* * *

One month later...

The past four weeks had been the busiest yet best weeks of Jen's life. The contract between Scythe Security and Counterstrike had been signed and their involvement with the protective details had been astoundingly successful.

So much so that Ethan, Milo, and Victoria were already onboard with having some of Razor's crew assist with the investigational aspect as well. Jen smiled at Bea as she passed her desk.

"Damn. I haven't seen you smile that big in a long time. You must've had a good weekend," Bea commented.

She had. Dating Razor was an eye-opening experience. She hadn't realized how stressed she'd always been, or how focused she'd been on work.

"I did. The cabin was amazing." Jen set her briefcase down. "How was your weekend?"

"Fantastic. Ryan was at a sleepover with Sam and the other boys all weekend. Tater and Mandy had a barbecue at their place that we were invited to. Quake brought his family." The woman smiled. "It was fun. Hazard and I are already planning to hold the next one, except maybe a bit bigger. A housewarming."

"Wow. Is it that ahead of schedule?" Jen couldn't believe so much time had passed.

"Yeah. Ryan is thrilled." Bea grinned. "And don't deflect. Things with Razor are going pretty good I take it?"

"They are." So much better than pretty good. Jen wanted to pinch herself because it was almost a dream. "I can't describe it. He's everything I needed without realizing. When I'm with him, I can just let loose because…" She swallowed. "I know he'll be there to catch me if I fall."

"It's scary. At least, it was for me," Bea admitted. "That's what I love about Hazard the most. He's always there, but he never stands in my way. He's always at my side."

Jen couldn't help but laugh. "The judges have finally

accepted there will always be a Scythe in the courtroom when I'm there. And they'll always be texting."

Bea nodded. "The fact your man makes that happen every time we have to go to court has really given Hazard a peace. He told me the other day that he doesn't worry as much as he used to when we go to court."

Scythe escorts for anyone Jen had to go to court with had become commonplace. The entire club was always present, offering a sense of security for whichever client Jen was helping that day. She wished she could say it wasn't necessary, but they'd intervened more than a few times and prevented a situation from escalating.

Jen's cell chimed with an incoming text. She pulled it out of her purse and read the message.

Zoey: Your man will need you at the compound. Incoming visitor in 20. No worries. It's all good.

Jen: Thanks.

Jen frowned at the vague message but didn't hesitate to grab her purse. "I've gotta get to the compound. Something's about to go down."

"You need backup? Travis and a few of the noobs aren't on the schedule for active cases." Bea pulled up Counterstrike's new schedule tracker. "Hiring Mandy was the smartest thing your brothers have ever done."

Jen couldn't agree more. The woman had singlehandedly freed up everyone to work the cases rather than slog through the administrative aspects. Not only that, but she was fierce.

She'd taken over initial greeting for the main headquarters, offering kindness and empathy to clients while activating the protective momma cub when an asshole abuser entered the office. She never hesitated to act, often using the drones in the lobby before anyone in the back ever realized there was a problem. Yeah, she was that quick because her asshole radar was solid.

Jen got to the compound faster than she'd expected and parked her BMW near the bikes, leaving enough room for a few to park where they normally did. Several people milled about in the picnic area. She waved at them.

Her gaze swept the main room of the compound. Razor sat in his usual corner with Anarchy, Sandman, and Frenzy. All their gazes moved to her.

"Everything okay?" Razor asked as he stood.

Jen pulled out her cell and handed it to him. "I wanted to be here, just in case."

His lips tightened as he passed her cell to Frenzy. The man growled. "Shit's never good if The Arsenal is giving us a head's up."

"Yeah, but they didn't," Anarchy commented. "Which means whatever this is, it's not a threat. I'll give everyone a head's up anyway. Just in case."

The man jogged toward the exit but froze when three men clad in military uniforms entered. Silence descended within the room. Jen shifted to place herself between Razor and the men as they approached.

Confidence exuded from them as they halted their progression. The one in the front cleared his throat. "You must be Ms. Davenport. Edge warned me you'd be here in bulldog mode."

Right. "I am. And you are?"

"General Thorne. Forgive the short notice. I was in the area and wanted to see this done immediately." His gaze cut to Razor. "The higher ups wanted to do this themselves, but I didn't think you'd want anyone higher than me intruding on your club. Do you have a moment?"

Razor's fists clenched. "What can I do for you, General? Whatever you have to speak with me about can be said here. I don't keep secrets from my brotherhood."

The two other men shuffled; their unease palpable. The

general's gaze cut to them both. "Of course. Why don't you two get the car cooled down? I'll be out in a minute."

"General..."

"I'll be out in a minute," the man repeated, his tone firm.

Both the men exited quickly. The general withdrew a packet from his briefcase and handed it to Razor. "I'm sure there'll be a formal ceremony or something else equally unwanted by you, so I wanted to give you what you deserve face-to-face. It's appalling, and frankly shameful, that it's taken us so long to formally investigate your allegations. You have my sincerest apologies for the horrifying way things were handled and my profound gratitude for your honor and bravery. You've been officially exonerated and cleared of all the trumped-up charges against you."

The general's gaze moved to Jen. She tightened under the scrutiny. "This isn't an official visit. Off the record, I'd highly recommend you demand more than whatever they've offered in that packet. We should never lose good men such as Razor." His gaze swept the room. "From what I've heard from Edge, we've lost far too many."

Razor's gaze turned misty as he extended his hand to the general. "Thank you, sir. And you're right. You have lost many good men, many of whom are now my Scythe brothers."

The general offered a tight nod to the room. "I'm sure we'll see one another very soon. The Arsenal is poring through many records with my full approval and protection."

Damn. Mary did not mess around. Jen stifled the amusement rolling within her. Laughing right now probably wouldn't be a good idea.

Frenzy threw his head back and laughed. The sound echoed within the room as everyone joined in.

The general grinned. "I see she's had the same effect on all of you. Have a good day, gentlemen."

Jen waited until the door closed behind him before she turned and leaped on Razor. Cheers erupted around them, but she ignored the revelry and kissed her man. He'd gotten his redemption.

"I love you," she whispered against his mouth.

"Fuck, beauty. You gut me when you give me that sweet in front of everyone," he growled in her ear. "I love you, too. So much it fucking terrifies me. Call your brothers and Bea. We're throwing a party here."

Shock rolled through her. "And you want them here?"

"They're always welcome, but yeah. This wouldn't have happened without them." He grinned.

Jen could argue the point. Counterstrike had nothing to do with clearing him, but for once, she didn't want to. All that mattered was the result—Razor was free from the unjust accusations against him.

"Think your crew could start that party without you?" She whispered the question against his throat.

A yelp escaped her when he lifted her up and headed toward the compound's bedrooms. Anticipation ignited along her skin. Yeah, they could. For now, Razor was all hers.

The relationship was new but stronger than forged steel because they supported one another. Better yet, their personalities complemented one another. She'd heard a few of the operatives at Counterstrike whispering about how quick she'd gotten serious about Razor, but they were the noobs—the ones who hadn't been in the trenches of the hells the organization fought daily.

They'd learn quick enough that life was too short not to embrace what you wanted out of life and hold on for the amazing ride.

~The End

OTHER BOOKS BY CARA CARNES

Counterstrike Series

Protecting Mari

Justice for Angie

Avenging Victoria

Loving Bea

Fighting for Jen

The Arsenal Series

Jagged Edge

Sight Lines

Blood Vows

Zero Trace

Battle Scars

Impact Zone

Hostile Ground

Lethal Echo

ABOUT THE AUTHOR

Born in small-town Texas, Cara Carnes was a princess, a pirate, fashion model, actress, rock star and Jon Bon Jovi's wife all before the age of 13.

In reality, her fascination for enthralling worlds took seed somewhere amidst a somewhat dull day job and a wonderful life filled with family and friends. When she's not cemented to her chair, Cara loves travelling, photography and reading.

Newsletter|Facebook|Twitter|Website|Bookbub

Want more of The Arsenal Series? Did you know there are free reads between all the Arsenal releases? Subscribe to my newsletter or join my Facebook group for the first peek at exclusive bonus content. Links to free short stories in the series can be found on my website at www.caracarnes.com

There are many more books in this fan fiction world than listed here, for an up-to-date list go to www.AcesPress.com

You can also visit our Amazon page at: http://www.amazon.com/author/operationalpha

Special Forces: Operation Alpha World

Christie Adams: Charity's Heart
Denise Agnew: Dangerous to Hold
Shauna Allen: Awakening Aubrey
Brynne Asher: Blackburn
Linzi Baxter: Unlocking Dreams
Jennifer Becker: Hiding Catherine
Alice Bello: Shadowing Milly
Heather Blair: Rescue Me
Anna Blakely: Rescuing Gracelynn
Julia Bright: Saving Lorelei
Cara Carnes: Protecting Mari
Kendra Mei Chailyn: Beast
Melissa Kay Clarke: Rescuing Annabeth
Samantha A. Cole: Handling Haven
Sue Coletta: Hacked
Melissa Combs: Gallant
Anne Conley: Redemption for Misty
KaLyn Cooper: Rescuing Melina
Janie Crouch: Storm
Liz Crowe: Marking Mariah
Sarah Curtis: Securing the Odds
Jordan Dane: Redemption for Avery
Tarina Deaton: Found in the Lost
Aspen Drake, Intense
KL Donn: Unraveling Love
Riley Edwards: Protecting Olivia

PJ Fiala: Defending Sophie
Nicole Flockton: Protecting Maria
Alexa Gregory: Backdraft
Michele Gwynn: Rescuing Emma
Casey Hagen: Shielding Nebraska
Desiree Holt: Protecting Maddie
Kathy Ivan: Saving Sarah
Kris Jacen, Be With Me
Jesse Jacobson: Protecting Honor
Silver James: Rescue Moon
Becca Jameson: Saving Sofia
Kate Kinsley: Protecting Ava
Heather Long: Securing Arizona
Gennita Low: No Protection
Kirsten Lynn: Joining Forces for Jesse
Margaret Madigan: Bang for the Buck
Trish McCallan: Hero Under Fire
Kimberly McGath: The Predecessor
Rachel McNeely: The SEAL's Surprise Baby
KD Michaels: Saving Laura
Lynn Michaels: Rescuing Kyle
Wren Michaels: The Fox & The Hound
Kat Mizera: Protecting Bobbi
Keira Montclair, Wolf and the Wild Scots
Mary B Moore: Force Protection
LeTeisha Newton: Protecting Butterfly
Angela Nicole: Protecting the Donna
MJ Nightingale: Protecting Beauty
Sarah O'Rourke: Saving Liberty
Victoria Paige: Reclaiming Izabel
Anne L. Parks: Mason
Debra Parmley: Protecting Pippa
Lainey Reese: Protecting New York
KeKe Renée: Protecting Bria

TL Reeve and Michele Ryan: Extracting Mateo
Elena M. Reyes: Keeping Ava
Angela Rush: Charlotte
Rose Smith: Saving Satin
Jenika Snow: Protecting Lily
Lynne St. James: SEAL's Spitfire
Dee Stewart: Conner
Harley Stone: Rescuing Mercy
Jen Talty: Burning Desire
Reina Torres, Rescuing Hi'ilani
Savvi V: Loving Lex
Megan Vernon: Protecting Us
Rachel Young: Because of Marissa

Delta Team Three Series

Lori Ryan: Nori's Delta
Becca Jameson: Destiny's Delta
Lynne St James, Gwen's Delta
Elle James: Ivy's Delta
Riley Edwards: Hope's Delta

Police and Fire: Operation Alpha World

Freya Barker: Burning for Autumn
B.P. Beth: Scott
Jane Blythe: Salvaging Marigold
Julia Bright, Justice for Amber
Anna Brooks, Guarding Georgia
KaLyn Cooper: Justice for Gwen
Aspen Drake: Sheltering Emma
Alexa Gregory: Backdraft
Deanndra Hall: Shelter for Sharla
Barb Han: Kace
EM Hayes: Gambling for Ashleigh
CM Steele: Guarding Hope

Reina Torres: Justice for Sloane
Aubree Valentine, Justice for Danielle
Maddie Wade: Finding English
Stacey Wilk: Stage Fright
Laine Vess: Justice for Lauren

Tarpley VFD Series

Silver James, Fighting for Elena
Deanndra Hall, Fighting for Carly
Haven Rose, Fighting for Calliope
MJ Nightingale, Fighting for Jemma
TL Reeve, Fighting for Brittney
Nicole Flockton, Fighting for Nadia

As you know, this book included at least one character from Susan Stoker's books. To check out more, see below.

SEAL Team Hawaii Series

Finding Elodie
Finding Lexie (Aug 2021)
Finding Kenna (Oct 2021)
Finding Monica (May 2022)
Finding Carly (TBA)
Finding Ashlyn (TBA)
Finding Jodelle (TBA)

Eagle Point Search & Rescue

Searching for Lilly (Mar 2022)
Searching for Elsie (Jun 2022)
Searching for Bristol (Nov 2022)
Searching for Caryn (TBA)
Searching for Finley (TBA)
Searching for Heather (TBA)
Searching for Khloe (TBA)

Delta Team Two Series

Shielding Gillian
Shielding Kinley
Shielding Aspen
Shielding Jayme
Shielding Riley
Shielding Devyn
Shielding Ember (Sept 2021)
Shielding Sierra (Jan 2022)

SEAL of Protection: Legacy Series

Securing Caite (FREE!)

Securing Brenae (novella)
Securing Sidney
Securing Piper
Securing Zoey
Securing Avery
Securing Kalee
Securing Jane

Delta Force Heroes Series

Rescuing Rayne (FREE!)
Rescuing Aimee (novella)
Rescuing Emily
Rescuing Harley
Marrying Emily (novella)
Rescuing Kassie
Rescuing Bryn
Rescuing Casey
Rescuing Sadie (novella)
Rescuing Wendy
Rescuing Mary
Rescuing Macie (Novella)
Rescuing Annie (Feb 2022)

Badge of Honor: Texas Heroes Series

Justice for Mackenzie (FREE!)
Justice for Mickie
Justice for Corrie
Justice for Laine (novella)
Shelter for Elizabeth
Justice for Boone
Shelter for Adeline
Shelter for Sophie
Justice for Erin
Justice for Milena

Shelter for Blythe
Justice for Hope
Shelter for Quinn
Shelter for Koren
Shelter for Penelope

SEAL of Protection Series
Protecting Caroline (FREE!)
Protecting Alabama
Protecting Fiona
Marrying Caroline (novella)
Protecting Summer
Protecting Cheyenne
Protecting Jessyka
Protecting Julie (novella)
Protecting Melody
Protecting the Future
Protecting Kiera (novella)
Protecting Alabama's Kids (novella)
Protecting Dakota

New York Times, USA Today and *Wall Street Journal* Bestselling Author Susan Stoker has a heart as big as the state of Tennessee where she lives, but this all American girl has also spent the last fourteen years living in Missouri, California, Colorado, Indiana, and Texas. She's married to a retired Army man who now gets to follow *her* around the country.

www.stokeraces.com
www.AcesPress.com
susan@stokeraces.com

Made in the USA
Coppell, TX
07 March 2022